PRAISE FOR KELLEY ARMSTRONG

"Armstrong is a talented and evocative writer who knows well how to balance the elements of good, suspenseful fiction, and her stories evoke poignancy, action, humor and suspense."
The Globe and Mail

"[A] master of crime thrillers."
Kirkus

"Kelley Armstrong is one of the purest storytellers Canada has produced in a long while."
National Post

"Kelley Armstrong is one of my favorite writers."
Karin Slaughter

"Armstrong is a talented and original writer whose inventiveness and sense of the bizarre is arresting."
London Free Press

"Armstrong's name is synonymous with great storytelling."
Suspense Magazine

"Like Stephen King, who manages an under-the-covers, flashlight-in-face kind of storytelling without sounding ridiculous, Armstrong not only writes interesting page-turners, she has also achieved that unlikely goal, what all writers strive for: a genre of her own."
The Walrus

ALSO BY KELLEY ARMSTRONG

Rockton series
City of the Lost
A Darkness Absolute
This Fallen Prey
Watcher in the Woods
Alone in the Wild

Standalone Novels
Wherever She Goes
The Masked Truth
Aftermath
Missing

Completed Series (fantasy)
Otherworld
Darkest Powers
Darkness Rising
Age of Legends

Completed Series (mystery)
Nadia Stafford
Cainsville

EVERY STEP SHE TAKES

KELLEY ARMSTRONG

Cover Image: SergeyChayko/iStockphoto

ISBN-13 (print): 978-1-989046-27-2
ISBN-13 (e-book): 978-1-989046-26-5

CHAPTER ONE

ROME 2019

Two FRAT BOYS jostle my shoulder as they tumble from the market shop. Their gazes brush over me. One realizes I'm ten years past his best-before date and pushes by without an apology. The other lets his gaze linger, considering.

"*Buongiorno*," he says, mangling it into something suspiciously close to "Bon Jovi."

"Hey," I say in English. "Watch where you're going, okay? These shops are really tiny."

My American accent dashes the poor boy's hope of a fling with a hot-blooded Italian, and he mumbles something unintelligible as he ducks past me.

An old man sitting at the counter glowers at the departing students.

"*Buongiorno*, Alessandro," I say.

He lifts his afternoon espresso in greeting and then compliments my sundress as his rheumy eyes linger on my bare calves before he mutters, "The tourists have come to Trastevere."

From behind the counter, Davide says, "The tourists have always been in Trastevere."

"They have always been over there." Alessandro gestures west. "This is not their side of the road."

"So, I should move?" I say.

"You do not count, Genevieve. You live here. You speak passable Italian. And you are a pretty girl, which they are not."

I laugh and accept the espresso Davide offers. Then I gather a few groceries as I chat with the old men. Davide rings me through, and I walk less than a hundred feet along the narrow cobblestone street to my apartment.

Alessandro isn't wrong about the tourists. They used to keep to the other side of Viale di Trastevere, but in the last few years, they've ventured farther afield. So have the restauranteurs, and as I approach my building, a young woman in a white shirt and black bow tie steps out to lure me into a new place. At the last second, she recognizes me and withdraws with a nod. The trattoria has been there six months, and my neighbors grumble that the hostess *still* calls to them every time they pass. It's one of the times I'm thankful for my memorable red hair.

I push on the heavy wood door to my building. It opens silently, and I step out of the hot June sun into the cool dark of the foyer. I glance at the glass front on my letter box. Empty as usual. Local friends text or e-mail, and most of my old ones have no idea where to find me. There was a time when that thought brought a wave of grief, but it's hard to mourn your past when your present includes a historic Roman apartment with a gorgeous terrace and a schedule that lets you spend the afternoon lounging on it. This isn't the life I envisioned, but I have fallen for it, like finding true love on the rebound.

Groceries in hand, I climb five flights of tilted, curving steps. There's no elevator. The building is five hundred years old. If you can't climb the stairs, you don't rent the place.

The stairs narrow as they ascend, and by the time I reach the top, they're so uneven that I slow lest I go tumbling down. I may have done that once or twice when I foolishly wore stiletto heels to a dinner that included a shared carafe of cheap house wine. Luckily, the first landing is only six steps down. Yes, I've counted.

With my grocery bag wedged between my shins and the door, I push the key into the lock and . . .

The door opens.

My heart stutters as the grocery tote drops to my feet. The key is only half-inserted, and the door is already cracked open. My muscles tense to run, but I roll my shoulders and take a deep breath.

Maybe I just forgot to lock it. At this time of year, I often leave the kitchen window and terrace door open. Everyone does in a country where the temperatures hit ninety by June and in-home air conditioning is uncommon. Whatever crime problems Rome might have, break-ins are rare, particularly in this area.

Then I remember that I definitely locked my door today. I'd dropped the garbage bag while locking it. With a four-hundred-square-foot apartment, you do *not* leave overflowing garbage until the weekly pickup. I'd taken a bag to stuff into the restaurant's bins. While locking the door, I'd fumbled the bag, and a wine bottle rolled out, tumbling over the edge—naturally—and shattering five floors below. Always a fun way to start the day. I was so annoyed that I heaved on the door, making damned sure it was locked after all that. It was. And now it is not.

I swallow hard and press my fingertips against the door. It creaks open farther. As I listen, my fingers fist against the wood, and I give a ragged chuckle at that. I'm a concert violist, not a barroom pugilist.

I take a deep breath, but my heart won't stop racing. My apartment door is open when I know I locked it. I should scramble down the stairs as fast as I can, phone at my ear as I summon the police. Yet my feet don't move. Calling the police means also calling attention to myself. I've spent ten years keeping the lowest possible profile, even here, thousands of miles from home.

I try to calm myself with the reminder that if it's a burglar, he'd better hope he plays the viola. That's the only thing of value in my apartment. I don't own a TV, or a stereo or expensive jewelry, and my phone and my laptop are in my bag, slung over my shoulder.

My viola *is* valuable, though, and I do play it in public—I'm in a small symphony orchestra and a classical quartet. If someone saw my viola and realized it was worth much more than any personal tech, that could be a reason for breaking in.

The other possibility is the one that must rise for every woman who lives alone. I've always felt safer in Rome than I ever did in New York, but that doesn't mean I *am* safe.

What truly sets my heart racing is the fear of a very different sort of intruder. As I stare at the open door, I hurl back into another life, one where I came home more than once to find my apartment broken into. It'd been ransacked twice, and once the intruder took nothing and left only ugly words lipsticked on my mirror. It's the words I remember, though. It's the words that have me swallowing hard, my hand shaking on the doorknob.

That can't be what this is. Too much time has passed, and I'm the only person who still cares what happened to me. Yet it takes only this unlocked door to slam me back to that life.

And *that* is why I decide not to call the police no matter how big a mistake that could be. I've clawed my way from under the shadow of my past, and I will not fall back into that pit of paranoia and grief.

I still unlock my phone, ready to call 113 at the slightest sign of trouble. Then I push the door open enough to peer inside.

The tiny kitchenette and living area are empty. There's no place to hide. Even the closet under the stairs is filled with storage shelves.

My gaze snags on a table. On it rests a cardboard box that I definitely didn't leave there. With an apartment this small, it must be kept spotless.

There is a shoebox-sized parcel on my table, wrapped in mailing-paper brown.

Bomb.

Even as I think that, my brain scoffs. A bomb? Really? I'm not a politician, not a person who has been in the news beyond the entertainment pages, and that was fourteen years ago. No one is going to send me a bomb.

Still, I inch toward the table, ears trained for any noise from upstairs. It's definitely a parcel. A courier package with all the appropriate labels and stamps for an overseas delivery. It's from the United States, and it's addressed to . . .

Lucy Callahan.

I haven't used that name in ten years.

CHAPTER TWO

NEW YORK 2005

I WAS REPLAYING the voice-mail message when my roommate walked into our dorm room.

Nylah waved at my cell phone. "It's called *telemarketing*, Lucy. Hang up."

I lowered the phone. "Hmm?"

"You looked confused, which means you're listening to some spiel about duct cleaning, making absolutely sure it's sales before you hang up." She paused. "No, actually, Lucy Callahan doesn't hang up on anyone. That would be rude."

I set the phone down and stepped aside so she could get to the coffee maker. No sane person came between Nylah and her 3 p.m. fix.

"It was actually a voice message from an old teacher," I said. "I took a summer film class with him a few years back."

"Ah, yes, film classes. Before you abandoned your Hollywood dreams for a musical career."

I rolled my eyes. While I loved film, I never earned more than faint praise for my directing and screenwriting. My viola playing, on the other hand, landed me here at Juilliard on a scholarship.

Nylah added grounds to her coffee maker. "Please tell me this former teacher called to say he's belatedly realized your brilliance and wants to offer you a paid internship." She paused, finger hovering over the Brew button. "Unless he's skeevy. Is there any chance he's been watching the calendar, waiting for you to turn eighteen? If so, do not return that call."

"First, he's in his fifties. Second, he's gay. Third, he's offering me a job teaching music."

Nylah sighed. Deeply. "The fact he's fifty doesn't mean he wouldn't hit on you, Luce. I'll accept *gay* as a potential disqualifier, but only if you've seen him with guys and he isn't just saying that to put female students at ease. And private music lessons?" She snorted. "It's not his flute you'll be blowing."

I shook my head as I sat at our tiny table. "Music lessons for *children*. Their parents have a beach house in the Hamptons, and I'd be there for the summer, teaching music while looking after the kids."

"Mary Poppins of the Hamptons? Not too shabby. So why the frowny-face when I came in?"

"Mr. Moore said I'd be working for 'Colt Gordon.' He repeated it three times like it was a big deal. Is that a person? A company?"

"C-Colt Gordon?" Nylah stammered. "*The* Colt Gordon?"

"You sound an awful lot like Mr. Moore. I should know the name, shouldn't I?"

"Did I just say you should go into film? I take that back if you don't know who Colt Gordon is. *The President's Wife*? *Fatal Retribution* one, two and three?"

"Oh, he's an actor, right?"

"That is like asking if Pavarotti is an opera singer. Colt Gordon is a bona fide movie *star*. Look up the top-grossing movies for the past five years. He starred in at least half of them."

"Wait! Isn't he married to Isabella Morales? Holy crap. I'd be working for *Isabella Morales*."

Nylah shrugged and spooned sugar into her coffee. "She's all right. I've seen her in a few things. Marrying him certainly helped her career."

"Helped—helped—?" I sputtered. "A pox on you and your

house, girl. Isabella Morales was a Mexican national treasure by the age of twelve. A freaking *legend* in the world of telenovelas."

Nylah rolled her eyes. "I'm about to get another lecture on the underappreciated art of telenovelas, aren't I?"

"Isabella Morales is a goddess. Started acting at the age of seven, and by eighteen, she was lead writer on her show. Totally self-taught. She began tweaking her scripts when she was a kid, and the writers humored her, but by the time she was a teenager, she wrote all her own lines and was drafting storylines, too. By twenty-one, she was directing."

"Then she married a huge American movie star and got to give up all that hard work for a cushy life raising his children." Nylah lifted her hands. "Kidding. Don't kill me. I just like to see that temper flare. You're a redhead and a Latina. You need to let that fire out more often. Live up to the double stereotype."

I'm only a quarter Latina. The rest is Irish and Italian, but if I point that out, Nylah claims that just gives me more reason to be tempestuous, one word that has never been used to describe me.

"Yes, Isabella did marry some action movie star," I said. "And she played a few roles in Hollywood movies, but she quit acting when she had kids. She continued writing for telenovelas, and she just started work on an American one she created herself. She'll be the producer."

"I get the feeling you're a fan of this Isabella chick."

I shot her a look.

"Which probably means you don't want to work for her, right?" Nylah said. "I mean, that'd be terrible, spending the summer in the Hamptons, living with a gorgeous movie star . . . and a woman you idolize."

Working for Isabella Morales.

I'd been offered a job working for *Isabella Morales*.

"I . . ." I swallowed. "That could be really awkward, with me being a fan, and—"

"Oh, my God, are you actually hesitating?" She shoved the phone at me. "Call him back, or I will."

I stared at the phone. Then I made the call.

CHAPTER THREE

ROME 2019

THE PARCEL SITS on my kitchen table, my former name screaming in block letters, and my past surges again, making my heart pound a drumbeat that steals my breath. My fingers tremble as I reach for the box. Then I remember the unlocked door. The courier service certainly doesn't have keys to my apartment. Does that mean whoever entered my apartment brought this inside for me?

Most considerate burglar *ever*.

I manage another weak laugh and roll my shoulders, struggling to stay calm. I made this choice. I came into this apartment, knowing the door was unlocked. If I'm really doing this, I need to see it through without collapsing in a heap on my kitchen floor.

My gaze slides to the stairs. It's a narrow flight, curving around to the loft bedroom. I back up and slide a knife from the drawer.

The problem with curving stairs is that there's no way to sneak up. The top of my head will appear before I can see anything.

I proceed slowly, holding my breath. I'll admit I'm starting to feel a little silly. I haven't heard even a floorboard creak since I've come in, and in a place this old, *every* board creaks.

The stairs open right into my bedroom. It used to remind me

of an attic garret, the sort of place I'd read about, where the family stores their crazy aunt, saving themselves the embarrassment she might cause. It's a little late for my family. Not that they'd ever complained. I stashed *myself* in Italy, and my garret cell has become a gorgeous nook instead, a cozy attic bedroom straight out of a little girl's dream.

From the stairs, I can see that my bed is empty. It's within arm's reach, a double mattress on the floor with no space for anyone to hide underneath. The minuscule bathroom is off to my right, and I can see it's empty. Across the room, the terrace door shutters stand open.

I didn't leave them like that.

I creep to the terrace door . . . which is actually a window. When I rented the place, the landlord told me to crawl through it to see the terrace. I thought he was joking. I'm accustomed to it now, and it's been at least a year since I bumped my head.

I crouch and peer through as I scan the sun-bright terrace. To my left, there's a pergola, the wooden frame lost in ivy and climbing flowers. Under that is a lounge chair . . . with a man sprawled on it, sunglasses propped on his head, his eyes closed as he dozes in the afternoon heat, wearing only his boxers.

I eye him, my head tilting. The incredible terrace view sold me on this apartment, but the current view under my pergola is even better. Marco lounges there, black hair curling over his forehead, brown skin glistening with sweat, athletic body showing off just the right amount of lean muscle. Excellent scenery, indeed. The problem is that he shouldn't be here. As I try to figure out why he is, my gaze crosses keys on the patio table.

As I set down the knife and lift the keys, they scrape over the glass top. My sleeping guest wakes, and gorgeous thick-lashed dark eyes travel up to my face.

"Forgot you gave me those, didn't you?" he says.

"No, I, uh . . ."

When I trail off, Marco sits up, legs swinging over the chair side.

"You do remember giving me your keys when you went home last month," he says. "But you forgot telling me I could hold on to them. Or that I could pop by if I had an extended afternoon break."

"Right. Sorry, I . . ."

He's on his feet, arms going around me, lips coming to mine. As I kiss him back, he takes the keys and tucks them into my back pocket.

"Yours, *dolcezza*," Marco says.

"No. I said you could hold on to them."

"Only because it was awkward taking your keys back from the guy you've been sleeping with for two years."

"I—"

Another kiss, cutting me off. "I'm teasing, Genevieve. For the past month, I've been telling myself you didn't really want me hanging out in your apartment, but today, my Colosseum tour was canceled, and I decided to test my theory."

I hold out the keys. "Keep them. I forgot, so I was surprised. That's all."

Which is true, but he *is* right. Taking the keys back after he house-sat would have been awkward, so I'd mumbled something about him using my apartment during breaks.

I also don't fail to notice he said we'd been "sleeping together" for two years. Not seeing each other. Not dating. Sleeping together. That isn't Marco being a jerk. He's phrasing it that way for my benefit, because every time he calls me his girlfriend, I tense as if he's shoving a diamond ring onto my finger.

In my mind, Marco is my lover, which sounds very sexy and European, when really, it's just me drawing a line. A meaningless line when we've been together exclusively for twenty-eight months.

I have relationship issues, and Marco respects that. But if I've fallen in love with this new life, a lot of it is due to the guy standing in front of me. I won't say I'm in love with *him*—I'm not quite ready for that—but if I deny this is serious, a little voice calls me a liar.

So I give him back the keys, and put my arms around his neck and whisper in his ear, telling him how sexy he looked in that chair. That makes him chuckle and accept the change of subject . . . and accept the keys.

"Sit," he says. "I have prosecco chilling, and I grabbed an antipasto tray."

"I'll get it," I say. "We won't deprive the neighbors of the lovely scenery." I waggle my brows suggestively.

His headshake teases me for my very American sensibilities. No one will be shocked to look out their window and see a guy in his boxers. They'll either enjoy the sight or ignore it.

Marco is very familiar with those American sensibilities, having lived in the US for a decade, going to college and then staying until . . . Well, I'm not sure what. Something brought him home, and I get the feeling it wasn't homesickness, but if I'm not going to discuss my past, I can't press him on his.

Having lived in the US, though, means that while he might tease me for my American ways, he never judges me for them. Nor does he need American idioms and pop culture explained. He's also been invaluable for improving my Italian and my accent, and when it's just us, we surf between languages, often switching midsentence.

I insist on bringing the snack and nudge him back into the lounge chair.

"Oh," he calls as I walk away. "There was a package at the door. I brought it in, but they have the wrong person."

I pause, having forgotten all about the parcel.

"It's for a Lucy Callahan," he says. "Someone must have looked up Callahan online and got your address. Not sure how you confuse Lucy and Genevieve."

"Weird," I say, crawling through the door-window before he catches my expression.

"I can drop it off at the mail depot tomorrow," he says.

"No, I'll handle it. Thanks, though."

I continue downstairs, where the parcel waits, my old name in those huge black letters. So I've solved the mystery of how it got into the apartment. The mystery of what's inside remains, but it pales next to the question of who sent it. The few people who know I'm here would never make the mistake of using that name.

Someone has tracked me down.

I approach the box and look for the sender. There's only an account number. When I gingerly turn the package over, I see the transit stamp. Originating in New York.

Has an enterprising journalist found me? That's always possible, but a journalist would send a letter, not a boxed gift as a bribe. They trade in the currency of promises and threats. Threats to expose me if I don't cooperate and promises to tell "my side of the story." I learned my lesson the hard way.

Thinking of New York and publishing, my mind moves to books. Did some enterprising junior editor dig up my story and see a tell-all book in it? Send me a box of their other books to entice me?

No, thank you, junior editor. My story is my own, and my past can stay buried.

I lift the box and shake it, listening for the heavy thunk of books. Instead, I hear the whisper of something light and soft shifting from one end to the other.

I set the parcel down. Stare narrow eyed, as if I can switch on X-ray vision.

Or I could, you know, just open the box.

I run a nail over the packing tape, creasing it. Then I tuck the box under the small kitchen table and head to the fridge for our midafternoon snack.

It's 2 a.m., and I'm lying awake, thinking about that damned parcel. I can't open it until Marco leaves. It's a lovely excuse. And total bullshit. Marco's so deeply asleep that if the apartment burst into flames, I'd need to fireman-carry him down five flights of stairs.

As a tour guide, he's the one who handles all the physically challenging excursions—from rowing the Tiber to climbing Mount Vesuvius. He also moonlights as a bike courier, which is still rare in Rome, city of scooters and mopeds and tiny trucks. When he sleeps, he's dead to the world.

As if to test my theory, I brush a curl from his face. His breathing doesn't even hitch. I smile and settle in, watching him sleep. His face would be model handsome if not for a broken nose that didn't quite set and an upper-lip scar from cleft lip surgery. Yet the flaws only improve the package, making him a real person with a face that tells a story. A face that also complements his personality—easygoing and authentic, relaxed and charming. Tour guides make minimum wage, but Marco's tips triple that with twenty-euro bills from the middle-aged men who enjoy his camaraderie, elderly women who appreciate his old-world manners and college girls who fold their phone numbers inside those bills.

I met him on a tour myself. It'd been the Pompeii and Mount Vesuvius one. I'd arrived late, and the only seat left on the bus was the one beside him. During the two-hour ride, polite conversation had turned real as we discovered shared passions for medieval history and old movies.

A week after that, I bumped into him at my favorite morning cappuccino spot. It wasn't until months later that he reminded me that he'd asked for coffee shop recommendations under the guise of passing them on to clients. Then he'd popped in for cappuccino every now and then, hoping for that "casual encounter."

The trip down memory lane, though, doesn't divert me. That package waits downstairs, and I could safely open it while Marco sleeps.

I need to open it. I won't rest until I do. I'm just afraid.

Afraid? No, terrified.

Ten years ago, I fled the US, planning to live a transitory life abroad. See the world while never settling in one place. I'd spend two years in England, two in France, two in Germany, two in Italy . . . That was four years ago. Rome stuck, and I will not allow that box to detonate my life here.

I didn't fight hard enough the last time. I was too young, too bruised. I will fight for this, and the battle begins with opening the damn package.

Marco doesn't stir as I slide from bed. I tiptoe down the steps. They creak, as usual, and I pause at the bottom, straining to listen as the apartment remains silent.

I lift the package and set it on the table. Then I ease a knife from the drawer, slit the tape and tug one cardboard flap. It opens to show another box inside. A glossy snow-white box with a crimson lid, wrapped in a thick, black ribbon shot through with glittering silver thread. In silver script, the lid proclaims, "Ainsworth & Kent." It's a gift box from a Fifth Avenue staple, one I wouldn't dare set foot in.

I tug one end of the bow, and it dissolves into a puddle of black velvet. Inside, bright red tissue paper is fastened with a silver Ainsworth & Kent seal. I peel back the seal and unfold multiple layers of tissue, first red and then gray and then white. The final layer reveals folded cashmere. I pull it out and find myself holding a silver-gray cashmere shrug with a single ebony button in the shape of a violin.

I lift the shrug for a better look. It's like hoisting a cloud, and I can imagine draping it over my shoulders when Marco and I go out at night. Light enough to tuck into a bag, the color suitable for any dress. The button shows this is no random present. Someone took great care with their selection.

I remove the gift box from the cardboard package. It seems empty, but as I lift it, something shifts in the bottom. It's a white envelope with "Lucy" written in looping script.

I touch my name, and a memory nudges. A letter with my name written in the same hand. The memory sinks leaden in my gut, and my fingers tremble. When I try to snag the memory, though, my mind slams shut and refuses to divulge a name.

I slit open the envelope. Inside is a folded sheet of paper. As I pull it out, my gut twists. That flash of memory again. My name on an envelope. Pulling out a folded sheet. Reading . . .

The memory reel snaps, leaving only my clenching gut and the smell of . . .

Jasmine?

I lift the paper. It doesn't smell of jasmine. Doesn't smell of anything. That's the memory, jasmine-scented paper, and I'd opened the envelope, my heart lifting, so certain that that letter would contain . . .

Again, the memory clamps shut.

Just open the letter, Lucy.

I still call myself Lucy. My full name is Genevieve Lucille Callahan, after my two grandmothers. According to family lore, my dad struggled with Genevieve. It didn't roll off his tongue, and he misspelled it on my birth notice even though it was *his* mother's name.

Dad used Lucy as his pet name for me. He died when I was five—T-boned by a drunk driver—and I started going by Lucy in tribute to him. I'd reverted to Genevieve when I decided to make a fresh start in Europe, but in my head, I will always be Lucy even if, at times, that feels like self-flagellation, the occasional lash to remind me I will never truly be Genevieve with her quirkily unorthodox and deeply satisfying life.

Just open the damn letter, Lucy.

Yes, I'm procrastinating. I know from experience that it does no good. How many days did I tell myself that if I just didn't look at the news, it wouldn't exist? The news exists. My story exists. This letter exists.

Deep breath . . .

I unfold it.

Dear Lucy

> I know I'm the last person you want to hear from—

I freeze. I'm not even certain I process the words. I see that salutation, in that script, and the memory slams back, that jasmine-scented letter in this same hand.

Dear Lucy,
> *I trusted you. With my children. With my home. With my husband.*

The letter falls to the floor as I clench the table edge. The floor seems to dip under my feet, and I want to drop to it. Drop and bang my head against it for not recognizing that damned perfect handwriting.

I snatch the letter from the floor, march across the tiny kitchen and yank open a drawer. I have to dig to the back of the assorted junk—paper clips, elastic bands, take-out cards—until my fingers close around a small cardboard box.

I strike a wooden match, flame hissing to life. Then I hold up the letter and . . .

I hesitate there, the flame an inch from the paper. Hesitate and then snuff out the match with my fingers and let it drop to the floor.

A fine sentiment, but if I burn this letter, I'll only spend more sleepless nights wondering what she'd said, what she wanted, what she was threatening to do if she didn't get it.

Isabella Morales knows where I am.

Of all the people I fear having that information, Isabella tops the list. I haven't heard from her since that infamous letter, and now something has happened to make her reach out, and that bodes no good.

I turn the letter over and begin reading again.

> Dear Lucy
> I know I'm the last person you want to hear from, but we need to

talk. While I understand you're in Italy, I'm hoping I can persuade you to come to New York for a weekend, at my expense, of course. If you would prefer I came to Rome, I'd happily do that, but I suspect you won't want me intruding on the life you've built there.

I have never forgotten what happened fourteen years ago. I suppose that goes without saying. But as time has passed, I've gained enough distance—and, I hope, wisdom—to look back on the events that transpired and realize you were little more than a child, and he took advantage of that. In my pain, I needed someone to blame. I should have aimed that anger at him. Instead, I turned it on you.

I know I cannot make amends, but I would like to talk. Please call me on my private cell so we may arrange a visit.

She gives her number and then signs with a familiar flourish.

This is exactly what I wanted to read fourteen years ago when my trembling fingers tore open that first letter. I hadn't spoken to Isabella since the incident a month earlier, and enough time would have passed for her to realize there had to be more to the story. She would contact me, and I would tell her everything. I would apologize—fall on my knees and apologize—and she would hug me and tell me it wasn't my fault.

Of everyone I'd hurt that day, this was the trespass that kept me awake at night. Isabella had been nothing but kind to me, and I'd made a stupid and juvenile mistake. She needed to know it wasn't what the tabloids said.

I hoped for an opening into which I could pour my apologies. Instead, her letter swam blood-red with hate and invective that sliced me open worse than any screaming tabloid headline.

And now, fourteen years later, she has sent the letter I dreamed of that day.

I read it again, and I do not fall to my knees with relief. I feel only emptiness edged with annoyance and, if I'm being honest, a hint of outrage.

Now she feels bad? *Now* she realizes she was wrong? *Now* she wants to talk to me about it?

I reassemble the package with the cashmere shrug and put it into the closet under the stairs. Then I strike another match, set the corner of the letter alight and watch it burn, charred bits dropping into the sink. When the flame warms my fingers, I drop what's left and watch the paper curl and blacken.

Then I run water in the sink and let the tissue-thin black pieces dissolve and run down the drain.

Footsteps sound on the stairs. I grab a glass from the drying rack and fill it as Marco descends. It's only when I turn that I see the opened envelope still on the table, with "Lucy" screaming on the front.

I dart between the envelope and the stairs.

Marco blinks at me. "Everything okay?"

I lift the glass, half-filled with water. He nods and yawns.

"You want one?" I ask.

He shakes his head. Then he sniffs. "Is something burning?"

"Outside, I think." I wave at the open window.

When he reaches for me, I hesitate. I want to go to him, to fall into his arms and take comfort there.

I have this new life, Isabella, and you cannot touch it.

Except she can touch it. The envelope proves that, and I cannot let Marco see it. So when he reaches for me, I lift the water glass. He takes it with a chuckle and says, "I'll put it on your side of the bed," as he retreats.

Once he's gone, I snatch the envelope and tuck it into a stack of music books for later burning. Then I follow him upstairs.

CHAPTER FOUR

THE HAMPTONS 2005

THE CAB DROPPED me off at the end of a long, curving drive. Nylah had joked about Mary Poppins, but that was who I felt like as the car pulled away, leaving me standing there, clutching my bag.

This couldn't be the right place. Admittedly, I didn't know much about Hollywood stars, but I was certain someone of Colt Gordon's caliber summered in a gated community, his house fenced and patrolled by gun-toting guards with Rottweilers. According to Nylah, this was a family who couldn't take their kids to school without attracting a conga line of paparazzi. Yet here I stood, at the end of a gate-free driveway, having passed through zero security on my way in.

It had to be the wrong address.

Or I'd been scammed.

I trusted Mr. Moore, but I'd had no direct contact with Colt Gordon or Isabella Morales. I'd only been interviewed by a woman named Karla Ellis, who claimed to be Colt Gordon's manager.

She certainly *seemed* like a celebrity manager, all designer pantsuits and cool efficiency. It also made sense that Colt Gordon and Isabella Morales would let their manager handle staff hiring —running background checks, getting NDAs signed—and Ms.

Ellis had done all that. I might feel inadequate for the position, but if I pushed aside my lack of confidence, I did have the experience: years of babysitting, children's music lessons and lifeguard summer jobs. Ms. Ellis had checked my references, so the job did seem real.

When she'd offered car service from the airport, I should have accepted. At least then I'd be certain I had the right place.

As I made my way down the long drive, I spotted a gardener. The front yard was clearly the work of experts—at least a half acre of rolling green lawn and gardens filled with tall grasses that swayed like ocean waves. In one of those gardens, a woman knelt, tugging weeds.

As I walked over, she twisted to toss a weed into the bucket, and I saw her face.

Isabella Morales.

I stood there, mouth opening and closing in the perfect imitation of a beached fish. She saw me—or heard the *gulp-gulp* of my fish breathing. As she turned, she fixed me with the smile that smote a million telenovela addicts, and I nearly did a schoolgirl swoon.

"Ms—Ms. Morales?" I managed. "I—I'm sorry for sneaking up. I thought . . ."

"That I was the gardener?"

I was about to say yes. Then I noticed her smile had dimmed, and I realized how that sounded—mistaking a Latina for the hired help. Which wasn't the case at all—I'd only seen her back and giant sun hat.

"No," I said. "I thought I had the wrong house. I expected . . ." I gestured like an idiot. "Armed guards and piranha-filled moats."

She chuckled and pushed to her feet. "We leave our piranha in LA, where they feel more at home." She peeled off her dirt-crusted gloves. "The security here is far more discreet. It's a very small community, and the summer residents contribute generously to the local law enforcement. The neighborhood also hires private security to patrol. I'd warned them you were coming today, but I still expected—"

The buzz of a cell phone. She took it out, glanced at the screen and smiled. "And there it is. A text telling me that your taxi was spotted." She tapped out a reply. "We're spoiled out here. It's a chance to give our kids the illusion of a normal life, but it really is an illusion. I'll need to send your photograph to the security firm and the local police department, or the first time you go out walking, they'll escort you to the village border."

As she pocketed the phone, I got my first good look at her. She was smaller than I expected. Maybe five feet two. A scarf barely contained her long black curls. Oversized sunglasses covered half her face, but the skin below it was flawless and makeup-free. She wore a sundress under a gardening apron, and the dress showed off the curves that were as much her trademark as that smile.

Isabella Morales had the kind of figure that shouldn't be possible—lush curves with a tiny waist. I'd read tabloid articles that insisted her waist was the result of industrial-strength corsets. Yet there was no way she had shapewear under that sundress, and the apron was cinched tight enough to show her waist in all its enviable glory. My waist might not be a whole lot bigger, but only because I had the narrow hips and chest to match.

When Isabella reached for the weed bucket, I picked it up and got a smile for that. Then she said, "The kids are out back. Colt's inside, I think. I suppose you'll want to meet him."

She said it lightly, as if aiming between wry and teasing, but a note of tightness cut through.

When I didn't answer, she glanced over, her brows rising. "Not a Colt Gordon fan?"

My face heated. "I . . . I've seen *Fatal Retribution*. The first one, at least."

Nylah had gifted me DVDs of the other two, and I'd meant to watch them, but I'd run out of time. I stumbled on with, "I liked it. I'm just not really into action movies. I'm more a telenovela fan.

Mi Hermana was just . . . It was amazing, and it got even better after you started writing for it and . . ."

My cheeks blazed, threatening nuclear-grade heat. "I-I'm sorry. I didn't mean to fangirl. I won't do that while I'm here. I promise. I know it'd be awkward. I'm just . . . My *abuela* got me into telenovelas, and I've followed your career and—"

I swallowed hard. "God, that sounds stalkerish, doesn't it? I'm so sorry. I'm just a fan of your career, what you've accomplished, and I didn't angle for this job. I didn't even know it was you. Mr. Moore said it was for Colt Gordon, and I didn't recognize his name and—" I stopped in horror.

She laughed, a throw-back-her-head laugh that echoed through the yard as I prayed for the earth to open up and swallow me.

"I'm sorry, Ms. Morales," I said. "I'm babbling, and I—"

She reached out and squeezed my upper arm. "You're fine, Lucy. We just won't tell Colt that you didn't know who he is." She grinned, dark eyes sparkling. "Don't worry—following my career isn't stalkerish. The real stalkers don't give a rat's ass about my actual achievements. Now, come and meet my family."

ISABELLA LED ME INTO A COOL, shady house, every window thrown wide to let the sea breeze waft through. There was nothing about the decor that screamed, "interior designer," but it was the kind of beach house that you saw in a magazine and tacked up on your dream-life wall. Every piece of furniture whispered a siren's call, inviting you to curl up with a book and a lemonade. Even strawberry lemonade would be fine. No need to worry about stains. This was a house for sandy feet and spilled wine and wet hair.

"Colt?" Isabella called as we walked through the living room. Then louder, "Colt?"

She turned to me and shook her head. "Either he's gone for a run, or he's in the exercise room. That's what happens when you hit forty and dream of being the next James Bond. Once again, I am grateful to be working off-camera."

Isabella opened one set of patio doors. The back wall was all window with multiple doors. She led me onto a stone deck surrounding an in-ground pool.

"Yes, we have a pool two hundred feet from the beach," she said, sounding almost embarrassed. "The water can be cold and . . . Well, while it's a private beach, the waterfront is public. We certainly do let the kids use the beach, but if passing boats linger, please let us know. And if you see a camera . . ."

"I'll bring the children in immediately and let you or Mr. Gordon know."

"Colt. He will insist on Colt, and I'll insist on Isabella. Now, speaking of the kids, they should be right over here."

We passed a low wall to find a boy swimming. That would be eight-year-old Jamison. He was reedy with sun-bleached hair and peeling red skin on his shoulders. The older girl reading on a lounge chair was Tiana. At ten, she had her mother's brown skin, sturdier build and dark wavy hair.

"Jamie," Isabella said with a sigh. "Where is your swim shirt?"

"Same place it always is," Tiana said without glancing from her book. "*Not* on him."

"I don't need it when I'm swimming," Jamison said.

"It's a swim shirt, dork," Tiana muttered. "When else would you wear it? While skydiving?"

He started to respond. Then he saw me, his freckled nose scrunching. Before I could say hello, he dove.

"That's Jamie," Tiana said, and now she looked up, her sunglass-framed eyes on me. "He's not being rude. He's just avoiding conversation, which sure, is kind of rude, but he doesn't mean it like that."

She set the book down and rose with a grace as mature as her words, and when she extended a hand, I hurried to shake it . . . and tripped over the leg of a lounge chair. As I stammered apologies, Tiana's lips pressed together. She lifted her glasses onto her head, and her eyes met mine.

"We're just kids," she said.

Behind me, Isabella admonished her daughter, but I knew what lay behind Tiana's very adult look of disapproval: years of people stumbling over themselves around her family, years of not being treated like a normal child. And oh, look, here was her new music tutor, starstruck already, stammering and stumbling, eager to e-mail her friends with "OMG, I'm here!!!" complete with surreptitiously snapped photos.

When she said, "We're just kids," I paused only a heartbeat before coming back with, "And I'm just a klutz." I took her hand in a firm clasp. "Lucy. Your Mary Poppins for the summer."

As I said it, I realized the reference might not mean anything to her, but she snorted and rolled her eyes.

"You gonna teach me to sing and dance on rooftops?" she asked.

"Sing, yes. As for dancing . . . you did notice me tripping over my own feet, right?"

Another snort, but some of the disapproval leached from her eyes. She lowered herself onto her lounge chair again and picked up her book. I glanced at the cover, expecting something suitably tween-friendly. It was *1984*.

"Nice beach read," I said.

The corners of her mouth twitched. "I thought so."

Behind us, Isabella held the swim shirt over the pool edge for Jamison, who was ignoring her by swimming underwater. I kicked off my sandals, took the shirt and jumped in, not even thinking of what I was doing until the water closed over my head.

I caught Isabella's laugh of surprise and Tiana's muffled voice, but I stayed under, holding the swim shirt out for Jamison. He saw me, his dark eyes widening. We both surfaced, and he took the shirt with a crooked smile.

"That's one way to do it," Isabella said, still laughing.

I swam to the side just as feet slapped on concrete, and Tiana said, "Hey, Dad."

I glanced up, straight into the sun, and squinted. I could only make out the shape of a man. I started to heave myself out. Then I realized I was wearing a soaking-wet sundress and dropped back into the water.

"Jamie was being a goof," Tiana said, "pretending he couldn't see Mom with his swim shirt. Our summer Mary Poppins fixed the problem."

A low chuckle. "I see that."

The figure bent at the poolside, and a hand appeared from the sun-shaded shadow. I squinted up into a face that sent a jolt of recognition through me. I might have blanked on Colt Gordon's name, but seeing that square jaw, the cleft chin, those bright blue eyes, I instantly recognized him.

Those eyes met mine in a direct look that only lasted a second before they moved on, to my relief. I was an eighteen-year-old girl in a movie star's house—I didn't *want* to catch his attention. But he met my gaze only perfunctorily, quickly shook my upheld hand, and then rose, calling to Jamison.

"Give me a minute to change, buddy, and then I'll join you while Lucy gets herself settled in."

Jamison nodded, and with a peck on Isabella's cheek, Colt strode into the house.

I exhaled and climbed out as Isabella handed me a towel.

CHAPTER FIVE

ROME 2019

Normally, Thursdays are my least favorite day of the week. It's my busiest, gone from dawn until dusk, with barely enough time to grab an espresso between gigs. Today, though, I thank God it's Thursday. It keeps me too busy to think of that letter.

The canary in the coal mine, warning of impending explosion.

I will not allow the explosion this time. I'll wait it out and pray Isabella takes a hint and backs off.

That day, I teach, and I play, and I teach some more and play some more. It's not the New York Philharmonic, but in many ways, this is better. Less stress and more job security.

At one time, I looked at musicians like me, hustling with side gigs, and I pitied them. They'd clearly failed in their chosen career. Now I know better. I am happier here than I ever would have been as first viola in a major orchestra. For every kid who sulks through my lessons, there's another who loves it the way I did or an adult who comes home from a long day and cannot wait to make music. Then I play with my small groups, all of us playing for the sheer love of it, with an audience who is there by choice, no one suffering through while reminding themselves that they're supporting the arts.

After an 8 p.m. outdoor performance, I should be dragging my ass home, but I'm floating instead. This evening, Marco has back-to-back tours through the Capuchin Crypt and Catacombs of Priscilla, and we're texting as I walk home. That's normal for us. When we're together, we talk as if we haven't seen each other in weeks. When we're apart, there's a casual back and forth that can last for hours, an unhurried exchange that'll go twenty minutes between responses while he's busy with his tours and I'm busy with my lessons or performances..

Tonight, someone suffered an emotional break down in the crypt bone chapel. It happens. The chapel is an artistic display of monks' bones with a singular message: someday, this will be you. It's a powerful memento mori. Too powerful for some. Marco handled the situation with grace, as always. He has a degree in psychology, and while he's never used it—as far as I know—he has a therapist's knack for dealing with stressed tourists.

As I walk, I pause on the Garibaldi Bridge to gaze out at the lights reflected in the Tiber below. Tourists pass, a dozen languages of excited chatter swirling around me. It's a gorgeous night, and I'm walking alone through the streets of Rome, and I have rarely been happier. My youngest student performed her first piece today. I got to play a solo in a historic Roman park. And my lover is keeping me entertained with amusing missives from tour-guide life. I fairly float over the cobblestone roads, and then swing up my endless flights of stairs and stumble into my apartment, where I will raid the fridge for a late dinner on the terrace. I'll also suggest that Marco stop by for the night since his tour ends a half mile away.

I'm barely through my apartment door when someone raps on it. With that knock, every good thing in my day evaporates, vaulting me back to the night before.

Another knock. I check the peephole to see a young woman in a delivery-service uniform. My gut twists, and I back away from the door. Then I steel myself and yank it open.

"Jenny?" she says.

I smile with relief, and she hands me a steaming box. When

she's gone, I open it. Inside is dinner—piping hot carbonara pizza from Dar Poeta. There's a receipt attached, with the sender's name, though I don't need to check it. Only one person knows that I use Jenny for deliveries. Say, "Genevieve," and you spend five minutes spelling it.

I send Marco a text.

Me: You're amazing. You know that, right?
Him: I do. Someone told me that just last night.
Him: Oh, wait. That was you.
Him: This is why I was being nosy, asking when you'd be
    home.
Him: I know you had a long day, and you seemed a little
    off this morning. I figured you could use a pick-me-up.

I start to type "Best boyfriend evah!" I delete it, and I tell myself it's because I'm fifteen years past being able to use *evah*, even jokingly.

Instead, I send "Thank you!!!" as if the multiple exclamation marks compensate for my inability to say the b-word.

Me: If you come by tonight, I can thank you properly.

I add a few suggestive emojis after that.

Him: You'll make me stuffed eggplant? Awesome.
Me: If you'd rather have eggplant, I believe I have one in
    the fridge.
Him: LOL. No, I'll take what you were really putting on the
    menu.
Me: Good, and I might even save you a piece of pizza.
Him: I'll understand if you don't.

As we sign off, I'm already slurping strands of gooey bacon-and-garlic-flecked cheese from my pizza. I cut off a slice and put it on a plate for Marco. Then I grab the pizza box, napkins and a bottle of fizzy water and head for the stairs.

As I'm turning, I spot a white envelope on the floor.

My heart thuds, and I cover the distance in two running steps, pizza box slapping onto the table as I dive for what I'm certain is yesterday's envelope, which I'd forgotten to burn. Even as I grab it, though, I know it's not the same one.

This letter hasn't been opened.

There's a new envelope on my floor. Under my table. I eye it and exhale with a soft laugh. Okay, a courier pushed it under the door, and it slid beneath the table. Mystery solved.

Sitting cross-legged on the floor, I turn the envelope over.

Lucy Callahan.

The name isn't in Isabella's handwriting. It's typed onto a label, cold and informal. No sender. No postage marks.

Two days ago, I wouldn't have opened this. At best, it would be the ravings of a crazed Colt Gordon fan, still determined to make me pay for my "sins."

After receiving Isabella's letter, I know the timing of this one is not coincidental. Is there some fresh threat that she'd been trying to warn me about? Is this envelope connected to her letter? Someone found out she was contacting me and did the same?

Colt?

Tiana or Jamison?

The last two make me shiver, hairs on my arms rising. I've spent fourteen years struggling not to consider what monstrous role I play in Tiana and Jamison's personal mythology. I might be furious with Colt and hurt by Isabella, but if you asked me who I most dreaded seeing again, it would be their children.

I open the envelope to find a typed letter. My gaze moves to the sender first. Isabella.

I curse under my breath. Then I pause. Is this really from her? A typed letter after a personal handwritten note makes no sense. Someone must be impersonating . . .

My gaze skims the first few lines, and my question is answered.

Lucy,

Please excuse the formality and impersonality of this letter. I know the package I sent was delivered Wednesday afternoon. It is now Thursday evening, and I haven't received a call, which suggests I'm not going to. So I've prevailed upon a local acquaintance to print this letter and have it hand delivered.

I don't blame you for not calling. I had hoped you would, but I can understand why you didn't. You may even have seen my handwriting and torn up the letter unread. I would understand that, too.

I really do want to put this right. Someone in my life has helped me to understand that what I feel is no longer anger. It's guilt. I did wrong by you, and I need to remedy that.

I realize it's selfish to ask you to come here. I'm still asking. Below you will find the number of a local travel agent who has been instructed to arrange for a first-class round-trip ticket to New York and a two-week stay, all expenses paid. Our meeting will not take two weeks, of course, but I thought extending your stay into a holiday might alleviate the inconvenience.

We must talk, and it will be worth your while. I don't mean the airfare or the hotel—that is incidental. I am going to repair the damage you suffered. I can give you back your life, Lucy. I just need to speak to you in person.

No, Isabella, you do not need to speak to me in person. You do not need to speak to me at all. I'm sorry if you feel bad about what happened . . .

Am I sorry?

No, actually, I'm not. That's the old Lucy bubbling to the surface. She's like a childhood friend I remember with alternating spurts of affection and exasperation. The Lucy who, as Nylah rightly said, couldn't hang up even on a telemarketer.

I'm not pleased that Isabella is suffering. I'll never be that cold or vindictive. Yet I won't fly to New York to clear her conscience. She says she can give me my life back, but I already have that. There's nothing more she can offer.

I'm still staring at the letter when a familiar *bang-ba-ba-bang* sounds at the door, and I scramble to tuck the letter, envelope and all, into my bag. Then I yank open the door, throw my arms around Marco's neck and pour all my frustration into a kiss that leaves him gasping.

"So . . . good pizza?" he says.

"I've barely started it. I was heading outside when I got distracted. E-mails."

He looks down at me. "Everything okay?"

"Just messages that needed an answer."

"Ah."

His gaze bores into mine, and I squirm under it. I replay my words, my tone, and it all sounds very normal. Even the kiss at the door isn't out of character.

I only need to see his expression, though, to know I've failed to pull off the "I'm okay" charade. As usual, Marco doesn't call me on it. I just get that searching look and a pause that I should fill with "Actually, yes, something happened." When I don't take the hint, he only gives me a smacking kiss on the lips, granting me my freedom and my privacy.

"All right, then," he says. "Let me rummage something from the fridge."

I hand him the plate with a quarter of the pizza. He smiles and accepts it with thanks. Then I miraculously change my water into wine—grabbing a bottle of red from the counter—as he gets glasses, and we head out onto the terrace.

NIGHT TWO OF NOT SLEEPING. This time, it's that letter calling my name. The more I think about it, the angrier I get. How dare Isabella invade my privacy? How dare she send anything under my old name? All it would take is for someone along the mailing route to say, "Hmm, why does that name sound familiar?" and follow it to a Colt Gordon fan board and post "Hey, I found where Lucy Callahan lives. Anyone willing to pay for that information?"

If Isabella wants to make amends, she can damn well leave me alone. That's what I want from her. *All* I want from her. Does she really think I'm going to squeal in delight at a cashmere shrug and a first-class plane ticket? I'm not that girl anymore.

And yet . . .

I've said I will fight this, and fighting it does not mean ignoring Isabella and hoping she goes away. If I even think that's possible, I've forgotten everything I know about the woman. To truly fight, I must go to New York. Take this meeting. Tell her I'm glad she has had this epiphany, but if she really cares about helping, she'll leave me the hell alone.

I could do that on my own dime. Lift my chin, buy my own ticket, reserve my own hotel room . . . and blow my meager life savings on this trip. That'll teach her.

If Isabella wants to throw blood money at me, let her. While I'd never be spiteful enough to rack up a bill with room-service caviar and champagne, I *will* enjoy the trip, and I will get what I need from it. Peace, at last. My past buried not in shame but in quiet reverence for a life I've left behind.

I send a message agreeing to the trip.

Sleep comes easily after that.

CHAPTER SIX

THE HAMPTONS 2005

AFTER TWO WEEKS at Colt and Isabella's place, I'd settled in enough that I even mentally referred to them by their first names. On that day, I'd taken my own role in the exact same scene I'd walked into that first day. Jamison swam in the pool while Tiana reclined on a chair with me lounging beside her, both of us holding novels while we talked about boys.

"You do know that's weird, right?" she said. "You should have a boyfriend by now." She lowered her glasses to look over them. "Do you like girls? It's okay if you do. We've got friends with two dads, friends with two moms, friends with two of each, even, all living together. It's Hollywood."

I chuckled. By now, I was past the point of being surprised by this ten-year-old girl. She'd been raised in a world where kids didn't stay kids for long, no matter how much their parents tried to shelter them. Part of this was an act, too—Tiana was playing the world-weary ingenue to impress me. Or shock me. If she hoped to do that with her talk of same-sex and polyamorous couples, she was barking up the wrong tree. I was a musician.

"I like boys, and I *have* dated," I said. "I didn't have a high-school boyfriend because I didn't want anything keeping me in

Albany after graduation. Now that I'm at Juilliard, I don't have time to date."

"Have you had sex?"

"Your parents would *love* it if I answered that."

"Actually, they'd be fine with it. You're a role model, and I have important life questions that require serious answers."

I snorted.

She grumbled. After a moment, she said, her voice quieter, "How did you know you liked boys?"

Resisting the urge to look over at her, I talked about my first crush—a bass player named Samson—and the telenovela stars whose posters decorated my wall, the boys I dreamed of kissing.

"Did you have any posters of my dad?"

"Nope."

"Did you ever dream of kissing *him*?"

Now I did look over, my nose wrinkling. "Eww, no. He's *old*."

She giggled, a true child's giggle, sputtering and snickering.

"What's so funny?" a voice asked, making me jump.

Colt strode off the patio. I'd come to realize that Colt Gordon did not "walk" anywhere. He strolled; he ambled; he sprinted. He was an actor—every movement and expression had to be imbued with meaning.

Today, he wore athletic shorts and nothing else. Well, I presume underwear, but trust me, I wasn't thinking about what Colt Gordon wore under his shorts.

I hadn't been lying when I told Tiana her dad was too old for my girlish fantasies. He *was* good looking. Criminally good looking, as Nylah would say. I could appreciate that, but it came with the mental corollary of *for his age.*

For his part, Colt never spared me more than a friendly smile. There'd been some initial discomfort, where he'd almost seemed to go out of his way to avoid me. I understood that. Every time he had lunch with a female co-star, the tabloids screamed that he was having a fling. People might say they love happy Hollywood marriages, but scandal is so much more delicious.

So Colt had been careful, making sure I wouldn't give off any flirty vibes myself. I must have passed that test with flying colors because he no longer walked out of a room if he found me alone in it. I didn't feel obligated to look away when he was dressed like this, either, which was good because he was almost always dressed like this.

When he repeated, "What's so funny?" Tiana glanced at me, her dark eyes twinkling. She opened her mouth, and I fairly leapt across the space between us. She rolled off the other way, giggling so hard she was snorting.

She looked at her dad, "Lucy said you're—"

I sprang at her again, half in mortification, half in jest, and she took off, grinning over her shoulder at me as she dove into the pool. I followed, and we horsed around for a few minutes before she swam to the edge and hoisted herself up in front of Colt, glancing back at me with a teasing grin.

"Lucy said—" she began.

"She said you're nicer than she expected," Jamison cut in. He'd been ignoring us, swimming laps, and I'd thought he hadn't heard anything. "You're scary in your movies, so she was worried. But she says you're pretty nice."

"Pretty nice?" Colt's brows shot up.

"Better than nice and pretty," Tiana said.

"Mmm, I don't know about that. I'm fine with pretty. I've been called worse." He looked at me, eyes twinkling exactly like his daughter's as he winked. A friendly wink, nothing more. Then he plunked into a chair. Tiana gave him a look, rolled her eyes at me, and we continued swimming.

CHAPTER SEVEN

ROME 2019

By morning, I have a message telling me everything has been arranged. I leave later today.

I tell Marco I'm going to New York for a few days, that something came up and a friend needs me.

"Nylah?" he asks.

I make a sound he can take as agreement.

"Everything okay?" he asks.

"Just stuff," I say. "I know it's very last minute . . ."

He tugs on his shirt. "I'm just glad you can help. I'd offer to come along, but this is obviously a girl trip."

"It is. I hope to see Mom, too, while I'm there."

"Good." He leans over to peck my cheek. "Tell her I said hi."

I nod, my face down as I button my shirt so he won't see my reaction . . . the one that says it's hard to do that when my mother doesn't know he exists.

"Got time for a cappuccino this morning?" he asks.

I smile at him. "Sadly, no. I'll just grab one on the way to my first lesson."

"Give me two minutes, and I'll walk with you."

• • •

As THE DAY WEARS ON, the deception pokes needle sharp. It's never *been* a deception before. Genevieve Callahan is my legal name. Marco knows I grew up in Albany and went to Juilliard. He knows I've never married, have no kids or siblings, just a mother in Albany, two grandparents in Arizona and a grandmother in Mexico. He's never pried into specifics of my past, and so I have never had to lie to him. Until now.

That evening, we're in a crowded airport taverna, leaning together so we can hear one another over the too-sharp laughter of tipsy businessmen. I've run out of time to tell Marco the truth, and this certainly isn't the place.

When I return.

I'll tell him everything when I return.

For now, there's something I can do, and even if he won't understand the significance, it is a silent promise to him.

I take out my phone and hold it up. "I want a selfie."

His brows rise.

"Of us," I say. "For my mom."

We put our heads together, and I snap pictures. In the last, he smacks a kiss on my cheek, and that is the best of the bunch—the unguarded delight on my face, the boyish glint in his eyes.

This photograph means that I will finally tell Mom about Marco. I will say, yes, there is someone important in my life, and here he is.

We finish our wine, and he walks me to the security area. Once he's out of sight, I zip over to the priority lane.

At the gate, I'm settling into a seat when I look up into the face of Colt Gordon, and every cell in my body freezes.

It's not actually Colt, of course. It's just his face—five times life-size, staring at me from an electronic movie poster.

This isn't the first time I've been confronted by his image. Colt is a Hollywood icon, and being male, his star didn't plummet once he hit middle age. At fifty-five, he's still an action hero though his love interests remarkably don't age at all.

On this poster, though, the second figure isn't a woman half his age. It's a young man who could have been Colt himself thirty years ago.

"Jamie," I murmur.

CHAPTER EIGHT

THE HAMPTONS 2005

A MONTH LATER, I was outside with the kids, giving them a music lesson. We were on the strip of land between the house and the beach, all sand and tall grasses. We'd pulled chairs out there to work in the morning sunshine, enjoying the sea breeze and ignoring the cacophonous percussion of the seagulls.

When footfalls thumped over the sand, I didn't even need to turn to see who it was. Sure enough, Colt appeared, dressed only in his shorts, a sheaf of papers in his hand.

"Where's your mom?" he asked Tiana.

"Internet sucks this morning. She went into town to send some e-mails."

Irritation flashed over his face. Then he spun on me and waved the papers. "You've done screenwriting, right?"

"Uh, a little, but—"

He shoved the script at me. "It's a fight scene, and I'm supposed to grab the guy like . . ." He finger waved at Jamison. "I need an assistant."

Jamison shook his head and focused on adjusting his tuning pegs. "No, thank you."

Colt strode over and took the violin sharply enough that I

cringed. He set it down and put a hand on Jamison's shoulder. "Come and help your old man out."

"I will," Tiana said, hopping to her feet.

"It's a fight scene," Colt said. "Jamie's my man for this. Aren't you, kiddo?"

"I would rather not," Jamison said in that quiet, formal way of his. "Tiana can."

"I'm not going to hurt you," Colt said with an eye roll.

"I know. I just don't like doing that."

"Don't like what? Helping your old man? It's a *fight* scene. It's fun."

"Not to me."

Silence. I opened my mouth to say something, but before I could, Jamison rose and said, "I'm not feeling very good. I'm going inside."

He took one step, and then Colt grabbed him in a headlock. Jamison yelped, and Colt laughed, flipping his son over and mock pinning him to the ground. And I . . . I stood there feeling sick and doing nothing. Colt was goofing around, not hurting Jamison, and I couldn't see Jamison's face. I glanced at Tiana, who cast me an uncomfortable look, paired with a nervous laugh, and then joined in, pushing at her dad and pretending to play fight him, and somewhere in the melee, Jamison ran for the house while his dad and sister roughhoused.

I slipped off after Jamison. I could hear him in his room, and I paced for a few minutes, hoping Isabella would return. I was just the music tutor, and I shouldn't interfere, but Jamison was upset, and I needed to do something.

If his bedroom door had been closed, I'd have retreated. It was cracked open, though, and from inside came the sound of crumpling paper. I tapped on the door, and it swung open, and there was Jamison, his face taut with rage as he ripped pages from a book, balling them up and whipping them at the wall.

Then he saw me and froze, and from the look on his face, you'd think I'd walked in to find him torturing a small animal. He quickly hid the book behind his back and stammered something unintelligible.

"May I come in?" I asked.

When he hesitated, I began to retreat. Then he said, "Yes," and I walked in and shut the door.

"I'm sorry," I said. "That was . . ." I stumbled because, again, this was not my place. So I only repeated, "I'm sorry."

Jamison nodded and took the book out from behind his back, and I could see it wasn't a book at all. It was a bound script.

Jamison's hands shook as he looked down at the script, at the pages across his room. The shaking spread until his whole body quivered with it.

"Hey, hey," I said, walking to him, my arms out. "It's okay. It's just a script, and you were mad."

He opened his mouth. Then he fell into my arms, startling me, his face buried against my side as he began to sob. I carefully embraced him, tensed for him to pull away, but he didn't, and I gave him a tight hug, letting him cry.

After a couple of minutes, he pulled away and said, "It's n-not just a script. It's—it's Dad's working one for *Fatal Retribution*. He g-gave it to me . . . A present because . . ." Jamison mutely shoved the damaged script into my hands, and there, on the first page, it read "To my son, who will be even more kickass than his old man."

I read that, and my eyes filled. It was a lovely sentiment from father to son. Heartfelt and true. But after what happened outside . . .

"*Kickass* can mean a lot of things," I said gently. "Your mom is a total kickass, and she doesn't do fight scenes."

"She's a girl. It's different."

"It shouldn't be."

"It is for Dad," he said, and my heart broke, just a little, at an eight-year-old boy who already understood so much about what was expected of him, the ideal his father—and the world—held for him to emulate.

"Tell me what I can do," I said.

He looked from the torn book to the pages littering his room. If it happened again, I would insert myself between Colt and Jamison—as Tiana did—but I couldn't actually interfere. This, however, was something I could do, and I picked up a page and smoothed it and said, "Give these to me, and I'll iron them later, and then we'll tape them back in."

"Iron them?" Jamison said.

"It's a secret method for fixing paper you've accidentally—or not so accidentally—crumpled." I winked at him. "Don't ask me how I know that."

"What'd you do?" he said.

"Help me gather these quickly, and I'll tell you."

He smiled, and we set to work cleaning up the mess.

A FEW DAYS LATER, I was on the patio tuning Jamison's violin while Colt took the kids to the ice-cream parlor. When the door slid open and Colt stepped out, I smiled, my gaze shifting behind him for the kids.

"Sorry," he said. "Just me. We bumped into Belle on her run, and the kids decided to postpone their lessons by running with her."

Belle was his nickname for Isabella. They met on a film where he'd been the star, and she'd been brought in as his secondary love interest to amp up the film's "international appeal." Colt had spent the shoot trying to impress Isabella, and she'd spent it with her nose in a book. So he'd started calling her Belle and teasing her about being a Disney princess. Colt said that's why they named their daughter Tiana—because it meant "princess" in Russian .

Tiana had told me all this, sharing her family legends with rolled eyes but obvious affection. I'd told her the one about my name and my father's inability to pronounce it. She'd declared Genevieve a very fancy name and said she liked Lucy better.

Colt slid the patio door shut behind him. In his hand, he held a silver bag that glinted in the afternoon sun.

"Your ice cream," he said. "Only slightly melted."

"Rocky road!" I crowed as I opened it to find a cone and tiny tub. "Thank you."

"Jamie said it's your favorite."

"It is."

"And Tiana insisted on the chocolate-dipped cone."

I beamed up at him. "Thank you. They're amazing kids. You don't need me to tell you that, but they really are. Jamison is so sweet and thoughtful, and Tiana's a firecracker."

"They both take after their mom." He settled beside me on the lounge chair. "Thank you for being here with them. I know you were hired as a music teacher, but Belle's been so busy with her new show . . ."

I bristled. Was he insinuating that Isabella wasn't fulfilling her maternal duties? Colt's only summer job was getting in shape for his next movie.

"Isabella's new show is important," I said carefully. "The studio is taking a risk launching a telenovela in America. I'm amazed she can focus on that while keeping her office door open, eating meals with the family, and swimming and playing board games in the evenings. By seven, I'd be sprawled on the sofa."

"Belle is a wonder," he said. "I don't know how she does it, either."

I relaxed and felt silly for defending her. She didn't need that. Colt and Isabella had my ideal marriage—interweaving melodies, always close, always harmonic, complementing one another yet able to stand on their own.

I assembled my cone and quickly licked off the drips. When I saw Colt watching, I hesitated and prayed that hadn't looked suggestive.

"Good?" he said. "I was worried it'd be melted by the time I got back. That freezer bag worked well. I'll reuse it tomorrow and grab Belle some on my run."

I relaxed again. I really needed to stop worrying whether I accidentally gazed at him too long or laughed too hard at his jokes or licked my ice cream suggestively. When he looked at me, he only saw his kids' music tutor.

While Colt didn't notice me, I couldn't help being physically aware of him. I was sitting less than six inches from the most attractive man I'd ever met . . . who was wearing nothing but a pair of athletic shorts.

"I should grab napkins before this drips," I said, rising.

Colt's hand clamped on my knee. My bare knee. My heart tripped, half sensual awareness and half panicked terror. It was only a quick grip, though, strong and firm, as he said, "Hold on," and held me on the chair as he slid across that gap between us. My heart slammed against my ribs.

"I really need—" I began.

"I'll get the napkins. Just . . ." He leaned in, close enough for me to smell raspberry sherbet on his breath. "I have a favor to ask."

I didn't move, *couldn't* move.

"I'd like music lessons," he said.

"What?"

The word squeaked, and all I could remember was Nylah and her warning.

It's not his flute you'll be blowing.

"I'm the only one in the family who doesn't play an instrument," he said. "Watching your nighttime jam sessions, I want to be part of that. Even if it's just beating a drum with some semblance of rhythm." His crooked smile reminded me of Jamison's, a little uncertain, even a little shy.

"Sure."

"One condition." He leaned in even closer, heat radiating over me, and I held myself still, focused on a shaving nick on his cheek, blocking out the rest as I struggled to breathe.

"I want it to be a secret," he said. "Belle and I have our

eleventh wedding anniversary in August. We'll be throwing a party. I'd like to surprise her then."

I looked up, and he was right there, those famously bright blue eyes locked on mine.

When I inched away, he seemed to realize how close he'd gotten and straightened. A quick glance toward the beach, and he lowered his voice. "They'll be back any second. We'll talk tomorrow afternoon when Belle goes for her run. That's when we'll do the lessons."

"The kids . . ."

"They can keep a secret. It's not like they won't hear me trying to play. They might even teach me a thing or two."

I exhaled. It wouldn't be *private* lessons, then.

"Deal?" he asked.

"Deal," I said.

He clapped a hand on my bare thigh, a quick squeeze, and then he rose and jogged off to meet his family.

CHAPTER NINE

NEW YORK 2019

THE FLIGHT IS UNEVENTFUL. My driver is waiting for me at luggage claim, and soon I'm in an Upper West Side hotel suite twice the size of my apartment with a king bed, a Jacuzzi tub, a kitchen and a luxurious sitting area. Isabella isn't just bending over backward —she's doing triple-flips.

It's midnight local time, so after brushing my teeth and popping off an "Arrived!" text to Marco, I fall into bed. I sleep for a few hours and then laze drowsily until the sun lights my windows.

After a quick shower, I pull clothing from my luggage to find a tiny white paper bag nestled between my folded shirts. I open it, and a string of silver rosary beads slides into my hand.

Vatican rosary beads. For my mother. Tucked into my luggage by Marco because he knew she'd asked for them, and her daughter had completely forgotten about it despite having been to Vatican City multiple times since being asked.

I joke that being half Irish, a quarter Italian and a quarter Mexican means I am one hundred and ten percent Catholic. While I'm not the most devout follower of the faith, living in Rome means I can't resist the allure of services at the Vatican. I mean, it's the *Vatican*. I get there maybe once a month, mostly so I can tell

Mom in our weekly calls, and then she can casually say to her church-lady friends, "Oh, my daughter went to services at the Vatican again."

When I'd said I was going to Easter mass, Mom mentioned she'd love a string of rosary beads. Believe me, Easter is not the time you want to brave the gift shop crowds. Getting into St. Peter's Square is challenging enough. I'd told Marco that I needed to grab her a string on my next visit . . . and then promptly forgot.

I text him a thank-you as I dress, and we continue text-chatting while I get ready and head out. When he asks whether my room is okay, I come close to telling him all about it . . . and then realize I can't.

So I lie. I lie, I lie and I lie again, each one heaving a brick into my guilt bag. There's only one way to ease it off my shoulders.

Me: Hey, when I get home, I need to talk to you.
Him: That sounds ominous.
Me: LOL Sorry. It's nothing bad.
Me: Just something we need to discuss, and if I tell you
    now, I can't duck out of it.
Him: Still sounds ominous, but okay. I'll hold you to it.

I tell him to do that, please, and then sign off as he gathers the flock for his next tour.

I CONSIDER ORDERING room service for breakfast, but Central Park summons me stronger. It's a gorgeous day, and I'm only a few blocks from Levain Bakery, which I used to walk to every Sunday morning when I went to Juilliard. A baguette with butter and jam is calling my name, paired with fresh roasted coffee. Real American coffee, not the "Americano" I get in Italy. A bakery treat, an extra-large coffee and a bench in Central Park. The perfect way to relax before I meet Isabella at three.

I thoroughly enjoy my morning. It's the first time post-scandal that I've been able to walk in NYC with my head high, zero danger of being recognized. I am no longer the girl that fled. I am the woman who returned, as anonymous now as I am in Rome, and it is glorious.

Which only reminds me of what I'm about to do this afternoon.

Unmask myself to the one person who can destroy me again.

I have questioned whether Isabella genuinely wants to apologize but only because I suspect it's more self-interest than altruism.

In the wake of the scandal, Colt's career exploded. *Exploded*, not imploded. He was a man, after all, slave to testosterone, and clearly, I took advantage of that. To the average fan, I'd tried to ruin his career, and by God, they weren't going to let that happen. The scandal only meant increased attention and sympathy for Colt, especially after his PR machine got hold of the story.

For Isabella, though . . . It's one thing for a husband to stray. Boys will be boys, and all that. For the woman he cheated on, the sympathy leans dangerously close to pity, underscored by whispered innuendo. *Why* had Colt strayed? Was she so wrapped up in her own career that he felt neglected?

Isabella had been bumped as showrunner on her telenovela. They said it had nothing to do with the scandal. Of course, it did. When the series later failed, they blamed her, ignoring the fact that the male showrunner took her concept and steamrolled over it. After failing to reestablish herself, she started script doctoring, which meant she could easily support herself, but to the average person, her career had failed, her name no longer in the credits.

What if she's still smarting from that? I have recovered from the scandal, and she has not, and she wants revenge?

What if she lured me here to expose me? What if I walk into that room and find cameras poised to record Isabella Morales's final takedown of Lucy Callahan?

It is perfect reality-TV fodder. *Wife wronged in the most famous celebrity scandal of the decade confronts the woman who ruined her career*. Fourteen years ago, people had been ready to paint Isabella Morales with the same brush they'd used on Hilary Clinton—a strong woman who "let" her husband stray with a young employee. Now, though, in the era of #MeToo, audiences are more ready to realize they're laying the blame in the wrong place. Of course, I could hope they'd lay it where it belongs—at the foot of the forty-year-old man who seduced a teenage girl—but I don't think we're there yet.

By the time I walk from the park to my hotel, I am convinced I'm being led into a trap. So what do I do about that? Run back to Rome, pack my things and flee into the night? Absolutely not. I came here to fight, and if that's what Isabella wants, that's what she'll get.

When the car service pulls up to our meeting place, I know I am truly heading into war. Isabella has chosen her battleground with care.

Do you remember this hotel, Lucy?

Do you remember that weekend?

Oh, yes, I remember it very well.

CHAPTER TEN

NEW YORK 2005

THE WEEKEND before the anniversary party, Isabella declared we needed a girls' getaway, so she took Tiana and me to buy our party finery. I tried to demur, but she was having none of it. The three of us were going shopping in New York.

I'd watched this scene in movies. The ordinary girl swept into a modern-fairy-tale day, where personal dressers rush about to choose her new clothing, stylists find exactly the right cut to suit her face, manicurists and pedicurists and aestheticians and masseuses primp and polish and pummel her until she collapses in a happy heap, eating bonbons and sipping champagne as the day slides into night.

That day, I lived the fairy tale. And Isabella was my fairy godmother, smiling over me and waving her wand and tut-tutting away my protests. Between her and Tiana, they even convinced me to get a bikini for the party.

At the end of the day, we did indeed collapse with bonbons and champagne. A tray of hand-crafted confections from the best chocolatier in New York and a bottle of Bollinger champagne. Even Tiana got a quarter glass of the latter.

As we lay sprawled across the bed—a California king, Isabella called it, big enough for a family of six—we lounged in our plush bathrobes and talked, and ate and drank.

After Tiana fell asleep, Isabella and I kept talking, and my half glass of champagne left me tipsy enough to admit that when I was twelve, I wrote her a letter.

"The only fan letter I've ever written," I said. "I didn't ever get up the courage to send it, but I wrote it."

She sat up. "To me?"

My cheeks heated as I nodded.

"Please tell me you still have it," she said.

I stammered and stuttered something about Mom cleaning my room when I went to college.

"If you find it, will you let me see it?" she asked.

"That depends on how embarrassing it is."

She laughed and stretched out again. After a minute, she said, "Would you come back next summer, Lucy?"

I rolled my head to look across the bed at her.

She smiled. "Yes, today might have been a teensy bit of a bribe. We would love to have you at the beach house next summer. The kids adore you. Even Colt is comfortable with you. I got more work done this summer than I ever did with nannies. And the kids certainly learned more. Not just music—you found what interested each of them, and you made their summer both fun and educational. They have both, separately, petitioned to bring you to LA with us. I won't ask that. You have your own career and talents far beyond playing Hollywood governess. But if you'd like to come back next summer . . ."

"Is it contingent on me digging up that fan letter?"

She laughed. "No, it is not."

"Then I would love to come back," I said, my voice cracking a little as my eyes welled. "Thank you."

"Good." She smiled at me. "And thank *you*."

CHAPTER ELEVEN

NEW YORK 2019

BEFORE THE CAR EVEN STOPS, I throw open the door and gulp exhaust-thick air, my stomach churning.

I have reason to be angry and hurt, but so does she. Grab a random passerby and ask them to judge who has been more wronged, and they would say Isabella, and I'm not sure they'd be mistaken.

I hurt her. I betrayed her. While my actions weren't as horrible as the world thinks, that does not leave me blameless. I was young, and I was naive, and I made a mistake, and the moment I realized it, all I wanted was to talk to Isabella. Beg her forgiveness, yes. But also make sure she knew I hadn't done what people said. I would never hurt her that way.

I wanted her to know the truth.

And she does. I sent her a letter of explanation, bleeding with every word, starting and restarting it until I hit the right note, the one that accepted my share of the blame and laid none on anyone else. She could infer where else that blame belonged and how to portion it. I would not wail, "It isn't my fault." I wasn't a child. I made a choice, and it was wrong, and possibly unforgivable, and I would not cower behind the shield of youth and naivete.

I told her the truth, and she spat in my face.

Actually, I wish she *had* spat in my face. Instead, she sent that letter, dripping with vitriol and heaping all the blame at my feet.

That is what pushes me from the car, staggering and woozy. When the driver hurries to ask whether I'm all right, the memory of that letter prods me to smile weakly and lie that I'm just feeling carsick. Then I take a moment to compose myself before striding into the hotel.

Chin up. Press forward.

Isabella's choice of hotel is an act of war, and I accept her challenge. First, though, I need a moment to prepare. I take a seat on a high-backed lobby chair and pull out my phone.

If I am about to walk into a trap—a reality-show camera crew or even a room of old-fashioned journalists—there are two people who must be warned.

I call my mother first. I haven't let her know I'm in New York yet. Sunday is Mass, followed by an afternoon of church socializing, and I didn't want to interfere with her day. Now, though, she needs warning.

Her phone rings three times before going to voicemail, which means it's sitting on her dining room table. Unless she's expecting a call, she often leaves it behind for church lest even a vibration disturb others. I tell her that I'm in New York and we'll talk this evening when she's home.

The next call is harder, and I hit the name twice . . . only to hang up before the first ring. What do I even say?

Hey Marco, it's me. So, first, I lied about why I'm in New York. Remember that package that came to Lucy Callahan, and I said I had no idea who that was? I lied there, too. In fact, I've been lying since I met you. I am Lucy Callahan. The name sounds vaguely familiar, you say? Ever heard of Colt Gordon? Er, yes, that Colt Gordon. Well . . .

There is no way to give that conversation the space it needs before I meet Isabella. Even if I could, this isn't a conversation for a hotel lobby. I want to at least video-call, so he can see my face when I give him the news.

I start a text, saying we need to talk, and I'll call in a few hours.

"Ms. Callahan?" a voice says.

I turn to see a stone-faced young woman. She's midtwenties, immaculately dressed, with a straight black page boy and bright red lips.

"Ms. Callahan?" she repeats.

I rise. "Yes."

"Follow me, please. Ms. Morales is waiting."

I look at my phone, text half-written. She stands there, her expression still as blank as a cyborg's, but in that blankness, I feel judgment. She knows who I am, and the longer I dally, the more uncomfortable this will become.

I glance up at a row of world clocks showing the time in Los Angeles, Sydney, Moscow and London.

It's already 9 p.m. in Rome. If anything does go wrong here, Marco will be asleep by the time it hits the news. No reason to worry him with another ominous "we need to talk" message.

I delete my text, pocket the phone and follow the young woman to the elevators.

THE YOUNG WOMAN escorts me to the penthouse suite—the same one Isabella rented all those years ago. Of course. Why bring me here and then pull her punch at the last second? Might as well follow through and hit me with all she has.

The young woman raps on the door. A moment passes. Then it opens, the figure obscured behind the door.

"Thank you, Bess." That voice, with its trace of a Mexican accent, slams me in the gut.

The young woman—Bess—says, "Is there anything else I can get you, ma'am?"

"No, you have the rest of the day off."

"That isn't necessary."

"I insist." While Isabella's tone stays warm, that steel thread is unmistakable. Bess tenses but only dips her chin and retreats without a glance my way.

Isabella stays behind the door, and I brace for a click of camera shutters documenting my entry. Instead, there is only Isabella and she is . . .

The word *old* springs to mind, but I reject it with a wince. I will not be cruel. I've hurt her enough. *Old* isn't the word, anyway. *Older* is correct, and it was only a shock, as if I expected to confront the woman I last saw fourteen years ago.

There's frost in her hair, artfully threaded through, as if she has declared herself past the age where dying it jet black would flatter her aging face. She *has* let her face age. I would expect no less. She's still beautiful, still bearing that impossible figure, if a little thicker through the middle.

"Isabella," I say stiffly.

She doesn't even seem to hear me, just stares, as if at a stranger.

"Yes?" I say.

I hear the bite in that word, like armor snapping around me. I shake it off. I need her to think I come defenseless, expecting a gentle, tear-and-apology-filled reunion.

I want to try for something softer, but standing in front of her, there's nothing soft in me.

That's a lie. There *is* softness—and every instinct screams to protect it. Shield myself before she can home in on my weak spots.

Forget subtlety, then. I'm in no mood to manufacture it. Too angry and too anxious, and I must focus on the former.

I stride past her and look around. "Where are you hiding the cameras?"

"Cameras?" Her voice crackles, as if she has to dig to find it.

I turn on her. "You sent a parcel bearing my old name into my new life. If you found me, you know I don't go by Lucy anymore. That parcel was a grenade lobbed over the parapet."

She blinks. "No, that wasn't— By using your old name, I only wanted to get your attention."

"Because otherwise, I'd ignore a parcel addressed to me? Who does that? Someone else found that parcel. Someone I haven't told about my past."

"Oh, I'm sorry. I didn't think—"

"You *always* think, Isabella." I walk into the suite. "I'm here because I recognize a threat when I see one. By using my old name, you reminded me that you know who I am, so I damned well better accept your invitation. After I arrived, I realized this might be more than a personal takedown. Then I saw the hotel you'd chosen, and that left no doubt."

Isabella walks to a chair and lowers herself into it. "I've made a mess of this."

"Only if you expected I wouldn't figure out what you were up to."

"There is no camera crew, Luc—Genevieve."

"Lucy to you."

She nods. "Look around all you like. If you're worried about hidden cameras, I'll phone down and ask for another room."

I almost say yes to call her bluff. But if we *are* being recorded, then she's miked, and moving venues won't help.

"No one is recording this?" I say.

"They are not."

"I have your word on that? The understanding that I've come in good faith, with no agenda of my own, simply to hear what you have to say?"

"Yes."

That's enough for me, considering my phone is also recording this conversation in case I need to prove I wasn't the doe-eyed idiot who bounded into her trap unaware.

"Why here, then?" I say.

She looks around the suite. "It was a good memory. I wanted to recapture that, to remind us both of a better time."

"I am well aware of the fact that you were kind to me, and you were generous, and I betrayed you. Bringing me here only salts the wound."

"Then I apologize. That was not my intention." She watches me as I take a seat. "You've changed."

I laugh. I don't want to—not this kind of laugh, harsh and bitter. I bite it off and say simply, "I had to. But if you truly wish to extend an olive branch, Isabella, then I'd like to begin by saying that I don't want to compare war wounds. You may accept the dubious honor of most-injured."

"I don't want it," she says softly. "I'm not sure I've earned it."

"Then let's put that aside. I'm fine. This is about you—what you need from this conversation."

She rises and pours coffee without a word. When she hands me a cup, I pretend not to notice her hands trembling as I take the bone-china mug with thanks.

"I spent a very long time hating you, Lucy," she says as she settles back into her seat. "I was hurt, obviously. Devastated. In my position, it's difficult to allow anyone into my house, around my family."

"You trusted me. I betrayed you. I understand that. I have never *not* understood it."

She nods. "Then perhaps you were the more mature one. I apportioned blame, and I gave you the lion's share. I took some, too, for allowing you in based only on Karla's recommendation. And I gave some to Colt, but not nearly as much as he deserved."

She tugs her skirt over her knees. "I made excuses for him. He was going through a rough patch. Roles were drying up. His body wasn't what it used to be. He was feeling old, and I brought a pretty girl into our home. What did I expect?"

"That he'd act like a forty-year-old husband and father and *not* see a teenage employee as a potential conquest?"

She flinches at that, but I don't withdraw the words.

"Yes," she says slowly. "I blamed myself for putting temptation in his way. I blamed you for falling under his spell. That's what we do, isn't it? Blame women for treating men like rational beings capable of controlling sexual impulses. Even in my bitterest anger, I realized Colt had done the seducing, and yet it was easier to blame you."

"You needed someone to hold accountable for your husband's infidelity, and I was the disposable person in your life."

She leans back in her chair. "There was no 'infidelity,' Lucy. Colt and I had an open marriage. For him, life has always included an all-access pass to sex. I used to joke that expecting monogamy was like expecting a man of appetite to refuse a buffet. I don't make that joke anymore. Appetite is an excuse. The truth is that he's a glutton, and he cannot look at the buffet and tell himself that he has better food at home."

She sips her coffee. "I offered him nonmonogamy because I knew he'd cheat. I had other reasons to be with Colt. We were good friends and good partners, and I knew we'd make good parents. Refusing his proposal because I couldn't expect fidelity would be like finding the perfect house and walking away because it lacked a master bath."

"Perhaps," I say. "But you could always add the master bath. Or you could ask your husband to look inside himself and figure out why he couldn't walk away from the buffet, what need it satisfied and how that hole could be otherwise filled."

Isabella's burst of a laugh flings me into the past. "I used to think you were someone I'd like to know when you got older. You've grown into a woman who is much, much wiser than I was at her age."

"Don't," I say and then add, softer, "Please."

She nods. "You are painfully correct about Colt, but at the time, I felt like such a progressive and modern woman, granting his sexual freedom to lift that specter from our marriage. Sex, then, was not the issue. The issue was that, when I married him, I had the wisdom to protect my future family and, yes, my heart. There were rules. Strict rules. He had to be discreet. He could have flings but not full-blown affairs. He would never bring that side of his life home—he wouldn't mention the women to me, and his children would not find out. Distance and discretion."

"A one-night stand with a fellow actor who would maintain his privacy," I say. "Not a fling with an eighteen-year-old tutor at your summer house."

After a moment, she says, quietly, "Yes."

"And that's why he did it, isn't it? Giving a child all the cookies doesn't mean he'll stop stealing them."

"Because it isn't just about the cookies," she says. "It's about the thrill and challenge of the theft."

I shrug and lift my coffee cup. "I won't presume to analyze your husband and your marriage, but you threw me into a position where I had to do that if only for my own understanding. Colt loved you very much. That was obvious. But he was bored and feeling old. I was a diversion. It had nothing to do with either of us. It was all about Colt."

"He's told me that many times. He accepted responsibility, but I still felt responsible. I was busy that summer, and he felt neglected."

"As if it was your wifely duty to surrender your dreams to nurse him through his midlife crisis."

Her lips twitch. "I could have saved myself a lot of money on therapists and just talked with you."

"I wish you had talked with me," I say, my voice low as I set my coffee down untouched. "That was what I wanted more than anything. To talk to you."

Tears glisten. Then she blinks them back and straightens. "I understand, but I also hope you understand why you couldn't. You were having sex with my husband."

"No, I wasn't. I was a virgin when I arrived at your home and a virgin when I left." I manage a wry smile. "I even went to the doctor afterward to see if my hymen was intact. Now we know that's bullshit, but at the time, I thought it was what I needed to clear my name. Yes, it was intact, but my mother rightfully convinced me that going public with that would only make things worse."

"Just because you didn't have penetrative sex—"

"There was no sex of any kind. Unfortunately, a doctor's note wouldn't prove *that*. My only hope was that you would believe me when I explained it in my letter. Obviously, you didn't."

She goes still, and something in her eyes . . .

"You *did* read my letter, right?" I say. "You must have. You sure as hell replied."

She flinches at the profanity, however mild, but then that look returns. Discomfort and dismay.

"You didn't read it," I say. "Not past a line or two. You didn't give a damn what I had to say. You had something to say. You had a *lot* to say."

"I . . ."

"You presumed my letter was excuses and apologies. *I'm so sorry, Isabella. I didn't mean to screw your husband. I just couldn't control myself. Please accept my deepest apologies . . . and is there any chance I can come back next year, maybe get an internship on your new show?*"

I look at her. "The letter was an explanation. Not an excuse. I wrote it and rewrote it until I'd erased any hint of self-pity or blame-laying. I made a mistake. But my mistake was not what you saw in the papers, and I needed you to know that. I would think you already did, considering you were still with Colt. Whatever he intended that night, he'd have made damn sure you knew he never got it."

Silence.

"What did he tell you, Isabella?"

She fusses with the coffee cup, and I'm about to prod again when she says, "We separated briefly after that night. I needed to get the children away before the media circus began in earnest, and I needed to make rational decisions, not emotional ones. Colt tried to contact me, of course. Tried many times in many ways until I said, if he kept trying, I'd respond with divorce papers. After that, he gave me my space. We reconciled. I suspect you know that."

"Kinda hard to miss," I say, "when every move you two made

brought a fresh invasion of paparazzi . . . and a fresh tsunami of vitriol from your fans."

God, that sounds bitter. Sarcasm sharpened on fourteen years of pain, and I am ashamed of myself. I want to be stronger, want to tell her none of it affected me.

How could it not affect me?

"You reconciled," I say. "Presumably then, he told you what actually happened."

"He said the papers got it wrong, that there hadn't been anything more than what I saw in those pictures. Which seemed convenient. He couldn't deny the photos, and clearly, nothing happened *after* you two realized you were being photographed, but the chance that some paparazzi just happened to be there to record your one and only encounter?" She shakes her head. "I wasn't that stupid. I told him that I wanted to set it aside and move on."

"And he wasn't going to insist on clarifying and jeopardize the reunion."

She says nothing.

"As for the chance that someone recorded our first and only encounter? It was a party. There were paparazzi skulking in the bushes and getting their long-range shots from the water. They certainly caught me swimming with Justice Kane. The guy who took those shots saw Colt sneak off with the nanny. Of course, he followed. Of course, he got the shots. That *was* our only encounter, Isabella. While I no longer care whether you believe that, at the time, I wanted nothing more than for you to understand . . . and you tossed out my letter and wrote me a reply that had me with a bottle of pills—"

I stop, biting off the words and shaking my head fiercely.

"Oh, Lucy," she says, and she stands and makes a move as if to cross the space between us.

I raise my hands, almost falling back in my haste to ward her off.

She settles into her seat again and says, "Will you tell me now?"

I lift my gaze to hers, my face as impassive as I can make it.

"Will you tell me what happened that night?" she says. "I would like to know, and I'd like to hear it from you."

CHAPTER TWELVE

NEW YORK 2005

ISABELLA KEPT STRESSING that the party would be a casual affair. As I discovered, that meant a whole other thing for celebrities. The patio and yard were transformed into a fairy wonderland of sparkling lights so expertly entwined that the trees and bushes seemed to glitter with fireflies. Our dresses may have been summer casual, but we had our hair, nails and makeup done by the same women who'd pampered us in the city, brought in for the day.

At six, the guests began arriving in a procession of chauffeured luxury cars and self-driven sports cars. Valets whisked vehicles off to some unknown location where they wouldn't clog the residential street.

Isabella had invited fifty guests. I counted sixty, presumably some unable to resist sneaking in a friend. Everyone was A-list. Actors, directors, musicians, producers, all flying from around the world to celebrate Colt and Isabella's anniversary.

The impulse to run and hide nearly overwhelmed me. It might have, too, if I hadn't kept reminding myself that, to them, I was the hired help. If Isabella took pains to introduce me, they assumed she was simply being kind, and they were kind in return, but they'd forget my name a minute later, and I was okay with that.

I mostly hung out with the children. Hid with them, really, taking refuge in my job. There were a few other kids to keep Tiana and Jamison company, and I played hostess to their corner of the party.

There were two guys my age. One was Parker Harmon, an actor in a hit TV series and the son of a director. The other was Justice Kane, lead singer of the Indigo Kings, the hottest boy band around, and the nephew of a family friend.

Earlier, Tiana had said Isabella invited Parker and Justice for me, and I will admit that I entertained a few fantasies of kissing a Hollywood prince that night. Those fantasies were dashed when Isabella introduced us . . . and I found an excuse to flee the moment she walked away. Kissing princes was one thing; talking to them was quite another.

As dinner got underway, I ducked into the house to prepare for our performance. Tiana, Jamison and I were going to surprise their parents with an after-dinner anniversary musical tribute. Of course, it wasn't really a surprise to Colt, but I was sure he could fake it, being an actor and all.

While the kids ate, I snuck the instruments out behind the hedge. Then, as Isabella and Colt dined on the beach with their guests, we came out playing. We started with the theme song to *Mi Hermana*, and then the theme for *Fatal Retribution* and, finally, the theme for *The President's Wife*, the movie where they'd met. Tiana played her sax, Jamison his violin, and I had my viola, and we serenaded the celebrating couple with songs from their past.

As we focused on Isabella, drawing closer to her, Colt slipped off. We swung into "Belle," from *Beauty and the Beast*, and Isabella clapped and turned to Colt . . . only to see his spot empty. Then he appeared from behind the boathouse, joining in with a guitar.

"She's going to cry," Tiana had said earlier, and Isabella did.

When we finished, she came to embrace the kids, and I slipped off to grab dinner, leaving them to their family moment.

I came back when Isabella brought out her flute, and we played impromptu tunes while the guests danced. Then Isabella pulled in Justice Kane, who took vocals. Guests danced on the beach, and champagne flowed. I had half a glass before Tiana backed into me, and I spilled it on my viola.

I excused myself, and I was hurrying inside to get a rag when Karla—Colt and Isabella's manager—appeared, towel in hand.

"Colt's right," I said as I took it and wiped down my instrument. "You really are a fairy godmother."

She chuckled. "No, I'm just not much of a party person, so I look for any opportunity to be useful. I've offered to serve drinks, but Isabella refuses."

Her eyes glittered with an almost self-deprecating amusement that was a far cry from the ultraefficient woman I'd come to know. Karla stopped by regularly, usually following a summons from Colt. He'd have some minor emergency, and she'd need to race up from New York, where she was stationed while they vacationed. She was indeed their fairy godmother, and judging by her tailored clothing and tasteful jewelry, they compensated her well for it, as they should.

We chatted for a few minutes, a lighter conversation than usual. She usually only talked about my job, making sure I was comfortable and happy, and I suspected, if I'd said I wasn't, she'd have waved her wand to fix that.

Karla wasn't exactly warm—at our first meeting, she intimidated the hell out of me—but she had a deep streak of compassion I'd come to appreciate. Between Karla and Isabella, I'd discovered two models of successful women to emulate, capable and caring in very different ways, proof that you didn't need to be a stone-cold bitch to succeed . . . and proof you *could* be a stone-cold bitch if the situation required it.

"I believe someone is waiting for you," Karla said, her eyes twinkling as she nodded toward the pool.

I looked over to see Justice with two filled champagne flutes in hand. He lifted one and smiled. I excused myself and walked over.

"To a successful concert," he said as he passed one flute to me.

I thanked him and took a sip. Then I glanced toward the beach.

"The music's done," he said. "Apparently, everyone's going swimming."

A splash echoed in the background.

"Right on cue," he said. "You've got a suit, I'm guessing?"

"Already wearing it."

He lifted a brow and looked at my dress.

"Underneath," I said.

"Good plan. I forgot mine. I'm hoping if I swim in the ocean, no one will notice I'm wearing my boxers."

I laughed softly. "Also a good plan."

He extended his elbow. "Will you join me? I hear you're at Juilliard, and I'm dying to pester you with questions. I figured I'd throw in a champagne walk on the beach to make it worth your while."

I nodded dumbly and took his elbow, and as we passed Isabella, she tossed me a wink. I was glad for the darkness as my cheeks flamed.

"Did Isabella tell you that I tried to get in to Juilliard?" he said as we wound our way through abandoned picnic blankets. "Twice. Didn't make the cut."

"And now look at you," I said with what I hoped wasn't a nervous laugh.

Justice grinned. "Well, that's what I say when I mention it in interviews. *Hey, kids, I couldn't get in to a fancy music program, either, and look where I am.* It makes a nice feel-good story, as my publicist would say, but the truth . . ." He shrugged and sipped his champagne. "There's a huge difference between being a talented classically trained musician and a guy who can strum a few chords. I grew up being told what an incredible musician I was, which I thought must be natural talent, since I never practiced." Another quick grin my way. "But the truth is that I was a cute guy with a guitar. Of course, the girls voted for me in the talent show every year."

I was about to say the expected thing—that I was sure it was talent that won him those accolades—but I'd sipped more champagne than I intended, and I heard myself say, "Nobody likes to practice."

A sharp laugh. "True enough. I still dream of Juilliard, though. What's it like?"

We talked as we strolled along the beach. Whenever we started getting too far from the house, he'd notice me glancing back and turn us around. The champagne buzzed through me, loosening my tongue, and we chatted away about the life of a music student versus the life of a pop star. At some point, we tossed our clothing onto one of the blankets and swam.

Isabella had invited Justice in hopes I'd have some flirty fun. And I did. I talked and swam and laughed with a twenty-one-year-old heartthrob who, in person, was as real as Colt or Isabella. Colt complained about how often people said he seemed like a real person.

"I *am* a real person," he'd grumbled. "Do they expect a talking mannequin?"

That was the allure of gossip rags. *Look, this actor eats at McDonald's, too! This musician's kids throw tantrums in the mall, too! They're just like us!* As if we thought they were another species, dwelling on some perfect plane of existence separate from our own.

Justice Kane was a swoon-worthy twenty-one-year-old who played guitar and sang lead vocals in one of the most popular bands on the planet. He was also a guy who liked bad puns, couldn't swim very well, and wished he'd gone to college.

I basked in the glow of Justice's attention, but even more than that, I enjoyed exactly what Isabella prescribed: time with a guy my own age.

Despite my hopes, there wasn't any kissing. I got flirting,

though, and glances of appreciation for my new bikini. We'd retreated to the beach to talk when a shadow blocked out the moonlight, and I twisted to see Colt looming over us.

"I'm behaving," Justice said, gesturing at the two foot gap between us. "We just snuck away from you old fogies."

Colt kicked up sand, and Justice dodged it, laughing.

"I need to steal Lucy from you," Colt said. "Tiana wants to talk to her."

"Sure." Justice held out a hand to help me stand, but Colt deftly moved into his way. I ignored both and rose to my feet.

"We'll catch up later," Justice said. "I think I saw cake. I'll grab you a piece before it's gone."

"Lucy has to put the kids to bed," Colt said, and I shot him a look—since when did I do that?—but he ignored it and started leading me away.

"I'll still see about the cake," Justice called after me. "I'd love your e-mail in case I have more questions about Juilliard."

Colt snorted and muttered something under his breath. He had his hand on my elbow as he led me away like a naughty child.

"We were only talking," I said. "We were in sight of the house."

Colt nodded abruptly and loosened his grip. "It's not you. I've known Justice since he was a kid, and he . . . has a reputation."

"He was fine," I said. "A perfect gentleman, actually." *Even when I would have been okay with slightly less gentlemanly behavior.*

Colt only muttered and led me to a side table where two glasses of champagne waited, still fizzing, as if he'd set them there. As he handed me one, I shook my head.

"I had one earlier, and it went straight to my head. I still feel woozy."

"Lightweight," he teased. "You're walking and talking just fine." He pushed the glass into my hand. "This is the good stuff. In thanks for helping me make Isabella very happy tonight."

"Doesn't Tiana need me?"

He leaned down and whispered, "I lied." He straightened. "That was about getting you away from the clutches of a very unsuitable young man." He enunciated the words in a proper English accent, and then his lips twitched in that crooked smile I knew well. "Do you forgive me?"

Not really. I'd been having fun with Justice, and I was irked to be pulled away, especially when Justice hadn't given off any *unsuitable* vibes. If Colt was right, though, maybe he'd been working up to that, lowering my guard so I'd let him lead me from the watchful eyes of my employers.

"You are forgiven," I said. "The surprise went well earlier. Isabella didn't suspect a thing."

He grinned as his eyes danced. "She didn't. And so we must drink a toast to our success, student and teacher."

We clinked glasses, and I tried to just take a sip, but he lifted the bottom of my glass, leaving me sputtering as champagne spilled down my throat. When he reached to do it again, I chugged it, which I was certain was entirely wrong for expensive champagne. He sipped a little of his and then set our glasses aside and took my hand, his warm fingers enveloping mine.

"I have something to show you," he said. "My secret stargazing spot."

He tugged my hand, and before I could protest, my feet were moving, following him as we jogged through the bushes that separated the beach house from the next property. The owners had left the first week of August, and the house was dark.

As we dashed onto the back deck, I giggled far more than necessary, the champagne making me so dizzy I could barely see straight. When I stumbled, Colt scooped me up, and I laughed, kicking half-heartedly.

He carried me across the dark porch to a gray square embedded in the wood floor. Then he kicked the square and managed to catch the edge on his toes, lifting what turned out to be a cover. Underneath, water glistened in the moonlight.

"A hot tub?" I said.

He hopped in with a splash that had me laughing anew as he turned and lowered me into the water.

"My secret stargazing spot," he said.

"The neighbors' hot tub? You just come over here and hop in?"

"Only when they aren't home. They never remember to turn off the heater."

As he sat, we sank into the warm water together, and I was dimly aware that I was on his lap, but my head swirled, thoughts flitting away before I could snatch them. I did manage to seize one long enough to realize I should move, but when I squirmed, he held me there, chuckling, until my struggles dissolved in giggles.

As I settled onto Colt's lap, he nuzzled my neck. Was he . . . *kissing* my neck? Whoa, no.

I struggled to move away again, and he let me get to my feet and slosh toward another seat in the tub. I made it two steps before he grabbed me, spun me around and pulled me to him, and this time, when I ended up on his lap, I was straddling him.

"You're so sweet, Lucy-girl," he murmured as he nuzzled my neck. "As sweet and delicious as cotton candy."

His hands slid down my sides. My *bare* sides. I was still wearing the bikini.

I was on Colt's lap, straddling him, wearing scraps of fabric, while he was in his bathing trunks, pushing up hard against me.

Pushing hard . . .

No, no, no.

He kissed my throat, whispering words I couldn't hear as blood crashed in my ears, my brain and body warring. I had to go, go *now*, but his hands felt so good. *He* felt so good.

Colt was kissing me.

Not just my neck. His lips were on mine, and I wasn't sure how they got there. Time had seemed to leap from his lips on my neck to his mouth on mine. His hands gripped my hips, and he ground into me, and oh, God, that felt so good.

No, no, no.

I went to shove his hands off my hips. Only they weren't there anymore. They were on my breasts. My bare breasts. Where was my bikini top? How did his hands get there? What the *hell* was happening?

Stop.

I needed to stop him.

Except I didn't want to. It felt so—

Isabella.

Her name was like a slap, and I reeled back, arching from the kiss, breaking it, pushing Colt, his hands gripping my breasts as something sounded behind us.

As a click sounded behind us.

A *click-click-click*, like the whirring of some giant insect. Light reflected off the side of the house. *Flash-flash-flash*, keeping time with the clicks.

I twisted out of Colt's grip just as the camera flashed again.

CHAPTER THIRTEEN

NEW YORK 2019

WHEN I FINISH, Isabella sits there, staring at me. "You're . . . you're saying Colt drugged you? Dosed your champagne and took advantage of you?"

"What? No. Don't put words in my mouth, Isabella."

"You said you were disoriented and confused after he gave you that champagne."

I pull back, coffee cup cradled in my hands. "I said I was *tipsy* after two glasses of champagne. You remember how I was after less than one glass, right here in this hotel room. Clearly, two was more than I could handle. That's not an excuse."

"If you were losing time, that means you blacked out—"

"Have I considered the possibility that *someone* put *something* into the champagne? Yes, I have, but there's no way of proving that now. It really might have just been champagne."

"Which Colt literally dumped down your throat."

"I—" I rub my face frantically, my gut screaming for me not to go there, not to remember that part. Chin up and accept blame.

"The point," I say slowly, "is that Colt kissed me, and I kissed him back. I was tipsy, and I was flattered, and I was an eighteen-year-old virgin with Colt Gordon kissing me in a hot tub. He didn't need to force me."

"He—"

"The *point*," I say again, more emphatically, "is that I stopped once I realized that what I was doing was wrong—horribly wrong—and a betrayal of your trust. That's when we discovered we'd been photographed. You have my version. Get Colt's. Believe me, I haven't spoken to him since that day. His will match mine."

"Except for where he *forced* himself on you after drugging you. If it happened the way you say, Lucy—"

"No."

"There was coercion there beyond Colt using his charisma and his fame, which I already knew was a factor. If he did what you say—"

"No," I say, sharper, gut twisting with anxiety. "You won't do that."

She looks at me in genuine confusion.

I continue, "I said that my mother wouldn't let me use that silly virginity proof. But when I first told her the story, she was furious with Colt. She wanted to call the police. Report him. Insist on an investigation. I was the one who talked her out of that. Begged her not to. Broke down in tears when she tried."

"If it happened—"

"And that is exactly why I didn't. Those words. *If* it happened the way you say, Lucy. *If* he did what you say. I had a friend in high school who went to a frat party pretending she was eighteen. Wore a miniskirt. Drank a beer. Smoked a joint. Wanted to have some fun and party with cute college boys. She passed out. Woke up to a guy on top of her with friends egging him on. She reported it. A year later, she killed herself. Do you know what she told me? That everyone—from the cops to the lawyers to her own parents—couldn't talk about it without saying 'if.' *If* you really were passed out. *If* the guy didn't know you were unconscious. *If* it happened the way you said. Even people who were trying to be supportive still said *if* just like you're doing. So I choose to excise that part of what happened to me. I will not say I was drugged. I will not say Colt used coercion. I will not say it was anything other than a drunk teenage girl letting her hormones run away with her and making an inexcusable mistake. That is where we will leave this. Insist on more, and I leave. Say *if* one more time, and I leave."

She looks at me. Stares, as she did when I first told the story, and I squirm under that stare and then hate myself for squirming. I want to be stronger. Not tougher, not harder, just stronger. Why is that so difficult?

Because it's Isabella, and every look, every gesture, every nuance feels like a needle pricking an open wound.

"What?" I say, finally, more peevish than I intend. I try to cover it with, "Can we just leave this and—"

"I'm sorry," she says, "for what you went through. I'm truly sorry, Lucy."

Now I squirm for real. "I don't need you to be sorry, Isabella. I don't *want* you to be."

"I still am. I thought I'd had this great revelation. With what's happened in Hollywood, Weinstein and the rest, I've had friends come forward, and I never doubted them for a second. I have my own stories. MeToo has been like a splash of ice water, waking me up and making me look back at what I endured and how we just accepted that's the way things were. The casting-couch jokes that weren't jokes at all. The casual misogyny that wasn't casual at all. We never stopped to ask *why* is it like this? Why do we accept this behavior? Why is it *our* job to overcome it? In the midst of all that, a friend told me a story about something that happened when she was a teenager, a one-night stand with a producer. Afterward, his wife came after *my friend*. I was outraged on her behalf. How dare this older woman blame *her* for her husband's actions. And then I realized I'd done the same to you."

I say nothing, just sit with my hands folded on my lap, my voice gone.

"I was so proud of myself," she continues, "for realizing I'd done wrong and resolving to fix it. To treat you to an all-expenses-paid trip so I can ask your forgiveness. How generous of me. Yet you come here, and you tell me your story, laying no blame, and when I see blame—squarely on Colt's shoulders—I still question. I don't mean to. I believe you. But I cannot help wording it in a way that implies doubt."

"He's still your husband," I say quietly.

She sits back. "In name only. We stayed together for the kids. A partnership rather than a marriage. I intended to leave once Jamie turned eighteen . . . but he's had some troubles, so I waited. He's better now, and I moved out last fall. That doesn't mean I spent fourteen years sharing my home with a man I despised. I love Colt. Always will. I still talk to him every day. We're friends. I won't make excuses for him. Or I'll try not to. He's flawed." A wry smile. "We all are. But do I believe him capable of exerting pressure on an eighteen-year-old girl he wants? Yes. Whether he'd have gone further once it was clear you didn't want that . . ."

"I don't think he would have," I say. "Men are accustomed to girls protesting. They're raised to think they have to talk us into sex."

Her lip curls in a sardonic smile. "We want it. We just don't realize it, so they need to show us."

"I dealt with that growing up. I'm sure you did, too. Not from every guy, of course, but there are always some. That night, when Colt kissed me, I kissed him back, and when I pushed away, he thought I was playing hard to get. That doesn't excuse what he did. But I think, once I clearly refused, he would have stopped."

She nods, her gaze down. She agrees he wouldn't have forced himself on me. Yet she fears defending him, so she only gives that brief nod.

"This isn't about what Colt did or didn't do," I say. "It's about me realizing I hurt you, which I do, and I apologize for that."

"And I realize I was wrong for not listening to you, for not reading your letter, for presuming you betrayed me, because that was easier than blaming my husband for his betrayal."

"I understand all that," I say. "It hurt, at the time, but even then, I understood. You had a family to protect. Maybe the truth could have helped, but honestly, the media circus was just about selling papers. We were the latest iteration of a popular tale. The wicked girl who uses her sexuality to tempt a good man, endangering his marriage to a good woman."

She nods. "Circe tempting Odysseus, while Penelope keeps the home fires burning. Never mind that Odysseus chose to stay with Circe for a year—and she was only one of many women he slept with on his way home. We are all Circe or Penelope. Whore or Madonna. Never Odysseus. Never the hero of the tale."

I shrug. "We can be. It just takes more effort than it should."

She moves to sit beside me on the sofa. Then she hugs me, and I try not to break down into that hug. I accept it. I embrace her back. Then I withdraw.

"I'm glad we had the chance to talk," I say.

"And now you're leaving as quickly as you can."

Before I can answer, she lays her hands on mine. "I want us to take control of this situation. Not at Colt's expense. He is still my children's father, and he's still someone I care about very much. This isn't about demonizing Odysseus. It's about excising him from our storyline."

"Okay . . ."

"I want to go public," she says. "The two of us with *our* story. The misunderstandings. The anger. You and Colt had a drunken moment together. Nothing more. If that's—"

She stops herself. "I'm sorry. Not *if*. That *is* the truth. I know it is. It makes sense for both of you. You were eighteen and unaccustomed to alcohol. We encouraged you to enjoy the champagne. Our marriage was nonmonogamous, and what happened may have been—*was*—a misstep on his part, but the media blew it out of proportion."

She gives a tight laugh. "Yes, I realize that doesn't eliminate Colt from our story, but he's only a side character. This is about us. Your misplaced guilt. Your experience with the press and the public. My misplaced anger. My experience with the press and the public."

"I . . . No." I pull from her grip. "This isn't what I want."

"It would help, though, wouldn't it? It's not what we necessarily want, but it's what we need. We can control the message. We'll make this about us."

"About us . . . or about you?"

She goes still, and I twist to face her.

"You feel guilty," I say. "You want to make amends. You want to give me this gift just as you gave me a weekend in this hotel fourteen years ago. But I'm not that girl. I don't need gifts. I don't want them."

I get to my feet. "I *am* glad we talked. I'm glad we cleared the air. But any attempt to fix this would be just as likely to blow up in my face. I don't want another fifteen minutes of fame even for the right reasons. I'm fine."

"You're living under an assumed name. You gave up your career, your talent."

"I'm living under the name on my birth certificate. No, I'm not a concert violist. I didn't graduate from Juilliard. Those are the dreams of an eighteen-year-old girl, Isabella. I teach music, and I play in a quartet and a small symphony, and I love it. I have a wonderful apartment and an amazing boyfriend. I won't lie—I would also love to be free from the lies. But I don't see a way to do that without risking the great life I already have. It's not a gamble I'm willing to take. I'm sorry."

I start for the door.

"Lucy," she calls.

I turn. She's still there by the sofa.

"Will you think on it?" she says. "I'll do the same. I understand your concerns, but I believe we could work something out. A strategy to give us what we both need."

When I don't answer, she sees opportunity and pounces with, "Lunch tomorrow. I know you're tired. You need time alone. Join me for lunch, and we'll talk, and if we can't come to a solution that satisfies you, then you'll go back to Rome, and I'll just be happy that we had this chance to talk."

I pause and then say, "I'll get back to you tonight."

"Thank you."

WHEN I GET DOWNSTAIRS, the car is pulling in, summoned by Isabella. I'm barely a mile from my hotel, and it's faster to walk. I *want* to walk. Even as I step out into a light rain, I don't change my mind. That car belongs to Isabella, and within its confines, I remain under her control. I need to get away from that and collect my thoughts.

I'm so wrapped up in those thoughts that I overshoot my street. As I take out my phone, I scan shop names so I can orient myself on my cell-phone map. The one right beside me proclaims Authentic Italian Iced Treats. One glimpse at the candy-colored gelato has me sniffing in disdain. I chuckle. I have become an Italian, who knows that this neon-bright whipped stuff is *not* proper gelato.

As I gaze at that shop, my mind tumbles back to an afternoon last month, meeting Marco after a Pantheon tour and having gelato at Giolitti. Sitting at a rickety table on the cobblestone street, we shared an insane dessert of chocolate ice cream and custard *zabaione*, entirely encased in a globe of whipped cream. Marco was telling me about studies that upend the prevailing theories on the Vesuvius eruption. The movie *Pompeii* shows people drowning in lava and perishing in a rain of fire, but any tour guide knows that's Hollywood hyperbole. It's long been presumed that people suffocated from the volcanic ash. New studies, though, suggest their brains may have exploded from the heat.

Marco was explaining this new theory to me, his enthralled audience . . . until we caught the horrified looks of the tourists beside us, who apparently didn't consider brain-boiling a proper dining conversation. So Marco switched to Italian . . . and got the same horrified looks from the locals on our opposite side.

Now I'm standing in the rain, staring at this fake gelato place, and I'm back in that sunny afternoon in Rome. I hear Marco's animated chatter, and then our stifled snickers and giggles as we realize we've inadvertently driven off our dining neighbors, leaving us free to continue the discussion.

I remember what that moment *felt* like. Sharing our crazy dessert. Basking in the sunshine. Enrapt in our conversation. I'd sat there looking at Marco and felt . . .

Happy. Giddily, unbelievably happy. I could scarcely believe this was my life. This beautiful, bewitching city? Mine. This gorgeous, fascinating man? Mine. All mine.

What I felt that day wasn't mere happiness. It was love, God help me. Love for that life. Love for that city. Love for that man.

I inhale so sharply I startle an old woman, who mutters at me in Korean before tromping into the gelato shop. I watch her go, and I breathe, just breathe, until the stabbing panic subsides. When it does, I know my answer for Isabella. I understand that she wants this thing, and I want to give it to her, in apology, but I truly cannot take the risk.

I will need to meet with her again, though. She has the power to upend my life, and I must talk to her face-to-face and bring her to fully understand what she's asking me to do and why I cannot do it.

I text her, warning that my position hasn't changed but accepting her invitation to lunch. We arrange to meet at her hotel suite at noon tomorrow.

Then I text Marco. As much as I'd love to call instead, tourist-season weekends are insanely busy for him. He won't be in bed yet, but he'll be exhausted.

Me: It's me. Busy day here, but I'm sure yours was busier!
   I just wanted to check in and say *buonanotte e sogni d'oro*.

The reply comes right away.

Marco: Yep, long day, but never so long that I'm not up for
   a chat. FaceTime?

I hesitate, my fingers over the keypad. I'm on a busy New
York street in the rain. Not the place for the conversation we need
to have. I can probably get to my hotel in about fifteen minutes
but . . .

My heart pounds, as if I've been asked to publicly perform a
new song from sheet music. I'm not prepared. I need to be
prepared.

Me: I'm out, having taken a wrong turn, and it's raining.
   Not a good look for me.
Marco: I'll be the judge of that.

I snap a photo and send it.

Marco: *Bellissimo*. But, yes, not the environment for a video
   chat. Tomorrow?
Me: I'll be up by six, and I don't have anything before
   eleven. That's between noon and 5 p.m. your time.
   Anything work there?
Marco: How about nine your time?
Me: Excellent. And . . . it won't be a short talk. I really do
   need to speak to you.

Silence. Then,

Marco: Those ominous words again. The same
   conversation, I presume? More urgent now?
Me: Just an overdue conversation that became more
   pressing after I left Rome. Nothing ominous, I promise.

I'm not sure he buys that. I've said it twice now, and a dozen
possibilities will be flying through his head.

We're getting too comfy — I need you to back off a little.
I'm moving to the US.
I've met someone else.
I love you and want to have your baby.
Okay, he knows me too well for that last one.

I try to reassure him by goofing around, asking for a photo of him now that I've sent one of me. He sends one of him reclining in bed with a book, and I tease that it doesn't show nearly enough. I get another picture . . . of his head and bare shoulders.

We go on like that for a while as I walk to the hotel, and ultimately, I get a full body shot . . . with the book strategically placed. I laugh at that, but I don't ask for more. We're old enough and savvy enough not to exchange X-rated pics. I'll reciprocate tomorrow with something equally sexy and PG-13. *After* we have the conversation, though. Better not to send him a boudoir photo right before telling him that, with the right online search terms, he can find pictures of me topless in a hot tub, straddling Colt Gordon.

I sigh. That is not going to be a fun conversation. None of it is, and I wish I could retract my promise to Isabella, fly home tonight and tell Marco in person.

I'll do it by video chat tomorrow, and maybe that's best, giving him time alone to assimilate everything before I come home.

Right now, though, I have another call to make. To my mother.

CHAPTER FOURTEEN

MOM and I talk for almost two hours. Her responses are as perfect as ever. She's concerned that I might be hurt again. Proud that I stood up to Isabella. Less forgiving of Isabella than I am, and let's face it, that's what every child wants, isn't it? The mother who will stand at your side, snarling in full Mama Bear mode, leaving you to feel proud of yourself for saying, "No, Mom, it's not all her fault—I accept responsibility, too."

That is hour one of our conversation. Hour two is quieter planning. Mom agrees I need to talk Isabella down from this mad scheme. She also agrees a public reconciliation would do me no good.

After that, we plan for her to come see me. She has a lunch engagement tomorrow that I urge her not to break. She'll arrive in the evening, and we'll enjoy three days of New York City before I go home.

That settled, I order room service for dinner and curl up on the massive bed to eat and watch a show on my laptop. I manage to stay up until ten, which is a miracle given the time difference. Then I sleep remarkably well . . . until my body jolts upright at four, shouting, "You've slept in!"

I force myself to stay in bed a while longer. It doesn't require much coercion. I slide between dreaming and waking. Then I admire the photos Marco sent. Indulge in a little sleepy daydreaming . . . until I'm awake enough to remember that call with him later this morning, the one I need to plan.

I'm doing that when my phone chimes with an incoming text, and I grab it, hoping it's Marco. Like when I'm waiting my turn to audition, and I get the chance to jump the line. I volunteer even as part of me screams that I'm not ready. Sometimes "not quite ready" is the best place to be, where you haven't reached the over-thinking and overplanning stage.

The text, though, is from Isabella. I wince, and I lie there, looking at her name, not opening the message, wondering whether I can text Marco instead and see whether he might be free before nine.

I sigh and open the message as I curse my mother for raising a responsible child.

Isabella: Is it possible to see you for breakfast instead?
Isabella: Jamie's had an episode. I need to leave this
    morning.
Isabella: Can you let me know when you're up?

Jamie's had an episode. Those words send a frisson of worry through me. I remember Isabella saying she'd stayed with Colt longer than expected because of Jamison. I know from that poster that Jamison is an actor, and honestly, that's a surprise. I remember a quiet, sensitive boy. Easily wounded, but kind to his core.

I google Jamison Morales-Gordon. The first few results are about the new movie, his second apparently, and the first with his father. I dig deeper, and when I do, it's like a punch in the gut.

Drugs. Alcohol. Rehab. Attempted suicide.

My eyes fill, and my heart hurts.

Oh, Jamie. Baby. What happened?

What happened? Well, let's start with his trusted tutor

allegedly sleeping with his father and nearly breaking up his family. I quickly text Isabella back.

> Me: Go to Jamie. We can talk another time.
> Isabella: I really would like to see you, and my car won't be here until ten.
> Isabella: Could you come for breakfast?
> Isabella: Please.
> Me: Of course.

I respond before I have time to consider. I still have one eye on that article, skimming it as tears brim.

What did you expect, Lucy? Didn't you just say he was sensitive, easily hurt? You befriended him, and he confided in you, and then you left . . . slicing a cleaver through his family as you went.

I tell Isabella I'm on my way, and she says to come straight up, and she'll have breakfast waiting.

I shower and dress as quickly as I can. As I'm roaring out the door, I catch sight of the bedside clock. It's 6:15. Will I get back before nine?

I send Marco a quick text saying I might call a bit late. Then I'm off.

For 6:45 A.M., Isabella's hotel is remarkably busy. People who flew in Sunday night for Monday morning meetings are now hurrying off to grab breakfast. I slip inside, and I'm on the elevator before I wonder whether I'll need a card to access the penthouse. I don't.

When I reach Isabella's door, it's not quite shut, as if someone dropped off breakfast and forgot to pull it closed. That gives me pause, and my skin prickles remembering another door left ajar just a few days ago. But there'd been an explanation for that one, and there will be for this one, too.

I ring the bell. Wait. Ring again and add a knock for good

measure. When she still doesn't answer, I press my fingers to the door and push it open an inch.

"Isabella?" I call.

Music plays upstairs, and I raise my voice, but I'm still not sure she'd hear.

I send a text.

Me: The door's open. I'm coming in.

She doesn't respond, and I push the door and slide through.

"Isabella?" I call.

Still no answer. I walk into the living area. There's no sign of breakfast.

I stop at the bottom of the spiral stairs leading to the second floor.

"Isabella? I'll just wait down here, okay?"

No answer. I check my phone. No reply to my text, either.

I call Isabella's number . . . and her phone rings right beside me. It's been left on the sofa. Well, that's not going to help.

I climb the stairs slowly, still calling her name. When I reach the top, I follow the music to the open bedroom door.

"Isabella?"

Nothing.

I peek through to see an unmade bed.

I pause as I remember all the times I'd walked past Isabella's open bedroom door to see her making her bed the moment she rose. A habit from her grandmother, she once said. So that bed snags my attention, but at fifty, she probably no longer feels quite so compelled to heed her grandmother's rules.

As I step back, I spot a slipper protruding from behind the bed, and I have to smile. It's a ridiculous novelty slipper—a giant bear paw, complete with claws. My mind trips back fourteen years to Isabella walking into the kitchen wearing them.

You like my footwear? she said with a laugh. *The kids got us themed slippers last year. Princess ones for me, and these for Colt.*

Beauty and Beast. He never wears his, so I stole them. Which one I'm wearing is a hint to my mood. She winked at me. *These mean I'm preparing for a call with the studio execs, and I'm summoning my inner Beast.*

That's when I see the angle of the slipper. It hasn't just been cast off. There's a sliver of leg visible above it.

"Isabella!" I tear around the bed to find her supine on the floor, her head against the base of the bedroom Jacuzzi. Blood haloes her dark hair, and there's a deep gash on her forehead.

I fall beside her and grab her shoulder.

It's cold. Her body is cold.

No. It's just chilly in here with the air conditioning pumping. She tripped and hit her head on the tiled step, and she's unconscious.

She isn't moving.

Because she's unconscious.

Her lips aren't moving. Her chest isn't moving. She's not breathing.

I can't be sure of that. I'm not a doctor.

You know how to check. Two summers as a lifeguard, remember?

I press my fingers to the side of Isabella's neck. Her cold, clammy neck. I tell myself it's just cool to the touch.

Unnaturally cool, you know that.

I swallow hard. My fingers don't detect a pulse, but with that voice of doom clanging through my head, I might not be checking properly. I try again. I watch for signs of breathing, of a heartbeat.

There are none.

Isabella is dead. She hit her head on the step and died here, alone.

That makes no sense. Look, Lucy. Think.

The gash is on her forehead, meaning she should be lying on her stomach. Instead, she's resting peacefully on her back with her eyes closed.

Someone put her here.

Someone all but crossed her arms over her stomach, leaving

her looking as peaceful as a corpse in a casket, with that halo of blood . . .

Why is there blood *behind* her head when the injury is on her forehead? There's no trail of it down her scalp.

I see blood under her nostrils, and I realize her perfect nose isn't quite straight. There's smeared blood on her cheek and chin, as if partially washed away.

She'd been facedown on the carpet. Facedown and bleeding, and then someone turned her over and cleaned her up and left her ready for her close-up.

I stagger backward. As I do, I bump the bed. I look at it again. Only the coverlet is pushed down, crumpled, the sheet still neatly tucked in. I catch sight of a gold square on the floor and bend to see a wrapped chocolate, the type left during turndown service.

Isabella didn't sleep in this bed. Someone just yanked back the covers and rumpled them to look as if she did.

This has been staged.

And I'm part of the setting.

Isabella is dead, murdered, and now my fingerprints are everywhere.

Yes, my fingerprints are everywhere . . . because I found her body. I just need to report this and explain. I have the texts showing that she called me here.

That niggling voice in my head clears its throat.

About those texts . . .

I grab my phone and skim the messages. The first came at 5:53.

I may not know much about forensics, but I've read enough mysteries to realize a body wouldn't go cold in an hour. Even if that could happen, it doesn't explain the bed.

I scroll through the messages. They don't *not* sound like her, but there's also nothing distinctly in her voice.

Did the texts actually come from her phone?

I race down the stairs so fast I tumble on the last three. Her phone still lies on the couch. I reach for it and then stop. I can explain away fingerprints upstairs, but not on her phone.

Did I leave fingerprints upstairs?

In my initial panic, I'd envisioned my prints everywhere, but I don't actually recall touching anything except Isabella herself, and I don't think prints could be lifted from that.

I held the railing, but I'd been here yesterday, and no one would have cleaned since then.

Why am I thinking this through? I'm going to report her body and admit I was here.

Is that wise?

Yes, yes, it is. Whatever my experience with the media and the police, I still trust them in something like this. Isabella's been dead for hours, and I only just arrived, and there will be no evidence I killed her.

Those texts . . .

If someone summoned me to this room, that means I'm being set up.

Maybe so, but it's poorly done. I'll be fine. I'm not about to leave prints intentionally, and the trail I *have* left supports my story.

I will call it in. I just want a look at Isabella's phone first. I need to know what I'm dealing with here.

I grab a facecloth from the main bath and lift the phone. Then I realize I can't check texts without touching the screen. I'll need to wipe it down afterward.

The phone tries to recognize my face. It can't, obviously. I glance upstairs and shiver.

I need to see the texts before the police get hold of this phone. I need to know if they came from it.

And I need to know what else happened last night, who the last person was that Isabella spoke to. Protect myself by having all the facts before I let the police take the phone.

Feeling like a ghoul, I slip back upstairs, bend over Isabella's body and unlock the phone. Then I go into settings, turn off the screen lock and—

The doorbell rings. I shoot up from my crouch, slip to the steps and creep down. The ring comes again.

Should I answer it? Throw it open and say, "Isabella Morales is dead!" Or casually open it and pretend I just arrived, and we'll "find" her body together?

Go away, please. Just go away so I can call 911 and do this properly.

Otherwise, how will it look? I'm found in the room with a dead body, a murdered woman whom I allegedly had every reason to hate.

My gut seizes.

I *must* be the one to report this. Anything else will heap suspicion at my feet.

I'm frozen between the living room and the foyer. If that door opens, I'll grab it and say I've found her. That's all I can do. Play this through with honesty. I found Isabella. I was just about to call 911 when the doorbell rang, and I raced down to answer it.

A keycard slides through the reader. I snatch my purse from the floor and lunge forward, ready to yank open the door and tell whoever's there—

As I reach for the knob, I see what's still clutched in my hand.

Isabella's cell phone.

CHAPTER FIFTEEN

I'M HOLDING A MURDERED woman's cell phone. I've unlocked it. My fingerprints are all over it.

The door starts to open, and I dive behind it. I don't think. I can't. I panic and scramble behind the door. Then I see the closet, its sliding door halfway open.

A woman knocks and calls, "Ms. Morales?" and as she does, I creep into the closet and ease the slider almost shut.

Footsteps sound.

"Ms. Morales?" a woman calls tentatively. "I am sorry to bother you, but we received a call that you were in trouble. I have brought security."

Someone reported a problem? How? I haven't made any noise.

No one heard anything, you idiot. You're here. That's what counts. You're here, and whoever killed Isabella knows it. Now you're about to be caught hiding in the damn closet. Are you trying to help the killer frame you?

Two people enter, one set of light footsteps and another heavier. The security guard and the staff member who brought him. They whisper right outside the closet, and I hold my breath. All I see is the front door, pushed against the closet. Then that closes with a whoosh as they decide the woman should lead the way in case Ms. Morales is still in bed. The guard will follow right behind.

As they head inside, I check my phone to see that my final text to Isabella—telling her I'm here—has been read.

Isabella's killer is in this suite. They picked up Isabella's phone downstairs while I was in her bedroom, and they read my message—

No, that's not possible. When I picked up Isabella's phone, my text showed as a new notification. Someone read it while I had her phone in my hand.

I'm about to say that's impossible when I remember one of my music students getting texts on her watch. I'd marveled at the technology, and she'd teased that I was showing my age. She'd shown me how messages from her phone appeared on both her watch and her tablet, and they could be answered from any of the three.

I stuff Isabella's phone into my purse as the stairs creak. I peer through the cracked-open closet door just as the security guard's pant legs disappear up the stairs.

Now's your chance. You have about twenty seconds between them finding the body and calling for help.

Run, Lucy.

I take a deep breath.

I will not run. I haven't done anything wrong. I was lured here, and I can prove it. I just can't afford to be found in this damn closet. Or found with Isabella's cell phone.

I consider my options and decide it's best not to be found in her room at all. Pretend I just arrived after receiving those texts.

I slip off my ankle boots and ease open the door. Footsteps overhead walk into the master bedroom. I brace for a scream. Instead, there's a gasp and then,

"Ms. Morales!" The man says.

"Is she—?"

"Call—"

I don't hear the last. I'm already out the door. I fly past the elevator, following the emergency exit signs to the stairwell.

Twenty flights of stairs. They're empty, and as I zoom down, I wipe off Isabella's phone.

I have to pause at the bottom to catch my breath and pull on my boots. Then I take out my phone. However bad this might look, I have proof that yesterday's talk with Isabella wasn't a heated argument. Proof that we'd parted on good terms, as supported by my texts.

I take out the phone and flip to the recording. I put it to my ear and press Play and . . .

I hear voices. Muffled and indistinct voices. I turn up the volume, and the distortion only comes louder as my eyes round in horror.

The phone didn't pick up the conversation through my purse. I never checked that it would work. I'd just blithely hit Record and left it in my purse, pleased with myself for being clever.

Not clever at all.

I don't have a recording of our conversation, just voices so muffled I can't even tell who's who.

Deep breath.

I didn't kill Isabella, and that's what counts.

I step from the stairwell with as much dignity as I can muster. There's no one in sight. I walk into the crowded lobby and take a seat in a plush chair.

With a tissue, I surreptitiously remove Isabella's phone and tuck it under the seat cushion. I'll come back for it later. Then I head onto the elevator and hit the button for the penthouse level.

It is only as the elevator doors open again that my brain screams a flaw in my plan. That final text I sent—the one saying Isabella's door was unlocked and I was coming in. It proves I didn't arrive just now.

I reach to stop the doors from opening, but of course, they still do. And there's a security guard standing right there, blocking the way to Isabella's room.

I could retreat. Pretend I have the wrong floor and . . .

He turns and sees me.

I step off the elevator. The door to the penthouse is open, and inside, people are talking, voices coming fast and urgent.

I look toward it. Before I can say a word, the guard says, "If you're here to see Ms. Morales, there's been an incident. You'll have to come back later."

Retreat.

Just retreat.

No, I need to be honest. Or as honest as I can be under the circumstances.

I cast a worried look toward the penthouse and then back to the guard. He's maybe forty. Bald with a beard that tries for trendy and fails.

"I was just up here," I say. "I was meeting Isabella for breakfast, and the door was ajar. She wasn't answering. I texted to say I was coming inside, but that felt weird, so I went downstairs and waited for her to call."

"You were up here earlier?" the guard asks.

I nod. "Maybe twenty-five minutes ago?" I check my phone. "Twenty-eight, apparently. The door was ajar. I figured that was accidental, and I shut it. She never did answer my text, so I came back up. Is she okay?"

He says nothing. Just studies me. A slow once-over—a little too slow for comfort—and then he eases back.

"What was your business with Ms. Morales?" he asks.

"Breakfast." *Like I said.* "We were supposed to have lunch, but she texted this morning to ask if she could switch to breakfast."

His eyes narrow. He checks his watch. "Awfully early, isn't it?"

"Her plans changed. I said I was up, and she asked if I could come over right away."

His lips purse behind the sparse beard. His gaze slides over me again, still slow, as if using the excuse.

"Were you the redhead in those *Jurassic* movies?"

I laugh softly. If the guy thinks I look like Bryce Dallas

Howard, he's clearly seen too many "celebrities without makeup" tabloid spreads. He must know Isabella is in showbiz, and Ms. Howard is probably the only red-haired actress he can think of.

The question does make me relax, though, and I say, "No, but thank you. That's very flattering. I'm just an old acquaintance of Isabella's." I cast an anxious gaze at her room. "*Is* she all right?"

The elevator opens. A gurney comes off, and I gasp, while mentally reminding myself not to oversell this.

"Did something happen?" I say.

The guard tugs me aside to make way for the paramedics though I've already moved. He uses the excuse to hold me there, his thumb rubbing my bare forearm.

"I'm in the way," I say. "I should go."

"Better give me your contact information first," he says. "In case they need it."

I glance toward the room. "She is all right, isn't she?"

"Give me your card, and I'll have someone get back to you."

"Thank you. I don't have a card, but I'll jot down my name and number."

I write *Genevieve Callahan* and my cell phone on a scrap of paper. As I pass it over, I add, "Isabella calls me Lucy, but Genevieve is my legal name." I don't want anyone claiming I tried to hide my identity, but nor do I want to write "Lucy Callahan" on anything involved with Isabella.

As he pockets the scrap, the elevator doors open, and he catches my arm again, using the excuse to pull me aside, though by now, I'm ten feet from the elevator.

"Are you sure you're not an actress?" he says. "I feel like I've seen you before."

"Excuse me," says a voice over my shoulder. I turn to see a woman about my age, wearing a suit. I think she's with the hotel . . . until I spot the two uniformed officers behind her. My gaze drops to her detective's badge.

"Is something . . . ?" I swing on the security guard. "Is Isabella okay?"

"Do you work here?" the detective says brusquely to the guard.

He straightens. "Yes, ma'am."

"Then you're supposed to be guarding this floor. It's a crime scene, and the media is going to descend at any moment . . ." A pointed look at me. "If it hasn't already."

"Cr-crime scene?" I say, my voice rising.

"She's not a reporter," the guard interjects. "She knows Ms. Morales. She was here for breakfast with the lady."

And with that, my chance to escape evaporates. Which is fine. I have to do this sooner or later.

The detective tells me that Isabella is dead, apparently from a slip and fall, and I pretend I just found out. I'm shocked, and . . . Oh, my god, was she in the bathroom? Showering for our breakfast? Maybe if I'd gone inside, I could have saved her.

I hate myself for my performance. Earlier, I'd thought this would be easy. A small lie. One little omission.

Yes, I came to the hotel. Yes, I went to Isabella's suite. But I didn't find her body.

It's not simple. I have to dredge up every film-camp acting lesson. Even then, I stand outside myself, critiquing.

You don't seem shocked enough to have just heard the news.

You seem too shocked for someone who already saw the EMT go into the suite.

You don't seem upset enough for having just found out an old friend is dead.

You seem too upset over someone you haven't seen in years.

Once I'm past my "Oh, my God, Isabella is dead" performance, the woman—Detective Kotnik—leads me into the suite, where she can speak to me in relative privacy.

I tell her everything, and I show her the texts. Those definitely catch her attention. Whatever the EMTs have said about possible time of death, she knows it's significant that I received these barely an hour ago.

That's when she sends one of the officers to look for Isabella's phone, and my moment of panic turns to one of relief. It may be a good thing they won't find it here. It'll look as if Isabella's killer took her phone to lure me in.

Detective Kotnik says nothing about the possibility that Isabella isn't the one who contacted me. I don't, either. I remind myself that if I hadn't seen Isabella's body, I'd be confused and concerned—and maybe a little curious—so I regularly glance toward the second floor, where the EMTs and Kotnik's partner work.

Kotnik takes my statement. When she asks what I was talking to Isabella about, I say it was a mix of personal and business, which is not untrue. I knew Isabella years ago, and we were catching up, and she had a business proposition for me. I'd initially turned her down, but I'd agreed to think it over last night and meet for lunch. I show the texts to support my story. I don't use the name Lucy, but I show my passport for ID, and Lucille is there as my middle name, which is good enough. I'm not hiding anything. Well, not hiding much, at least.

We're going through my statement again when Kotnik's partner calls her upstairs. She lifts a finger for me to wait.

As she leaves, I exhale. I've played it cool, even if my stomach hasn't stopped twisting the entire time.

The moment I saw Isabella on the floor, I should have summoned help. When the hotel staff arrived, I lost that chance.

No, I had that chance stolen from me. Intentionally. Whoever sent those texts was waiting for me, and I helpfully signaled my arrival by texting Isabella that I was coming in. Her killer gave me just enough time to be discovered with the body.

When I escaped, I should have just kept going, raced back to my hotel and . . .

And what? Pretended I never left it? This is a murder. They'll check Isabella's texts. For all I know, cameras caught me coming into the hotel, too.

You should have run. Just run.

No, that's the worst thing I could do.

What if they discover I've already lied? That I did come inside and find the body?

Someone set you up, Lucy.

You're being framed.

You need to get out of here.

They'll find out who you are, and that will change everything. You know it will.

But I didn't kill Isabella.

You didn't sleep with Colt, either.

A young woman's voice sounds in the foyer. Someone's trying to block her entrance, and she's blasting them.

I know that voice.

Do I? No, when I strain, it doesn't sound familiar.

I can't hear what she's saying, just a brief and angry interchange before she marches in and our eyes meet and . . .

I'm looking at Tiana Morales-Gordon.

It doesn't matter that I haven't seen her since she was ten years old. There is not a single heartbeat where I wonder whether I'm mistaken.

God, how much she looks like her mother.

That's my first thought, but then I realize it's not entirely true. Tiana is a taller version of Isabella, her dark curls cut shoulder length, her blue eyes flashing.

When Tiana sees me, there is not a moment's hesitation for her, either. Her mouth tightens, and those blue eyes blast pure hate. Then she pivots and marches upstairs, and even as her heels click toward the bedroom, she's already snapping, "What the hell is *she* doing here?"

There's a moment of confusion, and Tiana has to identify herself and be shooed out of the bedroom, which makes her forget about me as she argues that this is her mother, and she's not leaving.

A temporary reprieve.

Very temporary.

She will tell them exactly who I am, and I will leave this suite in handcuffs.

Stop that. You're overreacting.

Am I?

I need to get out of here. Not flee. Just get out and talk to someone. My mother. Nylah. Marco. Someone I can entrust with my story in case I am arrested. Someone who will tell me what I should do.

Upstairs, the police are still trying to keep Tiana from her mother, which is going as well as one might expect. Down here, the officer at the door is busy casting anxious glances up there, as if wondering how much trouble he'll catch for allowing Tiana inside.

I walk over and say, "I should probably go."

The officer cuts me a quick glance.

"Detective Kotnik got my statement," I continue. "I was just waiting to let her know I'll be at my hotel if she has questions, but there's obviously an issue up there, and she's going to be a while."

He nods absently, his attention slingshotting back to the argument.

"She has my contact information," I say.

Another nod. And with that, I'm free. Kotnik does have my contact information, and if that doesn't include my hotel name, well, she can remedy that oversight with a bit of digging. It'll give me the time I need to come up with a plan.

I pause at the door, listening to Tiana above. Then I'm gone.

CHAPTER SIXTEEN

ISABELLA IS DEAD, and I don't know how to process that, so I focus on taking action instead. Once again Isabella's phone is nestled in my pocket, and as soon as I reach the alley, I flip out the SIM card, snap it in two and stick that into my pocket. On the next street, I drop the broken SIM into a sewer grate. I know far too much about covering my tracks.

This isn't the same, though. I only discard the SIM so the phone can't be traced to me. I should just drop the whole thing down the sewer. I don't because my gut says I need to see who spoke to her last night.

Who do you think you are? Miss Marple?

No, but if the situation dives south, it'll help to know what else was going on in Isabella's life. It'll make me feel more in control, which I need right now.

I want to handle this on my own, quickly and efficiently clearing my name before anyone knows I'm connected to Isabella's murder. Is that even possible? I shiver just thinking about it.

It's happening again.

I'm going to be in the papers again.

My life will be ruined again.

The last snaps me out of it. *My* life ruined? What about Isabella, dead on a bathroom floor?

I can handle this. First, I need to notify my mother, who will understand the significance the moment she hears that Isabella is dead. When I call, I only intend to warn her. Instead, the sound of her voice unleashes all the panic and fear and grief and shock, and I have to veer into a building alcove before I break down sobbing in the street.

I don't tell my mother that I found Isabella's body. I can't tell her anything that could make her an accomplice.

Accomplice? You didn't kill anyone.

An accomplice to my lie. To what I'm sure is a criminal offense.

The full reality of that hits me.

I have interfered with a murder investigation. I have committed a crime.

Whatever I've done, I won't compound it by confessing to my mother. Nor do I lie. I just say that Isabella summoned me to breakfast, and now she's dead, and it wasn't Isabella who sent those messages. Someone's setting me up.

As I finish, I head back to the road, my eyes dry again.

"So now I'm heading to my hotel," I say. "I'm not certain the detective dismissed me. I just needed to get out of there and clear my head. I'll wait for them at my hotel."

"You can't speak to the police again without a lawyer."

"I'm a witness, not a suspect."

"You're being set up, Lucy. You need a lawyer. Now."

Her voice is firm, and let's be honest, despite my objections, I *am* worried. I'm scared, too. Every time I say I did nothing wrong, a voice whispers that it didn't matter before. This isn't the same thing—I was tried in the court of public opinion last time, and that bitch is stone-cold—but that voice still whispers.

I may be innocent, but I am not naive. I will never be naive again.

"I'm going to my hotel," I say. "I'll make some calls and find a lawyer."

"Thank you."

I WALK past the desk clerk and make a point of saying hi. I met him yesterday—he's a student from the Congo, and we'd chatted about coming to the "big city" for school as I'd done so many years ago. Now I must force myself to exchange pleasantries, as if I haven't just found the body of someone I cared about. Then I continue on to my room. I have not snuck in. I have not attempted to avoid security cameras.

I need to call Marco. I must warn him before my name hits the news in any way. I open my suite door and walk in, phone in hand, ready to call—

Someone has been in my room.

At first, I only stand there, clutching my keycard as if I've entered the wrong room. For a moment, I actually wonder whether I have.

It hasn't been ripped apart, as one sees in the movies. The opposite, actually. The sheets are pulled up, the pillows in place, the drawers all closed tight.

I'm not a messy person. I can't be, with my tiny Rome apartment. But as I tore out this morning, worried about Jamison, I'd glanced back at the room, shuddered and hung out the Privacy Please sign so the maid service wouldn't see the mess.

I exhale. Okay, there's my answer. Maid service. The sign must have fallen off, and someone came in to clean.

Except the room hasn't been cleaned. The sheets are pulled up, but the bed is not made. There's trash in the basket and a dirty mug on the night stand.

I check the door. The Privacy Please sign still hangs from the knob. I glance up at my room number, but that's silly. My keycard wouldn't work in the wrong door. Also, I can see my belongings scattered about the room.

Maybe the maid service came in and then noticed the sign and stopped.

Does that make *any* sense?

It doesn't, and I know the answer, as much as I hate to admit it.

Someone broke in.

It wasn't a random thief, either. Isabella's killer knew I wasn't in my suite. They came in and planted something. Planted evidence to frame me.

I hesitate, my brain insisting I'm mistaken, paranoid.

Someone's framing me for murder. How the hell can I *not* be paranoid?

But I'm overthinking this. Turning a casual redirection ploy into a full-fledged frame-up. Based on those texts alone, I would only be questioned. It would temporarily divert the investigation, setting both the police and the media on a juicy target. A serious frame-up requires a lot more than summoning me to the crime scene. It needs . . .

I look at the room.

Evidence. Planted evidence.

I lunge forward and start searching. Pull back the sheets, looking for . . . What? Bloodstains, as if I'd crawled in covered in blood?

Clothing. They could put blood on my clothing.

I grab yesterday's clothes from a chair, where they lie crumpled. As I'm turning from the window, I catch a glimpse of a police car. My breath stops, but again, I tell myself I'm being silly. It's a police car in New York, and it's not coming . . .

The car turns toward the hotel. I walk to the window and look down to see it pull into the loading zone. Two officers get out and head for the front door.

They're responding to an unrelated call. Maybe an early-morning disturbance. Just because you can afford five hundred bucks a night doesn't mean you won't smack your wife around.

I didn't tell the police where I was staying. Sure, they could get that information from Isabella's assistant, Bess, but it'd be easier to just call me and ask.

Hey, Ms. Callahan? You weren't supposed to leave. I'm sending a car to pick you up. We have a few more questions.

Even if they *are* here for me, it's just more questions.

Then why is it uniformed officers instead of detectives?

Well, that's proof they aren't here for me, isn't it?

As my brain argues, my body takes action without me realizing it, and I am startled to see myself stuffing the dirty clothing into my smaller carry-on bag.

Hiding potential evidence? No, not really. Not entirely, anyway.

My body continues taking action. More clothing into the bag. My laptop. My toiletry case.

What the hell do you think you're doing, Lucy?

What I must do. Being prepared.

You're not running. No matter what this is, you cannot run.

I don't answer the voice. My pounding heart won't let me. I methodically pack my smaller bag, and then take one last look around . . .

Something's wrong.

Yes, you're fleeing police who almost certainly aren't even here for you.

No, not that. Something . . .

I spot the charge cables plugged into the wall, and my gut says that isn't it, but I do need those. I grab them, stuff them into the bag and stride out the door.

CHAPTER SEVENTEEN

I HURRY DOWN THE STAIRS, each jarring step thumping a rebuke through me.

You're being silly.

You're being paranoid.

Isabella is dead. Murdered. Someone is hell-bent on framing me, and maybe the average person would trust that the truth will protect them, but I know better. It doesn't matter whether I'm guilty or innocent. The moment my name reappears in the papers, I will never go back to my peaceful life in Rome.

That thought sets my heart tripping so hard I can barely draw breath, and I allow the judgmental voice to return, telling me I'm overreacting. I want it to be correct. I would happily make a fool of myself if it meant I never had to go through the hell of another public scandal.

I walk slowly down the hall. By the time I near the lobby, I can hear the officers at the front desk.

"Do you have a room number?" the clerk is asking.

"No," one of the officers says. "That's why we're here talking to you."

"I'm afraid I cannot provide that information."

"Do you see this badge, kid?"

The "kid"—the Congolese college student—clips each word as he says. "I still cannot provide that information. If you would like me to ring Ms. Callahan, I can do so."

Ms. Callahan.

I back up two steps, where I can hear them but not be spotted.

"I don't want you to *ring* her," the officer says. "We're here to arrest her."

Wait. Did he just say . . . ?

No, it's too soon. I've misheard. I must have.

"Oh," the desk clerk says. "That's a very different situation."

"Good. So her room number?"

"As soon as I see the warrant. I'll need to photocopy it for my duty manager."

"Now you're just jerking us around, kid. Give me her room—"

"I am not 'jerking you around,' officer. I take your request as seriously as I take our guests' privacy. I need to assure my manager that I had a reason to provide Ms. Callahan's room number. A photocopy of the warrant will suffice."

"You know what will suffice—" the officer begins.

His partner cuts in with, "The warrant is on its way, Joseph. That's your name, right?"

"As it says on my tag, sir."

"Well, Joseph, we appreciate you protecting your guests, but Ms. Callahan is visiting from Italy, which means she's a flight risk. She fled a crime scene."

Fled?

Hell, no. I talked to that officer at the door. I provided my contact information.

The officer continues, "We'll have the warrant within the hour, and you'll get your photocopy then. Right now, we need Ms. Callahan."

"You can't arrest her without a warrant, officers, so I'm not certain I understand the rush. I saw her go to her room fifteen minutes ago. Our elevator and stairwell exit are both right there.

She can't leave without you knowing it. We'll wait for that warrant and do this properly."

The officers argue, but I'm out the side door before I hear the rest. As I stride from the hotel, I call Mom and tell her what just happened.

"They can't possibly have enough evidence for a warrant," I say.

"They don't need it. This is a high-profile case, and they want a quick arrest. You're their scapegoat."

"No, Mom. Even if they know who I am, it's a huge leap from that to a warrant. A judge won't give them one without evidence."

Mom says something, but I don't hear her over the voice in my head, whispering that they *do* have evidence if they know I was in Isabella's room this morning. My fingerprints are there.

And what did they plant in my suite?

Oh, shit. My room. I turn back toward the hotel. I shouldn't have fled. I should have gone back up and searched and found what the intruder planted, gotten rid of it and then waited for the police to bring their warrant.

Gotten rid of the evidence how? Hidden it in the hotel? What they planted is almost certainly forensic evidence on my clothing, which I have in this bag.

Still, whatever was planted, it doesn't explain the warrant. There must be more evidence at the scene. Unless they're bluffing about the warrant . . .

Enough of this nonsense. I'm not a fugitive. I'm not going to become one. I will dispose of my clothing and temporarily hide my backpack. Grab a coffee and head back into the hotel and "Oh, hello, officers. Did you want to speak to me?"

I need to confess to the crime I *did* commit. Tell them I found Isabella this morning, and when the hotel staff knocked, I panicked, realizing I was about to be discovered in a murdered woman's hotel suite.

That's understandable, isn't it? A very human mistake. If they charge me for it, I'll deal with that.

Unless the killer planted evidence in my hotel room. Something I missed.

Am I absolutely certain someone broke in? How likely is that? Joseph wouldn't cut a new keycard without ID.

What about the clerk at the desk earlier this morning? Could she have been bribed for a card? Or the housekeeping staff?

No. Stop this nonsense, and fix the problem. Trust the system.

"I'm going back inside," I say to Mom.

"What?"

"I didn't kill Isabella. She was dead when I got those texts. I'm very clearly being set up. I'll explain. It'll be fine."

"No."

"Mom, I won't run. I don't need to."

"I'm not suggesting you run. We need to take control of the narrative here, Lucy, the way we couldn't the last time."

Take control of the narrative.

I stifle a sound that is half laugh, half sob as Mom's words echo Isabella's from yesterday. She'd wanted to take control of our story, and I remember her eyes alight as she planned how to do that. Grief wells, but I have to tamp it down so I can focus on this.

"If you're suggesting I talk to reporters first—" I begin.

"Absolutely not." From her tone, you'd think I suggested summoning demons for help. "I read a case where a woman knew she was about to be arrested for murder, so she went to her lawyer, and they arranged to bring her in. You can do that. You were walking back to your hotel, and you called me, and I told you to get a lawyer. If I'm wrong, that's on me. You can't be blamed for listening to your mother."

"I'm pretty sure that isn't a legal defense."

"On my advice, you are turning around now and going to a coffee shop. I will find you a lawyer, and you will speak to them, and they will arrange for you to turn yourself in—after they've heard your story and given you all the advice you need to proceed." A pause. "How are you dressed?"

I tell her.

"Good," she says. "You'll look presentable and professional."

"Unlike the last time, when I looked like a slovenly little slut."

"Genevieve *Lucille*."

My eyes fill with tears as I force a smile. "Sorry, Mom. None of that. Yes, I'm dressed nicely, and I have my toiletries on me. I'll fix my hair and makeup because there may be cameras. Like you said, control the narrative, which means control the visuals, too. This time, I will choose the image I present in the media."

"Precisely."

I'VE BEEN in this coffee shop for an hour, and I'm already wishing I'd opted for water and bland oatmeal. Instead, I tried to cheer myself up with a cappuccino and something between a muffin and a croissant, filled with cherry custard. The caffeine swirls in my gut while the pastry lies leaden at the bottom.

Mom hasn't called back. I tell myself that's fine. I tell myself *I'm* fine. That's a lie. I'm confused, and I'm scared. No, I'm terrified. This morning feels like an anvil over my head, waiting to drop and crush me.

I've hidden Isabella's phone. I don't want to walk into a lawyer's office holding it, but I need to know where it is.

Seventy-five minutes after I talked to Mom, my phone rings. I go to grab it. Then I see Marco's number.

Marco. Oh, my God, I forgot to call him. I'd been about to when I realized someone had been in my hotel room. I need to talk to him. Really need to. But I'm waiting for Mom's call, and I'd rather be able to tell him I have a lawyer and everything is fine. Just get past that step, and then I'll speak to him.

I force myself to hit Ignore. A moment later, a text appears.

Marco: I just got a very strange message. Call me back ASAP.

I'm sure it has nothing to do with me. Nothing to do with my situation.

That now-familiar refrain takes on an air of delusion, but this time, I must be right. It's been three hours since the hotel discovered Isabella's body. There is no way anyone has tracked down Marco.

Of course, I also told myself there was no way there could be a warrant out for my arrest already.

I stare at his message.

ASAP.

Isabella tracked me down using a private investigator. If that investigator did a halfway decent job, they know about Marco. He must be warned.

I'm about to hit Call Back when my cell vibrates and Mom's photo appears.

I fumble to answer with a "Hey" that I want to sound nonchalant, but it's tight and high.

"Hey, baby," Mom says. "How are you doing?"

"You didn't find anyone, did you?"

Two heartbeats of silence. Then, "Not yet, but I will."

"What did they say?"

Three heartbeats this time.

"They're being silly," she says. "Absolutely ridiculous."

"They say I should have stayed at the scene." I lower my voice as I rise to leave the coffee shop. "Or at the hotel."

She sputters, but I know I've nailed it. The lawyers don't like the way this case smells, and they don't want to get tangled up with me after I've evaded police.

"I'll find someone," she says quickly. "It could be a career-making case, and someone will want . . ."

She trails off, realizing that I might not want to hear that this could make a lawyer's career. Not when it could also ruin mine. Ruin my entire life.

I am being accused of murder.

"I meant that it'll be high profile," she says quickly. "A decent lawyer will easily win a dismissal, and that's good business. The police have made a mistake, and a lawyer will benefit from that incompetence. They're about to learn the truth of the saying 'Act in haste, repent in leisure.' Someone will lose their job over this."

There's satisfaction in her voice when she says it. This time, someone will pay for hurting her baby girl.

"I'll handle this," I say. "I'm not eighteen anymore. I can find myself a—"

"Let me, baby. Please. Just let me do this for you."

I should resist, but I'm too numb. I might not be eighteen anymore, but I'm not in the mental state to do this.

Murder.

I'm being accused of murder.

Mom promises she'll find a lawyer, and I barely hear her. I disconnect and stand on the sidewalk, holding my phone.

I always thought that the one advantage to my Colt scandal was that it "only" involved actors. It was tabloid fodder, and respectable media steered clear.

Isabella's death is that perfect blend of scandal and news. A murder with a delicious backstory that will sell papers and earn clicks.

I stare down at my phone.

My finger touches a button. My browser springs open. I tap the search bar. A few keystrokes, half of them are wrong, my finger suddenly huge and clumsy.

I try again, slower, and I fill the bar with search terms. *Isabella Morales. Death.* I hesitate on the last, inhale, backspace and replace it with *murder.* My finger poises over the Go button.

Then I add two more words, as hard as they are to type.

Lucy Callahan.

I hit Go, and I pray—literally pray, something I don't believe in. I won't say I've lost my faith. There certainly were times when I swore never to set foot in a church again, but eventually I felt like a furious child, swearing never to talk to a friend again because she failed to come to my defense in a schoolyard fight.

The truth is that even without my ordeal, I'd still have become an Easter-and-Christmas Catholic. I don't pray because I don't think there's anyone up there actively listening. My God is not a genie who grants wishes. My God is not Santa Claus, rewarding me for good behavior.

In that moment, though, I cannot help praying just a little.

When I hit this button, please show me nothing.

I tap it, and a headline appears.

"Lucy Callahan Wanted in Murder of Colt Gordon's Wife."

There is actually a bizarre moment when the part that truly outrages me is the last three words. *Colt Gordon's Wife.* Even in death, Isabella is defined by that role.

Of course, then I see the rest of that headline. I read it three times and decide I'm still sleeping. Yep, very clearly, I am having a horrible and preposterous nightmare, and when I wake, I'll laugh at myself.

You dreamed that the cops had a warrant for your arrest a couple of hours after finding Isabella's body?

You dreamed that news of it hit the Internet a mere hour later?

That makes no sense. You do realize that, right?

My gaze moves to the article source, and I flinch. This isn't CNN, though the URL does share two letters in common. My mother calls CNR.com Celebrity Nasty Rumors, which is about as biting as Mom gets.

CNR actually stands for Celebrity News Reports, as if adding those last two words makes the site seem like a legitimate source. Nylah says CNR's tagline should read "Reporting the Stories Even TMZ Won't Touch!" CNR prides itself on beating other online tabloids, which means they'll jump on any rumor. They're also known to pay top dollar for exclusive firsts.

As Nylah also says, I should be an honorary CNR stockholder. Before the Colt-and-Lucy spectacle, they'd been a fledgling paper tabloid. Then their reporter—pushed aside by the "big boys" staking out the Morales-Gordon beach party—wandered farther afield and landed the infamous hot-tub shots. They'd been so eager to get the scoop that they'd uploaded the photos to their website instead, becoming one of the first celebrity gossip sites, with TMZ still a few months from launch.

Allegedly, CNR nearly bankrupted themselves getting exclusive interviews with staff and partygoers. The gamble paid off, and they're now the first place people go when they have a story to sell.

Stories like this one.

They reported Isabella's death within thirty minutes of the police arriving on scene. The clip states simply that Isabella Morales—wife of Colt Gordon—was found dead in her hotel room early this morning. It goes on to say that a source inside the hotel told CNR that Lucy Callahan had visited Isabella the day before and helpfully reminds people who Lucy Callahan is with links to past articles . . . and one photo. *The* photo.

CHAPTER EIGHTEEN

THE HAMPTONS 2005

THE CAMERA BULB FLASHED, and Colt was out of the hot tub in one action-hero leap, dumping me off his lap so abruptly I smacked down, my head slamming against the edge. I swallowed chlorine water and came up sputtering and gasping. As I start climbing out, cool night air hit my bare breasts, and I yelped. My arms slapped over my chest as I scrambled to find my bikini top.

I'd just gotten it back on when Colt returned. He grabbed my arm and hauled me from the water. Then he held me there, as if I were a burglar caught in the act, while he found his cell phone and speed-dialed a number.

"Karla? I have a problem." A pause. "A girl."

A girl? Shock snapped my head up, indignation filling me. I'd been living in his house, looking after his children and teaching him to play guitar. Now he called me "a girl," as if I were some crazed fan who snuck into the party.

I tried to wrench out of his grip, but he held me tight without seeming to even realize I was there, too intent on his conversation with Karla.

"Yeah," he said. "Yeah, okay. We're on our way."

She replied as he listened.

"I'm not stupid," he snapped. Then he hung up, turned to me

and sighed. His hand loosened, as he pulled me into a hug, cell phone clapping against my back.

"It's okay," he murmured. "Everything's going to be okay, Lucy."

Oh, so you remember my name now?

His hand moved to my chin, and he lifted my face to his. "You didn't do anything wrong. Champagne and pretty girls just don't mix." His lips quirked in a smile, and he leaned to kiss me. I jerked back, but it was only a brush of the lips, and he didn't notice me withdraw, just slung an arm around my shoulders and started leading me away.

"Karla will fix this," he said. "She always does."

WE RETURNED by circling around the front. When we saw Karla, Colt patted my back and nudged me toward her.

"You go on now," he murmured. "Let Karla take care of you. Just do as she says, and everything will be fine. Whatever happens, I'll look after you. Remember that."

He brushed his lips over the top of my head and propelled me Karla's way. Then he loped back to the party.

As Karla walked over, my legs froze. I stood there, knees trembling.

Karla gave me this job. She treated me like a valued employee, not seasonal student help. And now I'd been photographed in a hot tub with her client, the man whose children she'd entrusted to my care.

"Lucy," she said, her expression unreadable. She nodded curtly and waved for me to follow her. When I caught up, she held out a bag.

"Clothing," she said, "and a few things I could grab from your room."

"M-my clothing?"

She lifted a hand as headlights appeared. A wave, and the black SUV approached.

"Lucy?" a voice called.

Jamison stood on the front porch, still wearing his swim trunks, a towel draped over his thin shoulders.

"Lucy?" he called again.

"Hey, Jamie," I said, forcing calm into my voice. "Is it time for bed? I just need to talk to Karla for a second. I'll be right—"

Karla cut me short. "Let me get your dad, Jamie. I need to speak to Lucy."

"Is something wrong?" His gaze flickered to me. He knew the answer. Jamison read emotions as naturally as I read sheet music.

"Nothing that has anything to do with you," I said. "Just a little thing Karla and I need to talk about."

She was already on her phone saying, "I think your son would like you to tuck him in, Colt."

Her voice was pleasant, and she managed a rare smile for Jamison, but whatever Colt said made that smile vanish as she turned away, voice lowering.

"That is not as important as your son," she hissed. "Get inside *now*."

She hung up and took a moment before turning back to us. "Your dad is coming, Jamie, and I'm just going to steal Lucy away for a chat, okay?"

Jamison nodded, but his worried eyes stayed fixed on me as he backed into the house and shut the door.

When Karla caught me staring at the closed door, she put her hand to my back in an awkward pat.

"He'll be fine," she said. "Isabella will look after him."

I did not miss her wording. She might have ordered Colt to tuck in his son, but ultimately, the role of responsible parent fell to Isabella.

Isabella . . .

"I-I need to talk to . . . ," I began.

I needed to confess to Isabella. To explain. To beg forgiveness. But if Karla could fix this, as Colt promised, then Isabella never needed to know about the kiss.

I imagined going back into that house, waking up and acting as if nothing had happened. Shame and guilt washed over me. I wanted to come clean. That was best for me. Best for Isabella, though?

No. Unburdening my sins was for confession, and that is what I would do. Confess to a priest. Confess to my mother. Confess to Nylah. I had to respect Isabella enough to keep this from her *and* make sure it never happened again. I'd learned this lesson as surely as if it'd been branded on my skin.

Karla steered me to the waiting car. We climbed in, and she gave the driver instructions. Then she flicked off the intercom and called his name, watching to be sure he couldn't hear it. A nod of satisfaction, and as the car pulled from the curb, she turned to me.

"I have someone on this already," she said. "It will be handled, but if there is anything you can tell me about the man who took the picture, that will help. We need to offer him more than the tabloids will."

"I-I didn't even know it was a man. I just saw camera flashes, and then Colt took off."

She nodded. "All right. Then I need to ask you some uncomfortable questions."

I tried not to squirm.

"Colt may have said he used protection, but women cannot trust men in these matters. We need to take control of our reproductive choices. Are you on the pill? Please be honest with me, Lucy. If you aren't, I can get something."

"N-no. I . . . I'm not on the pill, but we didn't—" My face scorched. "We were kissing in the hot tub when the photographer showed up."

"And before that? The other times?"

"There were no other times."

I braced for her to argue. When she didn't, I collapsed forward, hands to my face. "I-I can't believe I . . . I . . ."

"Colt is a very attractive man. You wouldn't be the first girl to have a crush on him. I'm not judging you." She hesitated and then met my gaze as I peered over my fingers.

"I mean that, Lucy. If anyone's to blame here, it's me for thinking the man could keep his damned pants—" She inhaled sharply and looked away. "No, let's lay the blame where it belongs. I know who did the seducing, and I don't blame you for having a crush on him."

"I didn't. He's Tiana and Jamie's *dad*. He's old enough to be *my* dad. I never . . . I never felt that way about him, and I was careful. I mean . . ." My cheeks heated again. "I knew he wasn't going to fall for me. I'm just the tutor. But you hear things, so I was careful. I didn't want him thinking I liked him and then . . ."

My face dropped into my hands again as my stomach heaved. "I don't know how this happened. That sounds bad, but I really don't. It just . . . It happened and . . . and . . ."

"How much did you have to drink?" she asked, and her voice was softer than I'd ever heard it. "Again, no judgment. It was a party."

"I had champagne." I hesitated as I calculated. "Two glasses."

"Anything else?"

I shook my head.

"Are you sure? I'm not judging here. I know I keep saying that, but I also know that, at your age, I tried it all." A weak smile. "Booze, boys and bongs, as difficult as that may be to imagine."

I lifted my head to meet her eyes. "It was two glasses of champagne. Nothing else. I swear it."

She paused, and I thought she was going to push harder. Instead, she reached for my chin and gently lifted my face as she turned on the interior light. Then she swore, the oath so quiet I barely caught it.

"Did you pour your own drinks, Lucy?" she asked.

I shook my head.

"Who gave them to you?"

"Justice brought me the first, and Colt gave me the second."

"Justice . . . ," she whispered under her breath.

I realized what she was thinking. "No. He wouldn't—"

Her cell phone rang, making me jump. She answered it, and as she listened, her face darkened.

"How?" she said. "No, there's been a mistake. It cannot possibly be—"

A pause.

"Yes, I know how the Internet works," she snapped, "but this is a tabloid story. What's the point in putting it online where anyone can see it for free? Who has it?"

She listened and then sniffed. "Never heard of them. Get in touch with someone there, and offer them ten thousand. Let me know when—"

Pause.

"What do you mean they don't want to talk? They are a tabloid, correct? They want money. Now get on it, and let me know when that photograph is gone."

She hung up and took a deep breath.

"Someone posted it on the Internet?" I said quietly.

"Ridiculous, isn't it?" She shook her head. "They could have sold that to the *Enquirer* and made—" She stopped herself with a short laugh. "Well, they are fools, and that is all the better for us. It'll be down before anyone sees it. I'll get Colt's lawyers involved. I'm sure there's a law against posting things like that on the Internet."

She lifted her Blackberry and typed. I thought she was texting the lawyers when she stopped and inhaled sharply. As she composed herself, she lowered the phone to her lap. I could see the screen, and it took a moment to understand what I was seeing. I knew you could access the Internet with some cell phones, but I'd never actually seen it done. That's what this was. Her Blackberry browser open to a photograph . . .

It was us in the hot tub. Colt was lifting me out of the water, his hands cupping my breasts as I arched back, my eyes closed. The expression on my face—

"Oh!" I said, drawing back as if burned.

Karla looked down and realized what I'd seen. She snatched the phone up, as I heaved, gasping for air. She reached past me to put down the window.

"Breathe," she said. "It's all right. Everything will be all right."

"I . . . I wasn't. I swear." I swallowed. "It looked as if we were . . . But we weren't. I swear it."

She didn't ask what I meant. No one who looked at that photo would wonder what I meant. I was straddling Colt with my head thrown back, my expression looking as if . . . looking as if I were doing a lot more than kissing him.

"We will take care of this," she said. "They made a mistake putting it on the Internet, and we will take full advantage of that. However . . ."

She touched my arm, and I turned to look at her.

"This is going to be very difficult to hear, and I hate to say it," she said. "I take responsibility for you because I hired you and because I know you do not deserve this. My priority though . . ."

"Your priority is Colt," I murmured.

"Colt and Isabella. I need to handle this for them. I will give you advice, and I will give you money—"

"I don't want money." My chin shot up. "I don't need it."

"I don't mean hush money, Lucy. I mean compensation for your early termination. Covering your wages for the rest of the summer."

Wages? Did she mean I was fired?

A hysterical giggle bubbled up in me. Did I think I'd be going back? Living in Isabella's house? Caring for her kids? With that photograph out there for the world—

Oh, God, Isabella was going to see—

"P-please don't let her see it." My words tumbled out. "Don't let Isabella see that photo."

"I will do my best to prevent that," Karla said slowly. "For now, let's worry about you. I'm going to have the driver pull over at a bank machine so I can withdraw money. Then we'll find you a place for the night. Call your mother as soon as you can. Tell her what's happened. Once I leave, Lucy, as much as I hate to say this, you'll be on your own, and you'll need your mother."

But what about Colt? He promised to take care of me.

That laugh almost erupted again, and this time I had to cough to cover it.

You really are a little fool, aren't you? What did you think you'd do, run away into the sunset together?

Of course not. If Colt Gordon appeared right now, racing after us in his Ferrari to proclaim his love, I'd tell the SUV driver to hit the gas. I didn't want Colt. I just thought when he said he'd take care of me, he meant that he'd make sure I didn't suffer any fall-out. He'd protect me from that. He'd ensure I was okay.

Colt didn't mean it. He'd been playing a role. We got caught, and he was in damage-control mode, and that meant getting me the hell away from his family before I caused a scene.

I'll take care of this.

I'll take care of you.

Now go. Please just go.

"Lucy?"

I looked over at Karla. She held herself tight, but in her face, I saw genuine concern shimming under that careful facade. She felt sorry for me, but she couldn't afford to. I wasn't her client. I wasn't her boss. I didn't pay for that Blackberry in her hand or the diamond studs in her ears. I could be indignant about it. But I wasn't. This was her career, and I would never expect her to risk it for an eighteen-year-old who had willingly gotten into a hot tub with her client.

Karla *was* being kind, more than she needed to be, more than I'd have expected. She was withdrawing money for me, proper compensation for lost wages, not an insulting payoff. She would put cash in my pocket, set me on my feet, offer what advice she could, and then give me a gentle push into the world, where I'd need to fend for myself. I didn't deserve that consideration, and I would not forget her kindness.

"Thank you," I said, my voice as calm and mature as I could make it. "I understand, and I appreciate any advice you can give."

"Well, with any luck, you won't need it because this will all be over by morning, and you'll have the rest of the summer free along with an excellent reference from me and from Colt."

A note in her voice said he'd be writing it with her standing at his shoulder if necessary.

"Now, let's talk strategy," she said.

CHAPTER NINETEEN

NEW YORK 2019

I STARE DOWN at the photo on my phone. It's the one I'd seen on Karla's browser all those years ago. It didn't go away that night. Karla had been so certain it would, and that seems ridiculously naive now, but it'd been 2005. Scandals hit the papers, not the Internet. No one had ever seen such a thing before . . . until me. The first major Internet-driven celebrity scandal. Not exactly an achievement for my resume.

Every time I've caught an accidental glimpse of this photo, I've turned away in mortification. Now, though, I look at it with the eyes of an adult, and I am angry. I see a girl who was drunk, possibly drugged. An eighteen-year-old virgin in a hot tub with a gorgeous, famous older man who wanted her, *really* wanted her.

I'd dated before that. Had a couple of boyfriends. Made out and fooled around, but it always felt not-quite-right. Like cakes baked in a toy oven. Those few minutes with Colt had been my first mature sexual experience, and as much as I hate the thought, I can't deny it.

This is what enrages me about the photo. It has taken that moment and thrown it to the world for titillation and ridicule. I would always have regretted what happened, but I should have been allowed the memory of a regrettable experience, one I've learned from. Instead, that private moment is forever public, online for the world to see.

What makes it worse is Colt's expression. He's looking up at me like a quarterback who just scored the winning touchdown. Pleased with himself. Utterly and confidently and smugly pleased, grinning at my pleasure as if to say, "I did this."

It's a self-satisfied grin, and it's a proprietary one, too.

I won this girl. I'm going to have this girl, and I'm going to enjoy her, and I deserve this. By God, I deserve it.

Someone jostles me, and I glance up, startled. It's just a passerby, but as soon as my gaze tears from that photo, I remember where I am and what I was doing.

I scroll past the photo and continue reading the article. It resumes to say that I'd been at Isabella's hotel this morning, where I claimed to have been invited for breakfast.

Claimed? My hackles rise, but I smooth them down. This is CNR. Take everything with a ten-pound block of salt. I'll get this sorted as soon as I show those texts to a lawyer.

I read the next line and almost continue past it. Then I stop and reread.

Callahan claims to have left Isabella Morales's suite on finding the door open, but sources within the hotel say the police have evidence that she was inside when the hotel staff responded to an urgent call from Isabella.

The temperature plummets, goosebumps rising.

The police know I was in the room.

Did I really think I'd get away with that?

I didn't think. Couldn't, at the time, the primitive part of my brain screaming for me to flee. What I'd forgotten is that someone went to the trouble of luring me to the scene, which meant they'd find a way to prove I'd been in the room.

I need to admit to being inside before the police accuse me of it. Control the narrative.

As bad as this looks, I must remember that I was in my own hotel room when Isabella died. I arrived hours later after being lured to her hotel, which I can prove.

I've screwed up, and I may face criminal charges for my mistakes, but the murder allegations will be withdrawn.

I read the next line.

Sources at the hotel say Callahan and Isabella Morales argued yesterday during their afternoon meeting.

What? No. Isabella had met me with kindness and sent me off with a hug. There may have been tense moments, but even someone with their ear pressed to the door couldn't accuse us of arguing.

Why the hell didn't I test that recording? Why didn't I make sure it worked? Well, maybe because I'm a music teacher, not a secret agent.

I force back the seething regret and read on.

Police believe Callahan returned in the early hours of the morning to confront Isabella Morales. Hotel staff confirm she was seen exiting the hotel shortly before five a.m. She then returned at 6:45. It's believed she returned to remove evidence, most likely Isabella Morales's cell phone, which is missing from the scene.

Returned and exited hours earlier? Staff can *confirm* it? Impossible.

But the rest . . . I *was* at the hotel at 6:50—that's a matter of record. I thought that would help prove my case. Who returns to a murder scene hours later?

Someone who forgot something.

Like a cell phone.

The phone I *did* take.

I skim the rest of the article, which says that based on this and additional evidence, police have a warrant out for my arrest. Below that is a photograph. I look at it and blink.

The woman wears a pressed white Oxford blouse, slim-fitting black jeans and black ankle boots, with a chunky necklace and big-buckled belt. Her hair swings as she lifts a hand to remove her sunglasses. A woman on a mission, her mouth set in a firm line, as if daring someone to get in her way.

It's me. A photo taken by hotel security cameras. Yet for a moment, I don't recognize myself. It's the expression. It isn't resting bitch face. It's full-on active bitch face, and it's as foreign to me as my expression in that hot-tub shot.

We're accustomed to seeing ourselves in a very select number of poses. Smiling for photos. Or caught off guard for a photograph but still alert and calm.

This hotel photo shows a side of me I don't see. I wasn't angry. Not even annoyed. I was steeling myself to see Isabella again. Yet I look ready to mow down anyone in my path.

I look like a bitch.

I look like a woman who could kill.

I glance up to see a fifty-something man across the road, frowning down at his phone. He looks up at me. Back at his phone.

My heart stops. He's reading about me. CNR might get exclusive firsthand knowledge, but that won't keep others from reposting their article, linking to it, sharing it on Twitter and Facebook . . .

The man looks up again. He smiles. There's no fear or trepidation in that smile. It's interest mixed with hesitant flirtation.

He's not reading anything online about me. He glanced up from his phone to see a younger woman looking straight at him. Then he returned to his phone, only to look up and find her still watching him. He thinks I'm checking him out. I could almost laugh at that.

I give the man a quick wave with an embarrassed smile and shrug, which I hope conveys the message that I mistook him for someone else. I turn . . . and there's a woman about my age, staring at me. Showing her phone to her companion whose gaze rises to meet mine, her face slack with horrified recognition.

I turn on my heel, stride around the corner and duck into the first building I see. It's a housewares store. I move quickly down aisles of specialty peelers and designer juicers until I'm at the back with a view through the front window. The women do not walk past. Of course, they don't—they just spotted a murderer. They're on their phones to 911 right now, thirty seconds before posting #KillerSighting on Instagram.

I'd gone through hell in 2005, a mere year after Facebook launched, when social media wasn't truly a thing. What would it be like now in the age of Twitter and memes and hashtags? Even thinking of it, I have to bite my cheek to keep from throwing up on the housewares shop floor.

The store clerk is busy on the phone with a customer and didn't see me come in. I slip past a curtain into the hall. There's a door leading out the back. A sign reads Emergency Exit Only. Does that mean it'll set off an alarm? Only one way to find out. I push down the handle. No sirens sound, but I'm already gone anyway, darting past trash and recycling bins.

I'm quick-marching along the side street when my phone rings. It's Mom. I keep moving as I answer.

"I have someone," she says.

"Oh, thank God," I murmur. "It's hit the Internet. Well, CNR, but it's already spreading. My photo is out there along with the news that I'm wanted for Isabella's murder."

Mom has a few choice words for CNR. Epithets like "bottom-feeders" and "terrible people." After her G-rated tirade, she says, "I'm texting you the lawyer's address. A friend from church recommended him. She said he's one of the best criminal lawyers in New York City, and when I called, I left a message at the desk, but he phoned back two minutes later. He'd love to take your case, and he said I was absolutely right to tell you not to turn yourself in. You'll do that with him."

"Perfect," I say as I read her text with the address.

"He's expecting you at his office. He asked if you'd like a car to pick you up."

"No, it's about a mile from here. I can walk. Tell him I'm on my way now."

I TAKE a few basic identity-disguising steps along the way. I wear my sunglasses. I change into the lounging-around-the-hotel-room wear I'd grabbed from my suite—leggings and an over-sized off-the-shoulder tee. I also buy a floppy hat from a street kiosk and sweep my red hair under it. Good enough. It's not as if my photo is flashing across the screens in Times Square. Not yet, at least.

I make a wrong turn heading to the lawyer's office and end up at the rear of the building. I don't see a door, so I'm circling around when I'm passing the parking lot and . . .

There's a police cruiser just inside the garage entrance. I slow and then take three steps backward.

Once again, I tell myself the police aren't here for me, but once again, I decide to behave as if they are. I lose nothing by being cautious.

I head around the other way. As I do, I take a closer look at the building. It's in a decent part of town, but it's no executive office tower. Mom's friend seems to have exaggerated when she called Daniel Thompson, "one of the biggest lawyers in the city." Right now, though, I'm a beggar who can't be choosy.

I find a side door and slip inside. The lawyer's office is on the tenth floor. Mom said to text Thompson when I arrived, so he could come down and meet me. I decide to skip that step. If there are police officers in the building—for any reason—I want a low-key entrance. The stairs it is, then.

I'm passing the ninth floor when I hear my name. Of course, my gut reaction is "Paranoid much?" But I still step toward the door and ease it open.

"You're milking this for all it's worth, aren't you, Thompson," a woman's voice says.

"Of course I am," a man replies, "for my client's sake."

The woman snorts. "For *your* sake, you mean. You love seeing your face on TV."

"I am drawing necessary attention to my client's case. She's been wrongly accused of murder."

"Yeah, according to her *mother*. I could skin cats on national TV, and my mom would claim it was all a misunderstanding."

"Lucy Callahan is innocent, and I will prove it."

"Save it for the cameras. Just remember, you owe us one, Thompson."

"I owe *you*? I'm delivering the most wanted fugitive of the—"

"—morning?"

He continues. "You're getting the arrest, on camera no less. All I ask in return is that you stay here until I text you. I don't want to spook her. She'll notify me when she arrives, and I'll speak to her in my office. Once she's calm, I'll text you. You come to the door, and I'll persuade Ms. Callahan that it's for the best."

"And you'll claim you have *no idea* how we found her at your office?"

"Presumably, you tracked her phone."

"Yeah, it's not that easy. But whatever. Just hold up your end of the deal, or I'll report you to the bar association. Pretty sure this is a hanging offense with them."

Thompson tut-tuts her threat away. I withdraw and do what I should have done already. I search on Thompson's name.

The first thing that appears is an ad for his services, showing a man in his late thirties, blond with bright green eyes and perfect teeth. Then another ad. And another. Below that are articles on cases he's represented. He is a legitimate lawyer, one who seems to do well, but he's also the sort who advertises his services on the side of buses, his handsome face plastered larger-than-life.

Mom said her friend recommended him as one of the biggest lawyers in town. Probably because her friend saw his billboard advertisements or heard his radio jingle. He'll happily take my case and my money and probably do a decent job of representing me, but he'll wring every ounce of publicity from the job, and I'll be the one who pays *that* price.

I send Thompson a quick text.

> Me: It's L. Callahan. I'm stuck in a taxi on Broadway. The driver says I'm twenty minutes from you, but it might be faster to get out and walk. So sorry! Be there soon!

I actually hear his phone chime with the incoming text. A moment later, he replies.

> Thompson: No problem. Take care, and text when you're close. I'll come down to meet you.

The officer had grumbled about the bar association, but I'm not sure this is actually a violation. I suspect Thompson treads that wire with care.

Hey, no, I didn't breach confidentiality. She wasn't my client when I notified the police.

I don't care how legal or ethical it is. All that matters is that I got a heads-up before I walked through the front door. Score one for paranoia.

Speaking of paranoia, I take off my boots so I don't clip-clop down the steps. On the fifth floor, a man walks through the stairwell door. His gaze goes to the boots in my hand, only to nod and smile as he trusts in the logic of unknowable female fashion choices.

He climbs to another floor, and I don't encounter anyone else. At the bottom, I yank on my boots and fly through the stairwell door.

I can't ask Mom to find me another lawyer. She's a school teacher in Albany. Her contact list filled with church-lady friends and book-club friends and golf-game friends, plus a few discreet male friends that I'm not supposed to know about because God forbid I find out my mother is dating a mere quarter century after my dad died. Unless one of Mom's hook-ups is an NYC defense attorney, she's not the person to find me a lawyer.

I need to handle this myself. Yes, part of me wants to hide until my mommy sorts it out, but I'm not that girl anymore.

Take control of the narrative.

Go to the police. Not the ones upstairs. That would seem as if I tripped over them and went "Whoops, uh, so . . . I'm turning myself in." This must be a clear act of initiative. Find a police station. Walk in and announce who I am. Say that I wanted to find a lawyer first, but the one I contacted seemed shady—*there's your TV-ready soundbite, Daniel Thompson*—so I decided to do this on my own.

I'm heading for the side exit while searching my phone for a police precinct. The bathroom door opens. A young woman steps out. I see her pretty face, her perfectly coiffed hair, her equally perfect makeup . . . and the little microphone clipped to her lapel.

A reporter.

CHAPTER TWENTY

ALBANY 2005

OUR HOUSE WAS UNDER SIEGE. It had been three days, and yet, every morning, I looked out my window expecting to see a vacant street. Surely, they wouldn't keep this up for long. Surely there were bigger stories than mine.

Not right now.

I stood in my childhood bedroom, clutching Chopin, the ragged stuffed lamb my father bought for me. I squeezed him as I cracked open the side of the blind and inched just enough to see—

"There!" someone shouted, and a camera flashed, and I dropped the blind, scuttling backward so fast I stumbled over my open suitcase.

"Lucy?" Mom called.

Footsteps tapped down the hall, and I righted myself before she appeared in the semidark doorway. She was up and dressed, looking every inch the capable school teacher, hair done, light makeup already in place. The cordless phone was in place, too, at her ear, where it'd been for three days as she made endless calls, trying to fix this problem for me.

"Tripped," I said, nodding at the suitcase. "I really need to empty that."

"I'll do it. You just . . ." She struggled before blurting, "Practice. Why don't you get in some music time?"

My brows shot up as I forced a smile. "Did you just tell me to practice? The world really is coming to an end."

Mom always prided herself on not being one of *those* parents, endlessly pestering their musically gifted child to practice. Of course, as she'd also point out, she'd never had to nag me. I practiced on my own. Or I did until last Saturday night, when my world shattered, and music was suddenly the last thing on my mind.

"I'll practice," I said.

Her face lit up. "And I'll make breakfast. Right after I get off this dratted phone." She headed back into the hall. "They have to do something about those people. It must be illegal. I don't understand the problem."

The problem was that the media were on public property, careful not to set foot on our lawn or drive. The police couldn't do anything . . . and I got the feeling they didn't want to.

I didn't tell Mom that. She needed to do something, and if the endless calls kept her from feeling helpless, I would not interfere.

We will fix this, Lucy.

I will fix it.

It's silly, ridiculous. You're a child, and that man— That man—

It was a kiss. A kiss. People are dying of cancer. People are dying of starvation. People are dying in wars. And this is the story they're reporting? Ridiculous. Absolutely ridiculous.

The worst part was that Mom didn't know the half of it. All she saw was what was in the papers, on the radio and TV news. I'd only gotten her hooked up on e-mail this year. The world of the Internet was a mystery to her. I could tell her that the story "broke" online, but she didn't really understand. I certainly wasn't going to tell her what else I found online. The bulletin boards. The community forums. The comments.

I'd understood the concept of online bulletin boards and forums before now. We used them at school, but they were still relatively new. The ability to chat with total strangers online. The ability to comment about news online. The ability to talk about total strangers online. To call them a whore. To tell them they deserved what they got. To tell them they deserved . . . things that made me gasp and shake, that inner voice sounding exactly like my mother's, saying this must be wrong, must be illegal, there must be laws.

That hot-tub photograph wasn't just on CNR's website. People copied it and reposted it and . . . did things to it, things I didn't know were possible to do with photographs. They removed Colt's hands and pasted breasts on me. They took pornographic pictures from other sites and put my head on them, pretending they were real photographs they'd found. Fake photos of me in every porno-graphic pose possible, including some that scorched my eighteen-year-old virgin eyes.

I walked to my desk and picked up a CD. It was an advance copy of an album by a new band Justice Kane and I talked about on Saturday night. It arrived two days ago with a note. Seven perfect words.

This is bullshit. Keep your head up.

I'd cried. When I told Mom, though, she said if Justice supported me, he should come forward and say so. I disagreed. Justice knew nothing of what happened after Colt took me away at the party, so he couldn't clear my name, and I didn't want public support without proof. The media would have claimed I had sex with Justice first, and he was defending me because he didn't want to think he'd been the opening act for Colt Gordon.

I put the CD into my player. Before I could start it, my bedroom phone buzzed, I jumped for it. Nylah called three times a day to check in. A couple of other friends called daily. Then there were those I kept waiting to hear from, those who had not reached out, those I'd nudged with a quick text, only to hear silence in response.

I longed to hear from those friends. Not even so much to talk to them as to know they were still friends.

OMG, Lucy! I've been at my parent's cottage all week. I just saw the news. And OMG! Are you okay?

There were, however, people I wanted to hear from even more than those silent friends. Karla for one. She'd given me good advice—don't answer calls from numbers you don't recognize; don't talk to reporters; go home and let your mother help.

Since Saturday night, though, she'd been silent. She'd warned that she would be, and I understood why. She'd be putting in all-nighters trying to save her clients' careers. Still, I hoped for a call.

The person I most hoped to hear from, though, was Isabella. She would be furious, and I expected that. I wanted her to call to shout at me, and that would be the opportunity I needed to tell her the truth and beg forgiveness.

When I grabbed my bedroom phone, I glanced at the caller ID. If it was a stranger, on Karla's advice, I'd let it ring. The name came up as Maureen, and I knew a Maureen from Juilliard. It was only as I was hitting the button to accept the call that I realized the surname was wrong.

Karla would say to hang up, but that would be rude, and no matter what had happened, I still could not manage that.

"Hello?"

"Lucy? This is Maureen Wilcox from the *New York Gazette*."

"I'm sorry," I said. "I'm not giving inter—"

"Are you familiar with the *Gazette*? I know you were living in New York."

The *Gazette* was a relatively new paper. Not a tabloid, but not "establishment" either, like the *Times*. The *Gazette* had a younger, fresher vibe that I'd always enjoyed.

When I didn't answer, Maureen hurried on to say that she wanted to tell my story. Not Colt's. Mine.

"That's what's missing here," she said. "Everyone wants his side because he's the movie star. He's the man. His angle is the only one that counts."

Sarcasm leaked through every word, and I felt myself relaxing.

"But our opinions count, too, right?" she continued. "Women's stories. Girl's stories. This asshole screwed around on his gorgeous, talented wife with the *nanny*. Can you get any more cliché than that?"

"I wasn't actually the nanny," I said. "I know that's what the media has been calling me. But I was hired as a music tutor."

"Because you're a talented musician. A Juilliard student. Reduced to 'the nanny,' because that's the better soundbite. Or because they just presume you don't have a role beyond looking after the kids. And I just fell in that trap myself. We all need to do better, right?"

I wavered here. I was one hundred percent on board with feminism. Equal rights for women was a no-brainer. But something about her tone made me nervous.

Maureen Wilcox had a mission, and my story would help her prove a point. That made me uncomfortable and yet . . . Well, her "point" was telling my story. Giving me a voice.

All I had to do was be careful not to blame Colt. Don't give any quotes she could use to make me look as if I were embracing victimhood. Take responsibility and simply set the record straight. I didn't seduce Colt Gordon. I wasn't having an affair with him. I did nothing more than kiss him in a hot tub after a couple glasses of champagne, and I will never forgive myself for that, but my story wasn't one people heard in the news, and I wasn't the girl they saw there.

I took a deep breath. "Okay, I'll talk."

"Can you do it in person?"

I hesitated, but it would be better that way. If I was unsure after meeting her, I could change my mind.

"I know the vultures are circling," she said. "But if you can slip out the back after nightfall, I'll meet you close by."

I agreed.

. . .

MAUREEN SAID to expect the article in two days. That didn't keep me from sneaking out the next evening to grab a copy. I almost got caught by an enterprising young reporter who shone a flashlight my way, but I was already over the neighbor's fence.

Most of the media left at sundown, which was also when Mom's church friends came by to drop off casseroles and cookies. She insisted they were all on my side, but I knew that wouldn't be completely true. While Mom attended a progressive church, there would still be whispering, and I hated that she had to go through it. I hated that she had to go through any of it. With any luck, the *Gazette* article would make a difference.

I snuck out to get the paper on the proper day, and I caught a glimpse of my name on the front page. Resisting the urge to read it, I raced home and slipped through the back door, tiptoeing past where Mom was talking to Father Collins in the kitchen.

Normally, I'd pop in to say hello. I liked Father Collins. When Mom drove me home from New York after the scandal, I'd asked to stop for confession first. He'd taken mine, and I had felt seen and not judged, and that was what I needed. Right now, though, what I needed was to read this newspaper.

When a floorboard creaked, Mom called, "Lucy?"

I hid the paper behind my back and leaned around the doorway. "Hey, Father. Good to see you."

"And good to see you," he said, his lined face softening in a genuine smile. "How are you holding up, Lucy?"

"I'm managing."

"I'm sure you are. You're like your mother. Made of sterner stuff."

Oh, I wish that were true, Father. I really do.

"If you ever need to talk, you know where to find me," he continued. "But I'm sure this will all be over soon, and you'll be back to Juilliard."

"I hope so."

"You will," he said with Mom echoing his nod.

People talk about faith as a religious concept, but it was more than that. Sometimes, that sort of faith bubbled over into a general faith that the world would behave in ways that were good and fair and just. Mom had that faith, and she held fast to it, no matter how hard it was tested, first through Dad's death and now this. She believed, like Father Collins, that everything would be fine in the end. She needed it to be.

I retreated to my room and closed the door. Then I picked up Chopin, hugging him as I unfolded the paper. The first thing I saw was Maureen's photo, which made me smile. She looked open and earnest, and when we'd met for the interview, I'd instinctively known I'd made the right choice.

Her byline read "special to the Gazette." That gave me pause. I thought that was used when the writer wasn't staff, which Maureen said she was. It must just mean that the article was an exclusive.

The headline was a simple "Lucy Callahan Tells Her Story," so I zoomed past that, and started to read.

Lucy Callahan is not what I expect. I'm standing on this dimly lit corner in Albany, feeling like a john waiting for his underage "date." That's what I expect. Callahan will be gorgeous and sexy, a teenage Lolita. Instead, my first thought seeing her is "She's barely even pretty." Red hair. Unremarkable pale face. Skinny. I should say "slender" or "lithe," but she's just skinny.

This was the girl Colt Gordon endangered his career for? I'm thinking the movie star is in need of glasses. Then she starts to talk, and that's when I understand. For all her homeliness, there is a feral quality to Lucy Callahan. This is a girl accustomed to getting what she wants, a girl who got into Juilliard despite, as one fellow student said, her mediocre talents. This is also the girl who seduced Colt Gordon and now blames him for it. Blames Colt. Blames "too much champagne." Blames everyone but herself.

I slid to my knees, hands pressed to my mouth, still seeing the words before me, as if dancing in the air.

What have I done?

Oh, God, what have I done?

Karla warned me, and somehow, I thought I understood journalists better than a celebrity manager.

I forced myself back onto the bed, and I read it to the bitter end, and bitter it was, the portrait of a girl who was ugly inside and out, a stupid, thoughtless slut who seduced Colt Gordon and blamed everyone else.

Again, I heard my mother's voice, saying this wasn't right, and there had to be a law against the lies this woman spewed about me, the way she'd twisted my words, every quote taken out of context.

Unlike my mother's voice, mine took on a whine, the perfect tone for the girl in the article.

It's not fair.

Why is this happening to me?

I heard Karla's words again, warning me not to speak to the media, not to believe anyone who said they were on my side.

I'd been played. Maureen Wilcox knew exactly the face to show me, exactly the angle to take, exactly the words to say. She got an exclusive interview by promising to tell my side of the story.

The only story she told was her own. Whatever fiction would sell her article and get her own name in the news.

I stared down at the paper. Then I folded it and tucked it into a drawer.

Let this be a lesson to you, Lucy. Every time you open that drawer, remember and learn. Be smarter. Be stronger.

I took a deep breath. Then I went to the kitchen to warn my mother.

CHAPTER TWENTY-ONE

NEW YORK 2019

I STARE at the TV reporter coming out of the bathroom. She looks like Maureen Wilcox. Could be her if time had stood still, and I'm thrown back into that memory, the horror and humiliation and hurt.

Before the woman can look up, I stride past, and her heels click in the other direction. I zip out the back door, duck into an alley and jog behind a dumpster. An elderly woman peers down the lane, as if she saw me, but she doesn't slow for a better look.

I keep seeing that article, feeling as if I'm back there again, reading it for the first time, and I start shaking so badly I need to lean against the wall.

It's happening again. I'm going to see articles like that again.

I can't do it. I just can't.

I wrap my arms around myself, and squeeze my eyes tight and pull back into the present. I envision the article again through the eyes of Genevieve, older and at least slightly wiser.

I'd been so angry with myself for giving that interview. How could I be so stupid? Karla warned me. I knew better. Such a fool.

Looking back now, I don't see a fool. I see a desperate and confused girl taken advantage of by a predator.

I'm sure Maureen Wilcox doesn't see herself as a predator.

Probably gazes back on that younger version of herself and applauds her chutzpah. A few years ago, I looked her up. Her article about me didn't launch a career. She'd quit journalism school to work for the *Gazette* and was fired two years later for fabricating a story.

Maybe that should make me feel vindicated. It doesn't. She isn't the one who will come across the word *feral* or *homely* fourteen years later and feel physically ill. I trusted a young reporter who claimed sisterhood, and she publicly pilloried me for a byline.

I'll never be that naive again. Articles will come, and they will say horrible things that I'll feel fourteen years from now. That thought might make my stomach clench, but at least I know I will never be an active participant in my own humiliation again.

I've just fled a reporter. I made a clean escape, but I need to be more careful. More alert and aware in a way I haven't been for fourteen years. In a way I wasn't, even then.

I stand in that alley and take deep breaths, ignoring the stink of New York garbage bins in June. Then I send a text to Thompson.

Me: Your news crew has arrived.

Silence. I think he's going to leave it at that, which is fine. I just couldn't resist comment. Then my phone pings with an incoming text.

Thompson: I just spotted them myself. I am appalled by their audacity, and I apologize for not understanding how quickly they'd jump on this case.
Thompson: I know you've had regrettable experiences with their ilk in the past, and I don't blame you for being upset. Please allow me to send a car to retrieve you, and we will meet at another location.

I laugh, a burbling laugh that edges a little too close to hysteria.

> Me: A location where you can absolutely guarantee me that
> I won't encounter either media or police? Because if I
> do, I'll fire you in a heartbeat.

A long pause.

> Thompson: I can't guarantee anything, naturally, but I
> assure you, I will choose a place with as much
> discretion as humanly possible.
> Me: That officer was right. Screwing your client over like
> this should be a hanging offense. Or at least grounds for
> disbarment.

The pause stretches longer.

> Thompson: I don't think I understand your meaning.
> Me: You set me up. I overheard everything.

My phone rings. It's his number. I ignore it.

> Me: Don't bother explaining. And if you're telling the
> police to track my phone, I'll be trashing the SIM card in
> five minutes.
> Thompson: Are you intending to become a fugitive, Ms.
> Callahan? Let me assure you, that's a very bad idea.
> Professionals fail to pull that off. You are not a
> professional.

I bristle at that. He has judged me already and has decided he knows what I am—and am not—capable of.

I want to prove him wrong.

By what? Becoming a fugitive from justice?

No. His tone makes me grind my teeth, but he has a point. Running isn't smart. It's not what I have in mind, either. I'm only going to throw out my SIM card so I'm not picked up before I get to a police station.

Is that still my plan? To turn myself in?

Thompson: The more you run, the harder you make this on yourself.

Thompson: I am here to help you navigate this situation.

Thompson: At the very least, I would like the opportunity to discuss that with you.

The more you run, the harder you make this on yourself.

He's right about that, too. With each mistake, it gets more difficult to turn myself in and expect to be treated as innocent until proven guilty. My actions will scream *guilty*.

Yet while I might kick myself for every so-called mistake, I'm not sure I could have done anything different.

Should I have let myself be found at the murder scene?

Let myself be arrested before I could warn anyone?

Let myself be arrested on the news, duped by my new lawyer?

No to all of those.

So now what?

That's the question, isn't it?

With each passing hour, it will be harder to walk into a station and say, "Hey, weird thing, but I just saw on Twitter that you guys are looking for me. Here I am."

And is turning myself in the right move? This isn't a misunderstanding. Isabella's *killer* is actively trying to frame me for her murder. It's not just the texts luring me to the hotel. It's not just the fact I was on the scene that morning. It's the other evidence the police claim to have found in Isabella's suite. Also, someone broke into my hotel room and planted forensic evidence, and while it might just be on the clothing I took . . .

A niggle at the back of my brain whispers that there's more, that I overlooked something in the room. I try to chase it, but it only hovers there, vague and formless.

Even if this *is* the easily dismissed case my mother expects it to be, my name is already online. Memories slam over me, and I have to take deep breaths against the panic attack hovering at the edge of my consciousness.

I will not allow this to happen again. Yet I must acknowledge that the accusation is out there, and I know better than anyone that insinuation and gossip and innuendo are a miasma one cannot escape, a stain that truth never fully erases. But truth must help. I didn't get a chance to correct the story with Colt. I have that chance now. I don't want this accusation quietly dismissed. I want my name cleared with proof.

And how do you intend to find that proof? You aren't a private eye.

Thompson has texted me a few times since my last response. I don't read them. I just write my own.

Me: I'm being accused of murder. I'm not going to hire someone I don't trust.

Me: However, I do need legal advice, and I think you owe me.

Me: You might disagree, so don't consider this a request. It's a threat. I have a question. I demand an honest answer.

Me: Lie to me or refuse to answer, and I'll let everyone know what you did. Try getting clients after that.

It takes thirty seconds for him to respond, and I feel the chill in his words.

Thompson: What is your question, Ms. Callahan?

Me: If no one has attempted to arrest me or serve me a warrant, am I committing an offense by not turning myself in?

Thompson: No.

It takes a moment before he expands on that.

Thompson: If you resist arrest or flee an officer, that is an offense. If an officer knocks at your hotel door, identifies himself and you jump out the window, that is an offense. What you are currently doing is not. However, I wouldn't recommend it.

Me: Thank you.

Thompson: You will be arrested. The longer it takes, the guiltier you look.

Me: I know that.

Thompson: So what is your plan? Please don't tell me you intend to investigate and prove your innocence. No matter how many times you've seen that in the movies, I assure you, it never works in real life.

Me: I'm being framed.

Thompson: Perhaps. But that's something for me to investigate, as a lawyer with trained investigators.

Me: Goodbye, Mr. Thompson.

I open my phone, take out the SIM card and snap it in half. Then I toss it into the dumpster and stride away.

I FIND the nearest ATM and withdraw the limit from my bank card and my credit card. That almost empties both. For years, I kept every spare penny in my checking account in case I needed to flee at a moment's notice. But I got comfortable in Italy and started investing extra income and keeping my credit limit low. Excellent financial planning . . . unless you're a fugitive from justice, needing every penny before your bank records are tracked.

Am I a fugitive from justice?

No. I'm a conscientious objector to the misapplication of justice.

Right . . .

I *am* on the run. Even thinking about that, I want to flee and hide in a dark spot . . . and I want to come out swinging at the person who murdered Isabella. Murdered her and framed me.

I cannot afford to tear myself apart like that, lost in a maelstrom of terror and rage. So I focus on what I can do, starting with dyeing my distinctive hair.

I'm about to walk into a Duane Reade when I spot an advertisement for a museum exhibit on Marco Polo.

Oh, God. *Marco.* I haven't responded to his text, and it's been hours.

I grab my phone.

No SIM card.

Damn it!

I look around for a pay phone and then remember it's 2019. What I see instead are Wi-Fi hotspot booths. I can connect to Wi-Fi without a SIM card. However, that will not help me make a phone call.

I head into the drugstore and purchase hair dye and a cheap prepaid cell. Then I find a quiet spot, turn on my new phone and punch in . . .

I don't know Marco's number. I always just hit his contact info on my phone.

I pull out my cell, my heart pounding.

There, he's still in my contacts. I exhale and dial. It rings. Rings. Rings again. It's a strange number, and he'll think it's spam.

His voice message comes on in rapid-fire Italian, followed by English.

"Hey, it's Marco. As you probably know, I'm terrible at checking voice mail. Text me, and I'll get back to you as soon as possible."

There's no beep. Marco isn't going to warn people against leaving messages and then let them do exactly that. I knew this—I just forgot because, well, we always text.

I start a text . . . and then pause. A voicemail message can be erased, but if the police connect me to Marco and subpoena his phone records, they'll get his texts. If I'm on the run, I'm sure as hell not making him an accessory.

I try calling his number again in case his curiosity is piqued and he answers. He does not.

What I've done is an unforgivable breach of trust. I screwed up the moment that parcel arrived, and I pretended not to know who Lucy Callahan was. I could have fixed it then. Could have fixed it at any point thereafter. Now, though, it's too late.

I send up a silent apology to Marco with the promise of a full explanation, and I pray it's not too late for that.

CHAPTER TWENTY-TWO

BEFORE THE COLT GORDON SCANDAL, the worst thing that ever happened to me was Dad's death. Mom came to get me from my kindergarten class, and then I sat in my bedroom, waiting for the phone call that would tell us it was all a mistake. How could he be killed by a drunk driver in the middle of the day? The answer was three-martini-lunches, but I'd been five years old, and confident in my knowledge of the world, which stated that adults drank after dark. I only had to wait for him to come home and set this whole misunderstanding straight.

Dad did not come home.

That mistake didn't keep me from doing the exact same thing post-scandal. Mom found me with Nylah in my dorm room, holed up, waiting for the world to realize it had made a mistake.

I will not do that again. While I'm certainly hoping the police will realize they've made a mistake, I *do* plan to hole up in a hotel room, but only so I have a quiet place to dig for answers.

I dye my hair in a single occupant bathroom. Then I take the subway to a part of Queens that Nylah and I accidentally ended up in during our first week at Juilliard. I remember her joking about the rooming houses that rent by the hour, week or month. I find one of those places and walk in. A middle-aged woman sits at the desk, her eyes glued to Netflix.

When she asks for a credit card, I say, nervously, "My, uh, husband holds on to it. For safekeeping. I forgot to get it from him."

Her gaze flicks to my face and then my arms. She's looking for track marks, signs that I might be a difficult guest. Then she takes in my dark sunglasses and nods, accepting my story. Not the part about forgetting my credit card. That nod says she understands an older story, one that says I'm running away from the kind of husband who doesn't let his wife have her own credit cards.

"Can I pay cash?" I ask. "I'll only be here a few days. My sister's coming from Idaho to get me."

She quotes me a weekly rate, and I pay it. Then I retreat to my new room and take out Isabella's phone.

In the twenty-four hours before her death, Isabella had no fewer than a dozen text conversations. Most of them are business. She'd been texting with cowriters and others involved in a production. Two more seem to be friends. The "Hey, I'm in NYC for a few days. Lunch?" type of message.

There's one from Karla, who knows about Isabella's plan with me. She approves, while warning that Isabella needs to remember I have a new life, and she should do nothing to jeopardize that. My heart lifts a little reading that. Karla understood, and if Isabella had lived, Karla might have proved a valuable ally in my fight for privacy.

Could she be an ally now? No. Colt is still her client, and we are right back where we were fourteen years ago. Even if Karla didn't think I killed Isabella, her priority is the family.

Isabella's shortest text conversation is with Jamison. It's a simple "Call me" from her to him, sent at 8:03 last night. When I flip back in the thread, there's a lot of "Call me" and "Just checking in!" from Isabella with a one- or two-word response from Jamison. Not unlike my mom when I'd been away at Juilliard, a parent nudging her busy child for a call.

A quick check of her phone logs shows he did call after receiving that nudge, and they'd talked for half an hour.

By contrast, the longest text thread is from her other child. Tiana lives in New York. When she learned Isabella was coming, she offered her the spare room with a joke that she was the only twenty-five-year-old Manhattanite with a spare bedroom.

My heart aches, seeing those texts and recognizing the girl I'd known. It hurts worse, realizing she'd spit nails if she knew I was reading her private correspondence with her mother. And I wouldn't blame her one bit.

I shouldn't read those texts, but I cannot help it. A story unfolds here. A story I love. A different mother-daughter relationship that is as good as my own. This is mother and daughter as adult friends who flit in and out of each other's lives, grabbing cocktails and, I'm sure, talking deep into the night as we all had in that massive bed in the penthouse suite.

The suite where Isabella died last night.

I have to pause there to collect myself. Then I keep reading. Another answer comes soon, one that has me flinching again.

Tiana: Bess just called. She told me who you're meeting today, Mom.

Isabella: She shouldn't have done that. She seems to forget who pays her very well for discretion.

Tiana: She's worried about you.

Isabella: If I'm overworking myself or overstuffing my schedule, then as my PA she has every right to tell me so. I would prefer she didn't take an interest in my personal life, but I understand she might. She should not, however, be tattling on me to her ex-girlfriend.

Ex-girlfriend? Oh. She means Tiana. So the woman I met yesterday, Bess, is Isabella's PA and Tiana's ex. That explains the cold shoulder the young woman gave me.

Tiana: Does Dad know?

Isabella: I informed him today. I would prefer not to talk
about that.

I fast forward through texts I can read later. Then come ones
from late yesterday afternoon after I'd left Isabella's suite.

Isabella: Lucy just left. We need to talk.

Tiana: Why? So you can feed me whatever BS she fed you?

Isabella: Lucy explained. She didn't defend. She didn't
excuse. She just explained. You need to hear that
explanation. You need to see her, too.

Tiana: Oh, hell, no. Trust me, Mom, you do not want me
within fifty feet of that bitch. I will tell Lucy Callahan
exactly what I think of her.

Isabella: I don't think she'd have a problem with that. I'm
meeting her for lunch tomorrow, and I hope you'll
join us.

Tiana: Lunch? What game's she playing?

Isabella: No game. I want to go public with our story, and I
would like you to be part of that.

Tiana's answer is a torrent of punctuation marks, comic-
book profanity, to which Isabella says she'll call and
they can discuss it.

There are no texts from Tiana after that.

So TIANA KNEW about my proposed lunch with Isabella. She knew
about her mother's plan for us to go public. I will not consider the
possibility that Tiana killed Isabella, but if she knew—and was
furious about it—who else did she tell?

I open the next text thread. There's no name attached, so I
assume it must be business. It only takes a few messages for me to
realize my mistake.

Sender: I'd like to be there with you for this. I can be in
　　NYC in a couple of hours.
Isabella: I can handle this.
Sender: I know you can. I just don't think you need to be
　　alone while you do it. I'll get a room at the Baccarat,
　　and if you want to talk, I'm here. If not, that's
　　cool, too.

The conversation goes on from there. It's all very circumspect,
but there's enough in the careful and sincere texts to tell me this is
no mere friend. Isabella has a lover.

I skim down to texts sent yesterday evening.

Isabella: You're in NYC, aren't you? Damn it, didn't I say I
　　could handle this?
Sender: Yes, and that's why I'm staying four blocks away
　　with no intention of seeing you until you've worked
　　this through with Lucy.

He uses my name as if he knows me. Which means they've
discussed me often enough that he feels as if he does.

Sender: How did the meeting go? Better than you
　　imagined? Or worse?
Isabella: Both.
Sender: LOL So I was right, wasn't I? She didn't throw
　　herself into your arms for a good cry, all your
　　differences washed away in a sea of tears and shared
　　suffering.
Isabella: She told me the full story.
Sender: Was it anywhere close to what I guessed?
Isabella: You're enjoying this way too much. Jerk.
Sender: Jerk? Oh, come on, Izzy, you can do better than
　　that. Aren't you a writer or something?

The thread ends there, and the call log shows she called him and they spoke for an hour.

I search the phone for some clue to the mystery lover's identity. Isabella is careful, though. There is a phone number and nothing more. I make a note of the number, as I do with all the pertinent information I find in case I need to ditch the phone for good.

The texts suggest he'd guessed what happened between Colt and me. That could be useful.

And if pulling him into this exposes their affair?

I will avoid that if I can, but if the choice is one between "expose Isabella's affair" and "go to prison for life," there's no question of which I'll choose.

I brace myself to move on to the thread I've been avoiding.

Colt.

Deep breath and . . . I pause, finger over the phone.

Where's Colt's thread?

I'd seen it this morning when I'd skimmed the text threads before dumping the SIM. I can still feel the visceral blow of seeing his name. Now, though, I realize I haven't seen it since I opened the message app. There was a thread earlier . . . and now there is not.

Someone deleted Colt's thread before I removed the SIM card.

No, not someone. The person who has Isabella's tablet or other connected device. The killer who is framing me for murder.

All of these threads could have been deleted, yet only one was. The one belonging to the killer?

Part of me would love to think so, but again, I'm not convinced it's that simple. Did Colt's thread contain a clue? Or was the killer in the process of deleting them all when I removed the SIM card?

I don't know the answer here. I only know that I wish to hell I'd read that thread while I still could.

• • •

I SET the phone aside and stare at the dingy wall of my hotel room, as if a sign will appear to point me toward Isabella's killer. All I got from the cell phone was an uncomfortably intrusive look into her personal life.

As hard as I try to corral my thoughts, they keep running down unproductive lanes. Pain over the tsunami of hatred in Tiana's texts. Sympathy for Isabella's lover and the secret grief he's feeling right now. Suspicion over Colt's missing thread. But when I push past the emotions, memory steals in, memories of that night and the aftermath.

The best way to stop thinking about the past? Focus on the present, which is, at the moment, far worse. I need to see what's out there on the Internet now that a half day has passed.

I connect to the hotel Wi-Fi and open my laptop's browser. I'm typing in my name when I stop.

Is this safe?

I laugh at the thought. Am I honestly worried that someone will track me down for a search history that includes Isabella Morales's murder? At least one other person in this building will look up this story tonight. They'll have seen a headline flip past their newsfeed, and they'll idly search for details.

Still, I hesitate. I might know enough to throw out my SIM card, but am I completely certain that's the only way of tying a phone to me? It should be. And yet . . .

I head out in search of free Wi-Fi. I'd seen a Starbucks about a mile away. Guaranteed Internet service there.

I move fast along the empty street, still in my T-shirt and leggings, my purse swapped out for my laptop bag. Chin up. Walking with purpose.

A woman on a mission.

That bitch-face photograph from the hotel cameras flashes back, dragging with it the urge to pull into myself, look less certain. This is not the kind of neighborhood where that is wise, yet the memory of that photo leaches purpose from my spine, and I find myself moving even faster, a clipped pace that suggests I am not comfortable on this quiet street. I try to find that stronger stride, but it's gone now.

I glance at a window and give a start as I spot the reflection of a male figure across the road where the sidewalk had been empty a moment ago.

There's nothing on that side but vacant storefronts. The man didn't step from a shop or an apartment. He walked out of an alley.

Someone saw me walk past, a nervous woman alone, clutching a cell phone in one hand, laptop bag over her shoulder. I might as well just have a wad of cash sticking out of my pocket.

What if I was attacked? Mugged? Assaulted? Can't exactly call 911, can I? Not without turning myself in.

I steady myself and glance over my shoulder, as if I just noticed someone there.

The street is empty.

A car turns the corner, the sound making me jump.

I know I saw a figure reflected in the window. A male figure. That's when I spot the narrow alley right where I saw the man. He'd stepped out, and then seen me give a start, and eased back into the shadows.

He's there now, watching, evaluating.

Seriously, Lucy? No. He's an addict or a homeless person, and he stepped out to realize he wasn't alone on this street, so he retreated. Now he's just waiting for you to move along.

I take a deep breath and look both ways. I'm still a half-dozen blocks from the Starbucks. To my left, though, another street leads to a busier area, the dull roar of traffic audible from here.

This quiet road had seemed the right choice for a woman currently wanted for murder, but it seems a lot less wise for a woman walking alone carrying a couple grand in tech.

I head toward the sound of people. As I go, I cast one last glance over my shoulder, but the mouth to that narrow alley stays dark and still.

I walk three blocks and find a laundromat offering free Wi-Fi.

There are a half-dozen people inside, engaged in various stages of the laundry cycle—loading, folding and waiting. No one even looks up as I enter.

I pause a moment to regroup. The near-encounter outside unsettled me more than it should have, proving that I'm not handling this as well as I pretend. It only takes something like that to start my stomach twisting, my fingers trembling.

Once I'm calm again, I open my laptop, connect to the Wi-Fi and type in the search terms for Isabella's murder. My screen fills with results. I start with mainstream media, easing myself in. One mentions my name with a link to an old article in their entertainment section. Otherwise, articles only say that police are pursuing a suspect and an arrest is expected soon.

I move on to the tabloids and entertainment websites. They focus on Isabella's marital success as if it is the culmination of her career. The mainstream media deign to recognize her accomplishments, but even then, it's awkward, as if a Mexican television show was on the same professional level as an amateur web series.

I am angry for Isabella. I have always been angry for Isabella, and I wish I could have told her that. Now the outrage just festers on behalf of a woman who will never know that, even in my deepest hurt and anger, I sympathized.

The farther I venture beyond mainstream media, the more innuendo and lies I read about myself. One "source" claims I've been having an affair with Colt ever since the scandal, and when he refused to divorce Isabella, I took action. Another says that I've become a star in my own right . . . a porn star, trading on my notoriety. Another piece claims that I've spent the last fourteen years in a mental hospital, which I finally escaped to wreak crazed vengeance on my rival.

Post-scandal, I went through a stage where I'd force myself to seek out every article, read every comment on those old-school bulletin boards and discussion groups. I told myself I was building up a tolerance. That was bullshit. The girl who lashed herself with those whips is gone. What I'm doing now is wading through shit in hopes of stepping on diamonds.

Mainstream media won't speculate on the investigation. As much as I despise the tabloids, right now—God help me—I need them. I need to know what a hotel maid overheard the police say. I need to know what some guy in the lobby tweeted this morning. All that gives me a heads-up on what I'm facing.

From CNR and others, a picture emerges of Lucy Callahan. She's a class A bitch. The scheming Lolita matured into a ball-busting virago. Start with that photograph of me haughtily ripping off my designer sunglasses. Then get a quote from the driver who dropped me off yesterday. According to him, I staggered from the car, drunk. Not carsick. Not close to vomiting with anxiety. Drunk. Then there's the hotel staff member who saw Bess lead me upstairs. I'd ignored Isabella's poor PA as I swanned through the lobby. Then there's the guy who was guarding the penthouse. I came on to him, using my feminine wiles as I tried to inveigle information. More than one enterprising journalist has dug up Maureen Wilcox's old article and quoted the lines that painted me as a predator.

As for the murder investigation, cause of death is still unknown. "Sources" on the scene say Isabella was found dead in her bedroom from an apparent blow to the head. Another source overheard the coroner saying Isabella had been dead for a few hours.

I flip through the pages of search results. I skim comments, too, looking for particular keywords. There are those I wish I could unsee. Slurs and insults and suggestions for ways I should be punished. Post-scandal, I'd had to dig for those. I don't now. This is how the world has changed in fourteen years.

I used to think the world was becoming kinder, more compassionate, more open-minded. How many times has Nylah said that if my Colt scandal hit today, people would recognize my youth and his power and shift the blame to him? I used to agree, but reading these comments, I realize I'd been deluded.

People still hold those ugly and hateful opinions—they just know better than to unleash them outside their circle of like-minded family and friends. When those in power give free rein to their own ugliness, it's like uncorking a bottle. That's front and center in Italy, too, and honestly, the only thing that kept me from running home to the US was knowing things are no better here.

I'm already thinking of Rome when three words on my search-term screen stop me dead.

Via della Luce.

The street where I live in Rome.

I click the link. It's a poorly translated English version of an article posted a few hours ago. I type in the address for the Italian version. An amateur crime blog pops up.

My gaze goes straight to the embedded video. When I click Play, a shaky image appears, the familiar thick wood door of my building. With its huge round handle. A voice talks in Italian, so fast I struggle to follow.

It's a man saying he's tracked "Lucy Callahan" to this address, where she's living under the name Genevieve Callahan. He races through his amateur-sleuth findings—I'm a music teacher and musician, though he mistakenly says I play the violin. This is my home, and he's hoping to get access, and he's just heard footsteps on the stairs within.

Sure enough, the door opens, and one of my elderly neighbors appears. The man asks whether she knows me. Mrs. Costa hesitates, confused. When she starts to retreat, he grabs the door. She yelps. I watch in horror as this man tries to force his way into the building, and poor Mrs. Costa calls for help. A voice sounds off-screen, a man saying, "Hey, get away from her," in angry Italian.

I know that voice.

Oh, God, no.

The picture spins, as if someone grabbed the intruder. The videographer fumbles the camera, and when he rights it, the lens is pointing at an anger-flushed face.

Marco's face.

CHAPTER TWENTY-THREE

MARCO SNARLS at the man that this is private property, and he needs to get the hell out of here before Marco calls 113.

"Do you live around here?" the videographer says.

"No, and neither do you, so take that camera—"

"Do you know Lucy Callahan?"

Marco doesn't miss a beat. His brow scrunches. "Is that the old lady you just assaulted?"

"No, it's a woman who lives here. Around your age. Red hair. You might know her as Genevieve Callahan."

"Did you hear me say I'm not from this neighborhood? I'm looking for a cookie shop. My girlfriend sent me halfway across the city to buy cookies at some place around here. I'd like to get there before they close. I'd suggest you move along, because if you're still harassing old women when I come back this way, I'm calling the police."

Marco strides off in the direction of Biscottificio Innocenti, just down the street. The videographer resumes speaking breathlessly to his future audience, filling the video clip with all the details he knows about me as the camera pans the narrow street, winning glares from tourists and locals alike.

When someone opens a door, the videographer asks about me, but the man brushes him off and retreats. The videographer rounds the corner. He takes a few steps in one direction, then does an about-face to head the other way, as if he's lost in the cobbled streets. As he passes Via della Luce again, he swings the lens back for one more look at my building . . . just as Marco is walking inside, cookie bag in hand.

The videographer yells and races down, but the door shuts before he gets there. After some cursing, the videographer says to his audience. "I'm going to post a photo of that man from this clip. If anyone knows him, please leave his name in the comments. He ripped my shirt when he grabbed me."

Bullshit. The videographer is just trying to get a lead on Marco. Fortunately, this is just some random guy who fancies himself a crime reporter. His blog traffic barely hits double digits.

That's when I see the comment section. Other blogs—amateur and otherwise—ask whether they can post the video. The videographer requested links instead, and they obliged. In a few hours, the video has gotten five thousand views.

I'm scrolling through comments when I reach one that says, "I know that guy."

His name is Marco Alessi. He works for Romulus Tours. I did too, until he ratted me out for flirting with the tourists. Like he doesn't do the same. I was too much competition for him. That woman you're asking about is his girlfriend. She goes by Genevieve, like you said. She joined a few times when a group of guides went for drinks. He likes to show her off. I always wondered why—she's pretty enough but nothing special. Now I know. He was pleased with himself for dating the whore who screwed Colt Gordon. I hope you bring them both down. Anything I can do, just ask.

The guy leaves his e-mail address, which includes his first name: Giacomo.

I know Giacomo. Marco did indeed report him to the tour company and had been instrumental in getting Giacomo fired, but only because Marco had agreed to complain on behalf of his fellow guides.

Giacomo says Marco accused him of doing something that Marco himself does. Partly true. Marco said Giacomo gave tour guests his phone number with invitations to coffee, which is roughly how Marco and I met. The difference? I'm twice the age of the clients Giacomo targeted. Also, Marco really did want a coffee and conversation. The high-school girls who called Giacomo back showed up at the "cafe" address to find Giacomo's apartment instead.

I'm so busy being outraged that it takes a moment to realize Marco has just been identified as my lover. His name and place of employment are online in an article that is gaining traction by the second.

I start flipping through comments. Random people triumphantly announce that they've notified his employer. Someone found his address and posted that. Another posted his e-mail. Then his cell phone number. Finally, there's a link to an Italian tabloid news site. When I click it, Marco's face fills the screen. It's his professional headshot from the tour operator's site. I took it myself. Marco sits on the steps of the Fontaine de la place Santa Maria. He's grinning at me, his real smile, his dark eyes alight. He looks gorgeous and charming and personable all at once. It's no wonder Romulus Tours put it right on their website landing page.

Looking for a tour guide? How about this guy?

Now that picture has been stolen and plunked onto an article identifying Marco as the "longtime lover" of the notorious Lucy Callahan. As I read, my gut drops. Representatives from Romulus Tours confirm they are "reevaluating" his employment, as is the bike-courier service he works for. The tabloid is looking for anyone associated with Marco, particularly past girlfriends. There's a video, too. They caught Marco coming home. The reporter asks for a statement, and when Marco turns to the camera, his gaze is colder than I've ever seen it.

"No comment."

He says it in Italian and then English and then slams the door in the reporter's face. I rewind and freeze on Marco's face in that moment before he responds, and my eyes fill with tears.

Marco got his own personal glimpse of hell today. A peek into a world where he could lose his job, his credibility, his self-respect and his privacy. All because his girlfriend apparently played him for a fool.

He had no idea who I was, and now he's being cast as the hot but dumb-as-dirt lover of a scheming murderess. He could pretend he knew all along and suffer for that. He could also play to type and admit his ignorance, but there is nothing worse for Marco than being dismissed as an empty-headed pretty boy.

Tears well as I touch his face on the screen.

I'm sorry, Marco. I am so, so sorry.

He called me this morning. Tried desperately to get in touch with me, and I couldn't even bother sending a "Talk later."

I shouldn't have let myself get too distracted to reply. I should have e-mailed as soon as I realized I couldn't call him. He has no way of knowing that I desperately wanted to get in touch. All he knows is that I didn't.

I open my e-mail to send something. Instead, I find a message from him, and my breath catches.

Gen,

I know what's happening over there. We need to talk. Give me a # where I can reach you. Please.

xx Marco

I stare at that e-mail, and I can barely breathe. I blink, as if I'm seeing wrong. I reread, as if I've misunderstood. I even check the address, as if it might be a prank. It isn't. Marco is confused, but he wants to talk. He hasn't slammed the door. I have not completely lost him.

That's when I see the time stamp. Four hours ago. After the initial videographer, but before everything went to hell, his life exposed online.

Would you still send those kisses, Marco?

I want to believe the answer is yes while recognizing I'm probably delusional. Still, I respond to the e-mail.

> Marco,
>
> I'm sorry. That seems weak and trite. I wish I could be there, wish I could find the right words or at least let you *see* just how sorry I am.
>
> I should have told you the truth. I can defend myself and say that I never lied to you—that we don't discuss our pasts—but that's an excuse. When Isabella summoned me to NYC, I should have told you everything. I planned to earlier today and then . . . Well, then Isabella called me to switch our lunch to breakfast, and I learned of her death.
>
> I'm being framed. Maybe I'm naive, but I don't honestly think I'd go to prison. I just need to figure things out before I turn myself in, and I pray it won't even come to that, that they'll find the real killer first.
>
> I'm not hiding from the police as much as from the media. I can't have those arrest photos in the news, Marco. I know too well that is a stain that never comes out. I think you're getting a taste of that hell, and I am so, *so* sorry. All I can say is that I did not kill Isabella, and the truth will come out. I will fix this. For both of us.
>
> For now, though, I can't drag you into it. I don't have my cell, so there's no point calling or texting. You shouldn't respond to this e-mail, either. The less communication we have, the better it is for you. I will come home, and I will explain everything.
>
> In the meantime, I'm sorry. I'm so sorry.
>
> xx Gen

I hit Send and hurry from the laundromat.

I'M PUTTING away my phone when I see that I received an e-mail just as I was disconnecting the Wi-Fi. It's a stub, nothing downloaded except my name and the subject line: "We need to talk."

I can still reach the Wi-Fi signal, so I reconnect, my heart thudding. I'm certain it's Marco. While the martyr in me wants to protect him, the real me will leap at any excuse to communicate. I open the e-mail, and it's from Daniel Thompson, the lawyer who was going to turn me in to the police.

> LC,
>
> I apologize for the misunderstanding earlier today. Your mother was kind enough to give me your e-mail address when I explained the situation. I truly believe I am your best chance of avoiding these outrageous charges. Please allow me to prove that to you.

I let out a stream of profanity that has a passing woman veer away. I call a soft, "Sorry!" but she only walks faster.

I channel my anger into a very brief response. Only two words, initials *F* and *O*.

Before I can disconnect, Thompson responds with:

> LOL. Okay, I deserved that. Since we're being a little more casual in our correspondence: I screwed up. Give me another shot. No bullshit this time.

I linger over this glimpse of the guy behind that billboard-ready smile. The snake-oil salesman who's willing to admit he sells snake oil. The question, of course, is whether he actually has any product worth buying . . . or just another bottle of mineral oil laced with fragrant herbs.

You got me, ma'am. I can tell you're a discerning customer. I usually keep this under the counter, but for you . . . Wink-wink. Here's the real stuff.

I'm about to close my e-mail when he sends another one.

There's absolutely no point in me taking on a case I don't think I can win. It's like a minor-league pitcher trick-balling a scout. It might pay off in the short term, but they're going to figure it out, and then you're out of a job. If you're concerned about my ability to represent you:

A list of links follows. I click the first. It takes me to a first-degree murder case Thompson successfully defended. The next is the same. I don't bother with the rest. He's a good lawyer. He just isn't above lowball tactics to bolster his career . . . even at his clients' expense.

I send back a politer response.

I'm sorry, but no. I need someone I can trust. I can't give three strikes on that.

A reply comes moments later.

Understood. But I'm not convinced it's batter out just yet. I won't bother you again, but I am still here if you need me. You have my work number. Here's my private one. This is also a private e-mail address, should you have any questions. I believe I owe you that much.

I send back a thank you and log off.

SLEEP IS a bullet train to hell. That night, I am arrested five times and murdered twice. And once I do the murdering—I'm in Isabella's room, with her begging for her life as I rant about how she ruined *my* life before I smash her head into the tiled step.

I wake from that, gasping and clawing at the sheets. The smell of mildew hits, and I shove the sheets away, only to catch other scents, ones I'd been too preoccupied to notice earlier. The stink hits me, throwing me back through memories to another hotel room, another time waking from nightmares . . .

CHAPTER TWENTY-FOUR

ALBANY 2005

I LAY in bed and cried, shaking and shivering as a winter blast battered the thin motel-room window. I'd been dreaming. It had started as the most perfect dream. I'd woken in Isabella and Colt's beach house, the kids bouncing on my bed, telling me to get up and come for a swim. They'd be leaving later that day, with a car taking me back to New York City.

Isabella appeared in the doorway, shooing the kids out and asking whether I'd have breakfast with her so we could discuss next year. She also wanted to chat about her new show and the possibility of me looking over scripts in case, you know, I ever wanted to try my hand at working in a writing room.

It was just the three of us in the house. Colt was gone, and I was glad of it. I couldn't quite remember why, only that I was relieved he'd left for the West Coast already.

In the dream, I'd pushed back the covers, to be hit by the scent of mildew, which stopped me short. The beach-house sheets always smelled of fresh linen and coconut oil.

That's when I woke in the motel room, and I'd scrambled out of bed, tripping, and fell face-first onto the carpet, into the stench of stale beer.

This wasn't my room at the beach house.

This wasn't my room at Juilliard.

This wasn't my room at home.

It all rushed back as I struggled to my feet and found the bedroom lamp. I turned it on and looked around the cheap motel room. Then I crawled back into bed, sitting up, arms around my knees, and I started to cry.

It was November, and I should have been at Juilliard. I'd planned to go back. Well, more like Mom planned to make sure I went back. Then we got a letter suggesting I might want to take a term off to rest.

Rest? No. The letter contained enough vague "suggestions" that it was clear they didn't want me back. My notoriety would be too distracting for the other students. Mom was furious. I told myself I didn't disagree with the school—I'd hate to interfere with my fellow students' studies—but really, I just appreciated the excuse to keep hiding at home.

The media had wandered off as the weather chilled. We hadn't exactly been under siege even before that. Mom returned to teaching in September, and when we wanted to go out, we'd just climb into the car in the garage and back out with Mom honking the whole way. Reporters would take pictures and shout questions, but we learned to deal with it, much the way Floridians learn to deal with alligators in their yard.

Then they were gone, and surely that meant life would get back to normal. Except, I wasn't sure what "normal" was anymore. I was taking online classes—musical and academic—but I didn't dare enroll in college. I knew better than to try getting a job. The few local friends who stayed in touch had returned to college themselves. With the media gone, the gate to freedom was finally wide open . . . and I had nowhere to go.

Then came the fight. Mom wanted me to apply for winter term at a local college. I wasn't ready, and the harder she pushed, the more I panicked until I told her everything.

I told her about the forum comments. I told her about the online photos. I told her how many times I'd changed e-mails and the ugly things that I received each time someone tracked down my new address. I told her about the voice-mail messages and the texts until I finally had to tell my friends to only call our landline.

I spewed forth all the ugliness I'd kept inside, and Mom . . . Something in her shattered, and I had to watch my mother sobbing and shaking and blaming herself. Once, after Dad died, I saw Mom break down when she thought I was in bed. That was the worst thing I'd ever witnessed. Until this. And this was my fault.

I'd gone that night, leaving a note on the table that told her none of this was her fault. Told her I just needed to get away for a few days. I'd be fine. I had money for a hotel room, and I was almost nineteen. I could handle this.

I'd wanted to give her a break. I'd walked a few blocks, called a cab and directed the driver to a decent chain hotel, only to discover they required a credit card and ID showing I was over twenty-one. After two more hotels, someone took pity on me and suggested this cheap motel off the highway.

As I cried, an inner voice called me a spoiled brat. I only needed to glance out the window to see cars dotting the parking lot. People stayed in places like this all the time, and if my family could afford better, that was no accomplishment of mine.

But I thought of where I'd spent the summer, and I thought of my room at Juilliard, and I realized how much I'd lost. I wanted to scream that it wasn't fair, that I didn't deserve this. I wanted to cocoon myself in self-pity and—

A bell clanged in my room. I sat there, eyes round, as the sound continued, a reverberating *clang-clang-clang*.

"Goddamn it," a man's voice said in the next room. "Is that the fire alarm?"

Fire alarm? My head jerked up. That *is* what I was hearing, an old-fashioned fire bell.

It was almost certainly a false alarm. I'd been in hotels when the alarm went off, and while Mom insisted on leaving, most people didn't bother.

"Is that smoke?" the man's voice came again.

A woman responded, telling him to get his ass out of bed. I inhaled and caught the faintest whiff of smoke.

The motel was on fire. Really on fire.

I scrambled up. I'd gone to bed in a nightshirt, and it covered me well enough. I just needed my jacket. I spun around, searching for my coat, as the alarm clanged.

Well, you'll be warm soon enough, Lucy, if you don't get out of here.

I gave up, grabbed my purse and my cell phone and ran to the door. With trembling fingers, I unfastened the keychain, threw open the door and—

"Smile for the camera, Lucy," a voice said and a camera bulb flashed.

CHAPTER TWENTY-FIVE

NEW YORK 2019

I SIT UP IN BED, clutching my knees, the exact pose of that night long ago. I inhale the same stink of a cheap motel room, and the smell makes my gorge rise, but all I see is that photograph, sold to the tabloids within days.

Me standing half-naked in the doorway of a cheap motel room.

Oh, how far the mighty have fallen. One day, you're screwing Colt Gordon in a hot tub, the next, you're screwing God-knows-who in a highway motel.

It'd been a setup, of course. A trash can fire lit by an enterprising paparazzo to flush me out.

Now I'm in another cheap room, fourteen years later, clutching my knees, my stomach heaving as I shiver. There's no November breeze. If anything, the crappy air-conditioning leaves the room warm and humid. I still feel that frigid wind, though. Still hear the alarm bell. Still see the camera flashing and feel my stomach plummet as I realized I'd been set up.

I thought I'd come so far, and instead, I've traveled full circle. I am right back where I began, all my hard work erased.

As soon as the pity sparks, I reflexively force it back. I can still fix this. I'm no longer that girl, horrified at being photographed in a nightshirt. They can say what they want, post what they want, concoct whatever stories they want. I'm going to stay on top of this.

I will turn myself in. I just need to be prepared. I just can't risk being helpless again. I can't risk losing it all again.

Someday, I may look back on this as a tsunami of stupidity that washes Colt Gordon out to sea. I accept that possibility. I just won't let *myself* be washed out to sea, not without a fight.

I START my morning with a subway ride and a two-mile walk to a bus terminal, where I use a pay phone to call my mom. The police haven't been to see her yet, which is a relief. I won't tell her anything she can't pass on—and I insist that she be honest with the police if they show up.

I will not inflict any more pain on her than absolutely necessary. I'll never forget the woman who broke down that afternoon so long ago.

Next, I use an ATM. I only want to leave a record, pointing police to this bus depot. Yet when I check my bank balance, it shows over a thousand dollars. A care package from Mom? It must be. I withdraw my max—I'll repay her later.

Finally, I use my credit card to buy a ticket to Boston at the automated booth. Put that together with the cash withdrawal and the pay phone call to Mom, and I'm hoping the police will assume I've hopped a bus out of the state.

On the walk back to the subway station, I stop in a coffee shop to use the Internet. I open my inbox, telling myself that I hope Marco didn't respond, for his own good. I'm lying, of course, and when I see an e-mail from him, my heart leaps. Leaps and then plummets and then flutters there, uncertain, afraid of what the letter will say.

After last night, while I'm plowing forward internally, I am not in a good place. I've stayed offline because even the sight of a newspaper box nearly had me retching in the street. I have a sick headache that isn't responding to painkillers. I'm exhausted and shaky, and if Marco e-mailed to tell me that he never wants to see me again, I don't know what I'd do.

Gen,

I won't lie. I wish you'd given me a heads-up. But that's a conversation for another time. Right now, I just feel helpless. You're half a world away, and I want to fly there and help, but I'd only make things worse. I'm just a tour guide and a bike courier.

If there is anything I can do, say the word. I won't hold my breath for that call, and I won't look for another e-mail. Just remember that I'm here for you, and the moment you're out from under this cloud, I'll be there to bring you home.

xx Marco

I read it twice, my eyes filling. Part of me wants to reply and tell him to come, just come now, please. I know better. He's right that he can't help. I'd only be pulling him in as an accomplice. So I reply with a line of *x*'s. Then I sit there, reading his e-mail a few more times and committing it to heart before I reluctantly close it and move on. The following three e-mails are variations on "Is this Lucy Callahan? The one in the news?" I skim past.

The last one bears the subject line: "I Can Help," and I chuckle at that. *I'm sure you can, anonymous e-mail sender.*

I open it, expecting to find an e-mail offering Viagra to help me "with the ladies." Instead, after I skim the first few lines, I bite back the urge to curse aloud, lest I scare off my cafe neighbors.

Lucy,

Or do you prefer Genevieve? You don't know me, but I believe I can help you. I know about the warrant for your arrest, and I am convinced you're being framed. And, no, the next line of this e-mail is not "please send me $1000, and we can discuss your situation."

I'm a private investigator. I've worked for law firms, where I handled cases like yours. I've studied the timeline, and the police were far too quick to issue that warrant. Something's up. It's a high-profile case, so they have an incentive to find a suspect quickly, but they usually wouldn't risk the humiliation of arresting the wrong person. That makes me highly suspicious.

I'm not asking for anything from you just yet. I'm reaching out, knowing you may very well stop monitoring this address, which has already leaked online (see link at bottom). Please do keep it open, though, until I can send you something useful. Once I do, I'm hoping we can chat.

It's unsigned, but I know exactly who sent it. Well, maybe not *who*, but at whose instigation. Daniel Thompson.

Thompson has realized I'm not responding to yesterday's e-mail. He promised he wouldn't contact me again. So he's trying a different tactic.

I have to give him credit—the e-mail is pitch-perfect. A total stranger e-mails me from out of the blue to say they think I'm being framed, and this whole thing is suspicious, and by the way, investigating crimes like this is their job.

How awesome is that?

Too awesome.

Thompson knows I think I'm being framed. He's already told me I don't have the credentials to do this myself. I've refused his legal help, so he has set his investigator on it, and the guy—or gal —will dig up some tidbit of information that'll prove Thompson is the man to handle my case.

I'm tempted to say, "Screw you" and delete my account. I don't. Nor do I reply. I'll give Thompson a chance, through my silence. Let his investigator dig. If they actually do find something useful . . . maybe we'll talk.

The ball is in your court, counselor.

I'M ABOUT to leave the coffee shop when I remember to research

Isabella's mystery lover. Not surprisingly, his phone number doesn't bring up a name. The Internet tells me it's a cell phone—shock!—and an LA area code—double-shock!

On my walk back, I try the number. It goes straight to voicemail, where a cheerful male voice says, "Hey, you've reached me. Leave a message, and I'll get back to you!"

I hang up. Then I sit there, frowning.

Did that voice sound familiar?

Not exactly, but something in it . . .

I've heard that voice before.

An actor? That would make sense. It's the circle Isabella travels in, and I may have heard her lover in a movie or show.

I tuck the information away in hopes an answer will rise from my subconscious later.

THE PROBLEM with hanging out at my hotel is that it feels like a prison cell . . . which only reminds me of where I could end up. It drives me crazy, though, sitting there, trying to read a magazine when I should be doing something, anything. I'm wanted for murder, damn it.

So I should . . . start interviewing witnesses? Break in to the morgue to further examine Isabella's body? Call my nonexistent contacts in the police department?

I'm not a detective. Worse, as the actual prime suspect, I can't even play amateur sleuth beyond looking for clues on the Internet.

Or I can get a lawyer. The thought makes my gorge rise, thinking of Thompson. I can tell myself he was an exception, but he'd been the only one who'd touch my case, meaning anyone else who might could be Thompson 2.0.

Still, I should do some defense-attorney research. See whether there's anyone who looks like a possibility. I head out again to pick up the nearest source of free Wi-Fi and log on to find another message from TPI—my mental name for Thompson's private investigator.

TPI's e-mail comes with attachments. The first is a screenshot of Colt's Instagram post from yesterday morning. It's him on a veranda overlooking the ocean with the caption:

Early bird catches the worm! Or so I hear. Decided to try it once.
God, it's early. And I don't even get a sunrise on this coast.

The time stamp is 8:03 a.m. Eastern, meaning 5:03 a.m. in California. By 7:10 a.m. yesterday, Isabella's body had been discovered. Is that why TPI sent it? Suggesting this was Colt's reaction to the "your wife is dead" phone call? It's unlikely Colt knew by 8:03. He'd been relaxing on his deck with his first coffee, taking a selfie for . . .

No, it's not a selfie, which means someone else snapped it. Still, I'm not sure I get the point of Thompson's PI sending it to me. Does this imply Colt had a lover spend the night?

You know how you could answer these questions, Lucy? Read the damn e-mail.

Lucy

I hope you're someplace safe. If you need any advice on finding a spot, please let me know. I would like to speak soon. Speak online, I mean. I realize it will take much more than the contents of this e-mail to convince you that I can be trusted for an in-person conversation.

The attached photo was posted to Colt Gordon's Instagram account yesterday morning. I suspect he was informed of the murder and immediately posted this photograph to be clear he was on the West Coast at the time.

Twenty minutes later, this appeared on his Twitter:

This is Karla Ellis, Colt's business manager. He has received some terrible news this morning, and he will be withdrawing from all social media. Please respect the family's privacy at this time. Thank you.

I sent the photograph because it wasn't taken at 5:03 a.m. yesterday. It was pitch black in California at that time. I estimate it was taken closer to 7 a.m., on a different day, obviously.

I believe Colt received the news and scrambled to post a photograph "proving" he was at home when he was not. Does that mean he was at a lover's house that night? Or that he wasn't in California at all?

I'm still digging. I just wanted to send you this as an indication of what I can do.

Your first question will be why I'm doing this at all. Money. I'll make no bones about that. Fighting for a noble cause is laudable, but it doesn't pay my bills. However, I am not asking *you* for money.

As I said, I've worked for lawyers. In civil suits, they aren't paid unless they win their case. I believe this situation is similar. There is money to be had here for whoever tells your story. I will admit, I fancy myself something of a writer. My payment then is that I have your permission to tell this story once it is finished.

I will be blunt. If you are taken into custody and found guilty, your story has minimal value. If you avoid arrest and are ultimately vindicated, though? That is—pardon my language— one hell of a tale. I want to be the one to tell it.

So here is my offer. Talk to me. Allow me to continue working your case. At some point, I will ask for permission in the form of a binding contract. That contract, though, will stipulate that it is null and void in the event that you are convicted of this crime.

I could point out that I'm taking a chance on you, believing in your innocence. Sadly, I've never been much of a salesman. Instead, I'll point out that, considering the stakes for me, I'm fully motivated to prove your innocence.

Beneath that, he—from his use of "salesman," I presume he's male—gives me instructions on how I can talk to him via a messaging app. He's set up a new account for himself and provided his username. He's asked only that whatever username

I choose, it starts with an *L*, so he'll know it's me when I ping him.

He has a good story here. It's bogus, of course. But TPI—or his boss, Thompson—has at least come up with a more plausible explanation than "I'm offering to help you because it's the right thing to do."

Okay, Mr. Thompson. Let's see what you've got.

There's a sandwich shop a few blocks over, and I noticed it offered free Wi-Fi. I'll grab lunch there and contact TPI.

As I walk, I think about what TPI found, and I wish, for the hundredth time, that I'd read Colt's text thread before it disappeared. I'm so lost in my thoughts that I pass the sandwich shop and have to clear my head and backtrack. I arrive to find a tiny place ringed with counter seating, packed too tightly for privacy. There's also a lineup out the door.

I consider finding another spot to eat, but well, I only had coffee this morning, and I'm starving. I'll download the messaging app while I'm waiting, and if a seat clears, the sheer crush of people might mean no one will pay any attention to me.

I download the app and create a fake account using a new e-mail address. I choose Llamagirl as my username. Hey, he said to start it with an *L*. His own username is PCTracy. Is his name Tracy? Surname? PC makes me think *Police Constable*. That's British, though.

As I step into the shop, I pause to figure out what I want to eat. Italy might love its meats and cheeses, but sandwiches aren't its thing, and the second I see pastrami and rye on the menu, my mouth waters.

Back to the app. It pings him with an automated "Llamagirl says hi!" complete with my emoji—a blond cheerleader waving and grinning. Totally looks like me. A moment later, an emoji appears waving back . . . and it's a blond guy who looks like a high-school jock, the male equivalent of my choice. I have to laugh at that. Then I remember Thompson . . . who almost certainly *was* a blond jock in high school. Huh.

Llamagirl: Waiting in line for a sandwich. Chat in a
   minute?

PCTracy: Not going anywhere. So, llamas, huh?

Llamagirl: My secret passion. They're adorable.

PCTracy: They spit and bite, and they're bad-tempered.

Llamagirl: We have a lot in common.

PCTracy: LOL

Llamagirl: So Tracy, huh? Please tell me PC isn't Police
   Constable.

PCTracy: Nah. Plainclothes Tracy. Old comic.

Llamagirl: Any relation to Dick Tracy?

PCTracy: It WAS Tracy . . . before he became a dick.

I give a sputtered snort that has the guy in front of me
glancing over his shoulder. I also have to laugh because I'd been
thinking of him as Thompson's dick, the archaic name for private
investigators, which is where the *Dick* in *Dick Tracy* comes from.
It's like us independently choosing high school blond emojis—it
feels like a connection when I am desperate for one.

I remember Thompson's first e-mail, very professional and
formal, like PCTracy's. Then came the more casual ones . . .
exactly like the casual tone PCTracy has switched to here. More
proof that I'm actually talking to the lawyer himself?

I step up and place my order. As the young woman starts to
take it, a guy my age shoulders her aside with a murmured, "I've
got this. Filipe needs help in the back."

The new guy—the manager—asks for my order again. I give it,
and he takes forever finding it on the touch screen.

"Cheddar cheese?" he asks.

I correct him. His gaze scans the screen, frowning as if he can't
find Swiss. Maybe because it's the *default* for pastrami and rye?

"There it is," he says. "Now, mustard. We have . . ."

He begins rhyming off options. I stop him with "Dijon is fine."

Again, he takes forever to find it. Behind me, people start
grumbling. The second counter person frowns at his supervisor.

Typical management—jumps in when things get busy and actually slows the process.

"Pickles . . . ," the manager says, gaze on his screen. "Is that spears or whole?"

"Either is fine."

"Okay so . . . let's see." He reads back my order so slowly that I wonder whether I've developed an Italian accent and English seems like my second language. "Anything to drink with that?"

I'd love a Coke . . . but the people in my line may lynch me if I don't wrap this up fast. I whip out a twenty instead.

The manager lifts the bill and squints at it. Then he looks at me with exaggerated sorrow.

"I'm afraid this is counterfeit, ma'am."

"What? I got it from a bank machine. It can't—" I bite off the protest. "Never mind. Take this one, and I'll sort it with the bank."

I extend a second twenty.

He shakes his head. "I can't do that. Company policy. Let me take this into the office and scan it to be sure. Please wait here."

I stare at his retreating back, feeling as if I've stumbled into a comedy skit. Are there hidden cameras? I can see the headline now. *Fugitive Accidentally Caught During . . .*

I stop. This manager is stalling me. Actively and clumsily stalling me with what seems like a bad comedy routine, so over-the-top that it can't possibly be real.

It isn't real.

I've been recognized.

CHAPTER TWENTY-SIX

THE MANAGER HAS RECOGNIZED ME. That's why he came up front and took over. That's why he's stalling and dragging this out. He recognized me and called the police, and they're on their way.

Are you serious, Lucy? Do you realize how ridiculous that sounds?

Yep, but it's more believable than his screw-up-manager act. I open my mouth to call after him and tell him to forget it. Then I realize, if I'm right, that's a dead giveaway.

I exhale a dramatic sigh and look at my phone. The chat app is still open with PCTracy waiting.

LlamaGirl: I'm at the deli counter. I think I've been made.

There's a long pause.

LlamaGirl: The manager took over my order. He kept
   stalling. Now he took my money to "check" it in the
   back, saying it's counterfeit.
PCTracy: Get out.
LlamaGirl: It's packed, and they all just heard him say my
   bill was fake.

A pause. I start to lower the phone, ready to solve this on my own. Then he responds.

PCTracy: Put money on the counter. Fives, a ten, something small that'll cover it. No one counterfeits those.
PCTracy: Then move to the side. Tell the person behind you that you're getting out of the way so they can be served.
PCTracy: If it's enough of a crowd, slide toward any rear hall or exit.

I put down a ten and mutter, "Maybe he'll take this." Then I turn to the woman behind me and do as PCTracy said. She nods, obviously relieved to finally reach the counter.

As I slip to the side, someone says, "Hey, wait, didn't she just pass a fake bill?"

"No, asshole," a guy says. "That guy's screwing her around. Her money's right here. She's letting us get our damn lunches."

I join the crowd where the sandwiches arrive. I stand in one spot, and then I pretend to realize I'm in someone's way and move closer to the back wall. I keep that up. No one here is paying attention—these people are too far from the front cash to have overheard the counterfeit issue.

There's a back hall. When I peek into its shadowy depths, a woman says, "Yep, that's the restroom. Not sure I'd use it, though." She winks at me.

I make a face. "Desperate times . . ."

She chuckles as I slip into the rear hall. At the restroom door, I glance back. No one's watching. Two more steps, and I push open the exit and step out, exhaling as the door shuts behind me.

A delivery truck turns into the service lane, taking up the whole width of it. The driver motions, as if to say, "Wherever you came from, lady, go back inside."

I head the other way. Behind me, the driver taps his horn impatiently. I wave and pick up speed. A door slams, and over the patter of my sneakers, I hear the driver call me some choice names.

I duck into a passage between buildings. At the slap of boots behind me, I glance back, thinking the driver is coming after me, but he's heading for a delivery door, still grumbling. I wait there in the shadows as the door creaks open and then smacks shut.

I turn and—

Someone walking down the alley stops short, seeing me. I catch only a glimpse of a tall, broad-shouldered man wearing a hat and dark clothing.

The police.

I wheel and take two running steps, only to see the delivery truck blocking the lane. Blocking me in.

It's over. I am caught. Well and truly caught, and even as my stomach plummets, a frisson of relief darts through me.

Time to turn myself in.

My gut spasms. Not at the fear of a lifetime in prison. I don't honestly see that happening. No, the wild panic bubbling inside me comes from photographs that flash before my eyes.

Me in the hot tub with Colt.

Me in that motel room doorway.

And now me, being arrested for Isabella's murder. Photos of me, disheveled and exhausted. My mug shot plastered across the Internet.

It doesn't matter whether the case is dismissed tomorrow. I will already have been found guilty in the court of public opinion.

I want to say it doesn't matter. I survived before, and I'll survive again. Yet even as I think that, my body betrays me, shaking convulsively, screaming to run, just run.

No.

I am caught, but I will handle this. I will survive it.

Brave words, yet even as my body pivots toward the officer, hands rising, I'm half-blinded by sheer, gibbering terror, that voice screaming that I cannot do this again, cannot, cannot, cannot.

Will.

I will.

I'm turning to face him, my hands raised in surrender and—

A fist slams into my jaw. I stagger, so shocked that my brain only processes what just happened as pain explodes in my jaw. Hands grab me, and I scramble, clawing uselessly, my mind fighting for traction.

What's happening?

What the hell is happening?

Memory flashes, and in a blink, the alley is night-dark, and I'm walking from my job waitressing outside Syracuse. Someone grabs me and throws me against a wall.

The alley brightens again, shadowed light and the stink of summer trash. Hands pin me to the wall, and I struggle for that mental footing as the world threatens to dive back into that memory.

"I-I'm not resisting," I say finally. "I'm not carrying a weapon. Go ahead and pat me down. My ID is in my wallet. I'm Gen— Lucy Callahan."

There's a pause. Then a low, masculine laugh as lips bend to my ear. "You think I'm a cop, Lucy?"

I freeze.

Of course he's not a cop. He just hit *you.*

Which doesn't mean he absolutely isn't a police officer.

He's not a cop, Lucy. This is the important part. You are pinned to the wall by a man who is not a police officer.

I can't think straight. Memories surge, and all my energy goes to holding the dam against them.

Dark alley. Footsteps behind me. Hands slamming me into the wall.

This is not that. Focus on this.

"I-I have money," I say. "A few hundred in my wallet—"

"I think the price of freedom is more than a few hundred dollars, Lucy. I think it's more than you can afford to pay. Do you have any idea how much you're worth right now? There's someone who'll pay very well to—"

He whispers the rest against my ear, but I don't catch it. It's like a nightmare where you're struggling to hear what someone's saying because you know it's critically important, but all you hear is a buzz of words. He's leaning too close, his words garbled.

"Wh-what?" I say.

He pulls back and something presses against my spine. A gun, I think at first. But the moment it presses harder, I know exactly what it is. The cold tip of a knife digging in.

Dark alley. Footsteps behind me. Hands slamming me to the wall. Then a knife pressed to my throat as I stare into the eyes of my attacker, a woman my own age, her breath thick with booze.

I-I— I began. You were at one of my tables.

And I didn't leave a tip, she said. I decided to save that for later. Do you want it now, Lucy Callahan?

My throat closes, and I open my mouth, but nothing comes out except a low whimper as my insides convulse.

Here's the tip, she said, pressing the knife against my throat. You can't get away with what you did. You think you did. You think you got off scot-free after trying to ruin Colt's career, destroy his marriage. You think no one cares. But his fans do. I have been looking for you a very long time, Lucy Callahan. With a message from Colt's true fans.

The knife pulls away from my throat, and there is one shuddering moment of relief before I see her arm swing back, the knife slashing—

I let out a noise. I feel it, burbling up, an animal cry, and then I see the brick wall in front of me and shadowy daylight all around as I'm flung back to the present, and whatever noise I make, it is enough to startle my attacker.

I shove back from the wall as hard as I can, slamming into him. I don't know where that comes from. Perhaps ten years of replaying that night outside the bar, thinking of all the things I could have done, pierced by the humiliation of having only screamed for help.

This time, I act. I fling myself back into him, the old wound in my side seeming to flare white-hot. I hit him hard, and then I run. My brain mercifully clicks on, telling me that if he only has a knife, my best bet is to run.

What it fails to remind me of, though, is that the delivery truck blocks the laneway. I don't stop running. I race forward, and then I hit the ground in a dive and roll under the truck.

I crawl as fast as I can, ignoring the pain shooting up from my skinned palms. Move, just move. Behind me, my attacker's footfalls thunder down the lane. A thump, as if he's dropping to his knees to crawl after me. Then a door creaks open.

"Hey!" a voice calls. "What the hell are you doing with my truck?"

I send up a prayer of thanks for the delivery man as I scramble out from under the truck. Then I run.

CHAPTER TWENTY-SEVEN

I RUN as if I'm back in elementary school, convinced this will be the year I'll take first in the hundred-yard sprint. I never placed higher than fifth, and even that was pure effort and zero skill. I find that old willpower now as I sprint down the lane.

I turn the corner onto the street . . . clogged with traffic and pedestrians, and I'm a woman running for her life. Someone shouts. Car tires squeal. No one stops me, though. No one tries.

I run until I see an alley. I veer into it, duck behind a bin, wobble for a moment, and then double over and puke. I keep retching until nothing remains. Then I stand there, one hand braced against the brick.

At first, I think my free hand is clutching my stomach. Then I look down to see it clamped against the spot where the knife went in ten years ago. My breath comes fast, as if I'm back there, newly stabbed, struggling to breathe, my lung nicked by the knife.

I'm going to die.

The thought flashes, and even in the riptide pull of that memory, I know it's no longer true, but I still feel it. I am in that moment, stabbed in an alley, thinking I'm going to die. Back then, what flashed before my eyes wasn't a collage of my life. It was regret. A parade of regrets, starting with "Why the hell didn't I see this coming?"

Well, for starters, in a sane world, crazed movie-star fans don't knife people for kissing their idol.

I stand there, struggling for breath, hand pressed to that spot, slipping in and out of a world where I feel blood soaking my blouse, a world where I am certain I will die in a dirty alley behind a dive bar.

I did not die, obviously. A coworker heard my scream and came to my rescue. She called an ambulance, which took me to the emergency ward for surgery. She also called the police, who decided I'd been mugged. Forget what I said. Forget that my colleague—bless her—argued like a woman possessed, insisting she'd heard my attacker ranting about Colt Gordon. Nope, I was just mugged by some junkie, and now, attention whore that I was, I wanted another fifteen minutes of fame. When the police accused me of that, I'd laughed so hard I'd ripped my stitches.

This was the last straw for Mom, proof that I couldn't just wait it out and my life would miraculously return to normal. No one wanted Lucy Callahan teaching music to *their* kids, so I'd been working sustenance jobs that barely paid rent on a crappy apartment. I deserved better, she said. So she withdrew fifty grand from her retirement savings and came up with the European plan.

I could have argued. I didn't because all I could see was the carousel of regrets that had danced before my eyes. It was time to move on and move forward.

So I did. If I'd died in that alley today, I would no longer have seen regrets. My life truly would have flashed before my eyes, all the precious things I'd lose—my mother, Rome, my music, my friends, Marco.

I'm already losing them. I'm not sure I can recover my music career after this. Some of my friends will drift away. Marco . . . I have hope there, but he's only dipped his toe in the roiling cesspool of Internet hate. It will worse for him. Much worse. And Mom? My mother will never forsake me, but I'm no longer eighteen and living at home. She's regained her old life. I might never lose her love, but if I must, I will step away from it to protect her.

I stand at a crossroads here, and I keep going back to that moment where I thought my attacker was a cop, and I had been relieved. Ready to turn myself in.

What's the alternative? The realistic and unvarnished alternative? Keep running? Keep hiding?

What if it's more dangerous out here than in there?

I close my eyes, and I remember being thrown against a wall, the man breathing in my ear, threatening to . . .

I don't know what he threatened.

Didn't the knife answer that, Lucy?

He said something about me being valuable. Was there a bounty on me? He'd known who I was. He'd followed me to . . .

I pause and roll back the film to that encounter in the alley. I'd surprised him. I still can't see his face, but when I focus hard, I realize that his "hat" had been a hoodie. A white male in a hoodie. That's all I saw. He'd been coming down the alley and seemed surprised to see me.

He'd known me, though. He'd said . . .

No, I'd said my name. I'd thought he was a cop, and I said I was Lucy Callahan. That's when he mentioned the bounty . . .

Bounty? I snort under my breath. No, he'd said I was valuable.

He *could* have been following me. He could have been in the crowded deli when he saw me sneak out the back and circled around to cut me off. I surprised him, so he had to act fast, throwing me against a wall at knifepoint because he knew exactly who I was, and someone wanted to make sure I was turned over to the police . . . or *never* turned over to the police.

Option two, though? He was just a guy in an alley, not unlike the one from yesterday. I surprised him, and he saw the chance for easy money. Throw me against the wall and spout crazed nonsense about me being valuable.

Two ends of the spectrum with a million possibilities in between.

I don't know what just happened. I only know that, in fleeing once that deli manager called the police, I could have been stabbed in an alley. I also know that I am in no mental shape to deal with life as a fugitive. I'm a mess, cold sweats and nausea and nightmares and now actual flashbacks in broad daylight.

Turn yourself in, Lucy. Call Thompson, and let him take his shot. Or find another lawyer. It's the media you truly fear—the implosion of your life—but the longer you run, the more you risk it anyway.

My phone vibrates, startling me. I thought I felt it earlier, but I'd been a bit busy, running for my life, and tumbling into flashbacks and throwing up in alleys. Speaking of which . . .

I gaze down at the vomit pooled by my feet and stride onto the street before checking my phone.

It's PCTracy. I exhale in relief. Well, I wanted to turn myself in, preferably with Thompson's help. Here's my chance.

LlamaGirl: I'm here.
PCTracy: Good. What happened?

I hesitate. The encounter in the alley still has my stomach roiling, but I don't see the point in telling him about it. I keep remembering the doubt and mockery of the police after that knife attack ten years ago. If I'm not sure what happened, I should keep it to myself for now.

LlamaGirl: I got out of there as fast as I could.
LlamaGirl: But now I'm thinking I shouldn't have run. I
    should turn myself in, right?

When he doesn't answer, I realize what I'm doing.

LlamaGirl: Sorry. I'm asking you for advice on a decision I
    need to make myself. I don't believe I'll end up in

prison. Well, not for longer than it takes to set a bail hearing if they even go that far. There's no actual evidence against me, right?

Again, he doesn't answer, and I exhale at that. Okay, PCTracy wasn't disagreeing with his silence. We've disconnected. I'll go to my hotel room and wait—

PCTracy: Where are you right now?
LlamaGirl: On a street, catching my breath. I'm not sure where the nearest police station is, but I can look that up. I just need a lawyer.

Hint, hint . . .

PCTracy: Yes, you do. Right now, though, are you someplace safe and private where we can talk?
LlamaGirl: What's up?
PCTracy: You returned to your hotel room yesterday morning, right? After finding Isabella?
LlamaGirl: Right.
PCTracy: Did you see any sign of disturbance?

My heart pounds.

LlamaGirl: Someone had broken in. I should have mentioned that.
PCTracy: It's fine. But you noticed the room had been entered. Did you notice anything else?
LlamaGirl: I took my clothing, thinking someone might have left evidence on it. Took my toiletries and tech. I don't think anything else had been—

Shit. Oh, shit. The memory slams back, the thought that's been niggling at me since yesterday.

My towel. The one I used in the shower that morning. I'd just gotten out when Isabella texted, and I'd tossed it on the chair as I hurried to blow-dry my hair and get ready.

The towel had been on the chair with my dirty clothing when I left to see Isabella.

It was not on the chair when I returned. I grabbed my clothes, and the towel wasn't there.

> PCTracy: The police found a bath towel stuffed into the vent.
>
> PCTracy: It had Isabella's blood on it.
>
> LlamaGirl: I didn't do that.
>
> PCTracy: Of course not. No one is going to commit a murder, stuff the towel in a hotel vent and leave it behind when they flee. The problem right now is that it's forensic evidence. The police claim to have more, but I don't know what that is.
>
> LlamaGirl: You're saying I really could go to prison for this.
>
> PCTracy: I can't answer that without knowing the other so-called evidence. The towel isn't enough. The texts were obviously sent from a linked device. That can be tracked. Someone let the killer into your hotel room. That leaves a trail, and once I can prove someone got access, all evidence found in there becomes inadmissible.
>
> LlamaGirl: You sound like a lawyer :)
>
> PCTracy: Just too much time working for them. You do need a lawyer, like you said. As for turning yourself in right now, if that is what you want to do, then I will help with whatever you need.
>
> LlamaGirl: But you wouldn't recommend it.
>
> PCTracy: My honest advice is to stay out until I can find enough proof to make the DA think twice about proceeding with charges. But that's easy for me to say. I'm not in your shoes.

LlamaGirl: Just give me data. Pros and cons.

PCTracy: I don't think there's significant danger in you staying free a bit longer. Could it harm your case? No more than it already has, to be blunt. But clearly, we'd argue that you were frightened.

Frightened. I think of what just happened in that alley. PCTracy says there's no significant danger in me staying free, but he's speaking from a legal perspective. He doesn't know what happened a few minutes ago.

Except I don't really know what happened, either. Was I attacked for being Lucy Callahan? Or just the victim of big-city violence?

PCTracy: If you do turn yourself in, I can keep working on your behalf. There's also an advantage, though, to me having full-time access to you. And to you assisting in your own investigation, which you seem willing to do.

LlamaGirl: Absolutely. I'm not looking for a white knight here.

PCTracy: I know. My advice then is to give me twenty-four hours. If you want to turn yourself in then, I'll guide you through it.

LlamaGirl: Shouldn't I have a lawyer for that?

PCTracy: Absolutely, and I will make sure you do.

Because he is Thompson. Or works for him. The more we talk, the more certain I am that I don't need to find a lawyer. I already have. I just need to be sure I can trust him.

LlamaGirl: Fair enough. What are my restrictions, though? I just got caught buying lunch. Can I go back to my hotel and get my things?

PCTracy: If you don't need your belongings, skip it.

LlamaGirl: I need them.

PCTracy: Okay. You'll have to find a new place to stay,
 though. Do you trust me enough to arrange that
 for you?
LlamaGirl: No. Sorry.
PCTracy: Don't apologize. The problem, though, is that I
 presume you're paying cash and not showing ID. Even
 at the seediest hotels, you're calling attention to
 yourself. I can book you a room and leave the key
 where you can find it.
LlamaGirl: Not yet.
PCTracy: The alternative would be finding a place to spend
 the night out-of-doors. A park or such. That would be
 far from comfortable.
LlamaGirl: That's fine.
PCTracy: Let's talk specifics, then.

AFTER I FETCH MY BELONGINGS, I stop at a library. I'm not even sure
which one. It's a big branch, quiet on a Tuesday afternoon. I find a
study carrel and log onto the Internet. PCTracy has asked me to
give him twenty-four hours, and I'm giving myself the same.
Twenty-four hours to make headway, or I am turning myself in.

Making headway means diving into the Internet cesspool
again. Even thinking about it makes me shy away like a spooked
horse. No, that analogy puts a pretty gloss on the truth. I'm not
merely skittish about seeing my life dragged through that muck. I
am viscerally sick, physically and mentally. I want to be stronger
than this, to tell myself that people have endured far greater
trauma. Yet my body doesn't care for distinctions. This *feels* like
trauma, slashing open life-threatening wounds that had finally
begun to heal.

I can tell myself that words can't hurt me. I can tell myself I
will survive this. Whatever happens, I will rebuild my life again.
None of that matters, though, when I feel as if I'm watching it all

burn to cinders around me, and every time I try to throw water on the flames, I dowse them in gasoline instead.

So here I go, wading in, water hose in hand. Again, I find myself grudgingly relying on the entertainment tabloids. I focus on the Morales-Gordon clan and quickly discover that I'm not the only one being burned at the stake in a public spectacle.

They've zeroed in on Jamison. In and out of rehab since he was seventeen. Two suicide attempts. A "beautiful wreck of a boy" with "deep-rooted psychological issues" that can stem from the trauma of his beloved nanny turning into a Lolita hell-bent on destroying his family.

Then there's Tiana. A young woman who spurned the family business and got her master's in political science and became an activist. In the words of one right-wing publication, she's a professional shit-disturber, a whiny millennial malcontent. Ultraconservative blogs make a big deal of her sexual orientation, too, snarking that for someone like Tiana, being gay is a career requirement. Others speculate that her experience with me and her father "turned her gay."

Next up is Colt. After the scandal, a couple of his past lovers talked to the media. There are whispers of him being seen at sex parties. Also a paternity claim from a nineteen-year-old ingenue. Nineteen, Colt? Jesus. You learned nothing, did you?

Then there's Isabella. No one has a bad thing to say about her . . . which is exactly the ammunition they use against her. Poor, long-suffering Isabella. Gave up her career for her man. Stuck by him when he screwed around with the nanny. Pathetic, really. Isabella may be the Madonna in our drama, the faithful Penelope to my seductress Circe, but that doesn't win her anything except contempt.

I dig for rumors of Isabella's potential lover. Of course, any search on her name fills the page with news of her death. Even as I try to filter out keywords, I find myself reading the most up-to-date stories on her murder.

Colt arrived in New York yesterday. Tiana was rumored to be

picking up her brother yesterday from rehab, but she was spotted having dinner last night with her father, and there was no sign of Jamison. Lots of speculation there, everything from "he had a relapse, and he's in emergency detox" to "he attempted suicide, and he's in hospital."

Guilt and grief wash over me. Yet there's no way Tiana would be seen having dinner out with her dad if her brother was in the hospital. If she's not with him, there's a reason. I just don't know what it is.

I start to dig deeper and then stop. Where is this getting me? I can tell myself I'm hoping to find a clue that will help my case, but really, I'm just checking up on Tiana and Jamison, worrying about them.

What might help me is finding Isabella's mystery lover. I know he was in New York the night she died, which makes him a suspect, but I can find nothing online suggesting Isabella *had* a lover. Part of the issue is keywords. No matter how I phrase it, I end up with references to my fourteen-year-old scandal and Colt's alleged subsequent affairs.

I call the mystery lover's phone number again. Voice mail picks up immediately. I could text him, but I'm not sure what I'd say. I'm not even sure what I'd have said if he answered my call.

Frustration buzzes through me. My only lead is this dead end. Getting more will have to wait until I'm ready to share Isabella's secret with PCTracy.

When I consider reneging on my decision to not tell him, I realize, to my shame, that I'm looking for an excuse to talk to him. I'm unsettled, and he settles me, and that's a weird and uncomfortable thing to say.

I'm staring at my phone when he messages, as if he sensed me debating.

PCTracy: Just checking in. Everything okay?
LlamaGirl: All good. Found a spot to hang out and do
    some research.

PCTracy: Anything?

LlamaGirl: Nope. Just busywork. I am not a PI.

PCTracy: Well, I am, and it's still slow going. I might have something, but I need to check a few things first.

LlamaGirl: Tease.

As soon as I hit Send on that, I deliver a mental head smack. He responds with a simple "LOL. Sorry." and then I feel silly for worrying that it sounded flirtatious.

PCTracy: Soon, I promise. But you're okay? Need anything?

LlamaGirl: Work. I'm running in circles. Is there something I can do? Something I can research for you? I feel useless.

PCTracy: I understand. Right now, there's nothing, but if I have anything, I will let you know.

LlamaGirl: Thank you. In the meantime, I have to contact my mom and a friend. Is it safe to do that on a prepaid?

PCTracy: No, sorry. If they monitor your mom's calls, an NYC prepaid cell number would be a giveaway. They could get your location from the GPS.

LlamaGirl: Right. Duh. Stick to pay phones, then?

PCTracy: You found one? Are you sure you're not a detective?

LlamaGirl: I saw one downstairs by the restrooms. Otherwise, yeah, they are in short supply.

PCTracy: Use that for now. I have an idea for options that might be more convenient. I'll investigate and let you know.

I work in the library for another hour. Then I head down to the pay phone. I call Nylah first. As I hoped, the police haven't reached out to her yet. I give her a quick update. Basically, *I'm fine. I didn't do it, but I'm afraid to turn myself in after my scandal experience, so I'm giving the police time to realize they've made a horrible mistake.* All true, and also all things she can tell the police if they contact her. Nylah wants more, of course. What was I doing in New York? What happened? How can she help?

I answer the first two honestly. For the third, I pretend I'm fine and everything's under control. I stop myself before reassuring her that I have professional help. I need to protect everyone. Protect Nylah and my mom from keeping secrets. Protect PCTracy from getting in trouble for aiding a fugitive.

I insist that Nylah tells the police everything if they do get in touch.

"Can I tell them that they're idiots, too?" she says. "That they should have been there for you ten years ago when you were stabbed in an alley? That if they think you'd kill Isabella Morales, they need a brain transplant?"

"That seems unwise."

She snorts. "Too bad. I'll tell them anyway." Her voice lowers. "You are okay, right, Luce?"

"I didn't do it."

"Stop saying that. Of course you didn't. But you're on the run and . . . you aren't exactly fugitive material."

"I've spent fourteen years running from something I didn't do. That's gotta count for something."

She goes quiet. Before I can speak, she says, "I hate this, Luce. You don't deserve it. No one would, but you least of all."

I assure her I'm fine, and we talk for a few more minutes before I sign off.

CHAPTER TWENTY-EIGHT

I CALL MOM. Our conversation is strained. She wants me to turn myself in with the help of "that Mr. Thompson." I long to tell her that I suspect I'm already working with him, but I can't say anything she'd need to keep from the police.

"I know there was a misunderstanding, Lucy," she says. "He made a mistake. I really think you should give him a second chance. Have you heard from him?"

I hesitate. "Not since last night. I'm sure I will end up hiring him. Right now, I'm working a few things through and giving the police time to figure out they made a mistake."

We talk more. I stick to the script I used with Nylah. No mention of PCTracy. No mention of what I'm doing or where I've been or what my plans are. Nothing Mom would hesitate to tell the police. I finish the call, and then I head out.

I'LL BE SPENDING the night in Central Park. That's not as easy as it once was. The park is closed from one a.m. to six, when it's patrolled by park police, who'll roust and fine trespassers. If I'm caught, well, then I guess I'll turn myself in.

The Ramble is the obvious place to sleep. It's a forest within the park, thickly wooded, with plenty of hidey-holes. It also has a reputation for being the most dangerous spot after dark, and while it's much safer than it was twenty years ago, I'm not taking that chance.

While power walking, I survey possibilities and choose a place near Belvedere Castle, where I can sleep along the back of a building, tucked into the shadows, dressed in dark clothing.

It's still not late enough to take up position, so I find a hidden place and work. I'm all set with a newly purchased notebook and pen. No more aimlessly wandering the Internet. It's time to get organized.

First, I build a timeline.

Sunday, 3 p.m.—4:15 p.m.: visit Isabella
    5:02 p.m.: text Isabella to agree to meet for lunch Monday
    Head back to hotel after that, and stay in my room until morning.

Note: Can they confirm my comings and goings with keycard access? My door didn't open after turndown service. Check this with PCTracy.

Monday 5:53 a.m.: first text from Isabella
    6:15 a.m.: leave hotel and walk to Isabella's
    6:45 a.m.: arrive at hotel
    7:05 a.m.: staff enters hotel room
    7:20 a.m.: talking to security guard before police arrive

I'm pleased at myself for thinking of the keycard question. Yet deep down, I know that, while this would be the exonerating evidence in a TV legal drama, it won't be enough to prove innocence.

On the park Wi-Fi, I search for time of death and end up on a website that tells me, firmly but gently, just how inexact a science "time of death" is. It'll be a time frame of hours, not minutes.

Helpful if you're trying to decide whether a victim died on a Monday or a Tuesday. Not so helpful if the critical question is whether she died at 5 a.m., 6 or 7.

Next, I map out Isabella's timeline. No one has reported her receiving visitors to her room. Would the hotel know? I suspect not. While cameras place me in the lobby, none report me in the elevators or the stairwell or on the penthouse floor, which I suspect means the old building doesn't have cameras beyond that lobby.

So the killer arrives. He or she goes straight up to the penthouse, and Isabella lets them inside. They fight, and she dies. That seems the most likely explanation, but I can't rule out premeditated murder.

Who would want Isabella dead? I list my suspects, their motivations and alibis and start with the easiest: Isabella's children.

Jamison. In rehab out of state. There's a check-up text from his mom Sunday evening and then a phone call. No sign of trouble between them. No sign that he knew I was even in New York.

Tiana. In New York. Knew I had visited Isabella. Knew I would return for lunch. Motivation for murder? None.

I pause there. This is the problem. Knowing the suspects blinkers me. PCTracy wouldn't write "none" after Tiana's motive. She's Isabella's daughter. Surely she'd stand to gain something on her mother's death. So would Jamison. PCTracy would dig deeper into their finances and their relationship with Isabella.

He can do that; I won't.

Colt. Possibly not in California at the time of the murder but pretended he was. Knew I was here meeting Isabella. Did he know about my lunch plans with Isabella? Unknown. Motive? Yes.

A lawyer would laugh at that last part. Can you elaborate? I only know that I can come up with a half-dozen reasons why Colt might kill Isabella, and I'm sure there are more. They were married; he was chronically unfaithful and unhealthily dependent, and she was about to divorce him.

Mystery lover. Definitely in New York at time of murder. No one knows this (presumably) except me. Knew about my meeting with Isabella. Motive? Yes.

Again, I don't have a clear motive; I only know that, as a secret lover, he would have at least one.

Others: business associates. Personal assistant—Bess—knew I was in NYC, wasn't happy about it and told Tiana. Manager—Karla— knew and was cautiously ready to move forward with the "go public" plan.

If Karla knew, other staff likely did, too. Isabella would open her hotel door to any of them. I don't know her current staff and business associates, though, and the more I think about it, the more I realize I know so little of Isabella's life these days. There could be a dozen other people who belong on this list.

I'm tired, and panic is creeping in. Time to get to my sleeping spot and settle in for the night.

I SLEEP BETTER than I expected. I feel oddly safer here than I did in my hotel room. The building hides me, and after an hour of lying awake but hearing no one on the nearby paths, I drift off.

When I wake to a touch on my cheek, I don't jump up. I think only of the man who has shared my bed for hundreds of nights in the past two years. My eyelids flutter, and I stretch and smile up at a dark-haired figure.

"Good morning, sunshine."

My smile freezes. It's a flat American accent in a voice deeper than Marco's musical contralto. I blink, and a man in his late thirties appears. A very average face with short hair and twinkling hazel eyes.

I scramble up, realizing where I am. I see his dark jacket and that short hair. Park police.

"I—I'm sorry," I stammer. I'd come up with an excuse last night, but now my sleep-sodden brain can't locate it. "I . . . I was with a friend and . . . we'd had a few drinks . . . and I just sat down for a minute . . ."

The flimsy excuse rolls out, and the guy nods sympathetically, as if it's perfectly plausible.

"Is there a fine?" I say. "I'll pay it if there is."

He hems and haws, and I babble nonsense about how nothing like this has ever happened to me before, and I'm so embarrassed.

Even as he's nodding, something pings deep inside me. The faintest warning chime.

I look up at him. Really look at him. He is terrifyingly bland. Average age. Average appearance. Clean-shaven. Well-dressed. Looks like a cop.

A memory flashes. A man in an alley, dressed in dark clothing, who'd seemed to be wearing a hat, which turned out to be a hoodie, and afterward, I'd wondered how I'd mistaken a guy in a hoodie for a cop.

Because he seemed like one. I might only have caught the briefest glimpse of a face, only enough to recall that it was a white guy. Something deeper, though, mistook him for a police officer because he had that look.

Clean-shaven. Well-groomed. Solid build.

Not a guy you'd mistake for an addict shooting up in an alley. Not a guy you'd mistake for a homeless person.

A guy you might mistake for a cop.

I look down at this man's outfit—a dark jacket, dark jeans and sneakers. Then up at his face, and that alarm screeches.

I know you.

Oh, shit. I know you.

I scramble up, but he's on me in a second, grabbing my arm and expertly pinning it behind my back. Then he leans in, and his voice loses that midwestern accent and rises an octave to a voice my gut recognizes with a breath-stealing twist.

"Hello, Lucy," he says. "You aren't very good at this fugitive nonsense, are you? Grabbed in an alley, and what do you decide is your next move? Sleep in an empty park." He chuckles. "Not exactly a criminal mastermind. Lucky for me."

"Who are you?" I say, my voice rising, shrill and shaky. "What do you want?"

He laughs at the movie-cliché dialogue and relaxes his grip just a little, reassured that I really am an idiot. It's the opening I want, and I yank from his grip, spinning around to slam him with my backpack as I knee him between the legs. He staggers, and I run.

If you'd asked me whether I ran as fast as I could earlier today, I'd have said obviously I did. I did not. My attacker had been thwarted by the delivery driver, giving me the time I needed to get to a public place.

I'm still in a public place . . . only this one is completely empty, and there's nothing to slow down my attacker. I run, skidding and sliding at first, the backpack thumping against my side. Then I manage to sling it over my shoulder as I find my footing.

The man comes after me. He is not on the ground, writhing in agony after that knee between the legs. He's frothing-at-the-mouth furious, screaming epithets, his average-guy mask shredded.

I start down the footpath and then veer with a mental reminder that, when running for one's life, one does not need to stick to the paths. I run, blinking against the darkness until I spot the Delacorte Theater ahead. I race toward it and swing toward the first building I see.

As soon as I slow, I hear his pounding footfalls, and I plaster myself to the wall and squeeze my eyes shut to listen.

Run past me. Just run past me.

There's a chance he will. There's also a chance that he'll look over his shoulder as he passes, and he'll spot me. I will be ready for that. I'll run if I have time. I'll fight if I do not.

I keep my eyes shut, tracking his progress. When I pick up a second set of footfalls, my eyes fly open.

Is that the actual park police? There's no way I could be that lucky. I'm hearing an echo. I must be.

Unless my attacker isn't alone.

Dear God, what if he has a partner?

I brace myself. He's drawing closer. He's still running full out, not slowing as he nears the building. He's going to run past. Please, let him run past.

A yelp rings out. A high-pitched squeal of surprise. Then "What the—?"

The sound of a fist striking. A thump, too hard to be someone falling. Someone being thrown to the hard earth.

Another smack. An animal yowl of pain.

Run!

What's going on? What just happened?

Does it matter? Run.

I want to look. I so badly want to peek out and see what's going on, but the audio will have to be enough. Someone chased my pursuer. Either the park police or a stranger who saw him coming after me. Now there's a fight, and I have a chance to escape.

I creep along the theater. It seems to take forever, but finally, I see the Great Lawn ahead. I race toward it as the sounds of the fight fade behind me.

CHAPTER TWENTY-NINE

When I exit Central Park, I check the time. Three a.m. My stomach twists. This might be the city that doesn't sleep, but it does hit a point on weekday nights where the only people out are . . . not people I want to meet. I feel as exposed as a lone antelope at the watering hole.

I duck into an all-night diner, buy pie and coffee, and sit in a corner booth. If the server or the cook recognizes me and calls the police, I'm done. I won't flee. I won't fight. I'm casting my die here. Fate will have her way, and I'll think, *At least it's not as bad as what could have happened tonight.*

What did happen tonight? I'm still unpacking that. I made a mistake this afternoon when I told myself that the alley attack was a crime of opportunity. Ten years ago, I'd have berated myself for that as much as I did for the knife attack. How could I be so stupid?

I'll be gentler with myself tonight. Kinder and more understanding. I did not want to seriously entertain the possibility that this afternoon's attack was targeted because the online vitriol has ignited old memories. Memories of my self-worth being ground into dust. Memories of being stomped into ignominy even as my picture graced a thousand newspapers. Who did I think I was?

Just some girl, some nanny, some homely nobody. Attacked in an alley by a crazed fan? Don't be silly. That doesn't happen. Do I really crave attention that badly? Do I really think anyone cares enough to do that?

Paranoid. How often have I chastised myself with that word? I'm being silly, being paranoid. It felt like common sense, but the root of it was that insidious whisper from the past, telling me I was nothing, wasn't even pretty enough to snare Colt Gordon for a night—God, did you see her? How drunk and horny was he?

I didn't want to think I'd be targeted because it made me feel as if I was thinking too highly of myself. Thinking I was important enough to be attacked.

Do you have any idea how much you're worth right now?

That's laughable, of course. This isn't about me. It's about me as a potential fall guy for Isabella's murder, and in that, hell yes, I'm valuable. Someone has gone to a lot of trouble to frame me. Am I questioning the possibility they'd hire someone to find me?

I'm almost certainly not dealing with a crazed fan here. Whoever killed Isabella has money, and that means they could hire someone to do the police's work. Because, let's face it, the cops aren't exactly putting up roadblocks to find me. I'm not public enemy number one. They'll just track my banking cards, and block my passport and remind the public to call if they see me.

That isn't enough for the killer.

The guy in the park was the same one who attacked me in the alley. Yes, I'd surprised him there as he'd been following me, but he'd acted swiftly as he had tonight. That arm hold told me he knew what he was doing. He wasn't some random guy who made it his mission to find me in hopes of a reward.

And he *has* found me. Twice now.

Or is it three times? I keep thinking of that first night, the man I'd briefly seen step from an alley and then sink back into the shadows when I spotted him.

He hasn't "found" me three times. He's never lost me. He's

been tracking me from the start, waiting for the right moment to . . .

To what? Turn me in to the police? That only takes a phone call.

The killer is framing me for Isabella's murder. Yet, being innocent, I would fight like hell.

What if I never get to trial? What if I die in an alley? In Central Park? Die with further evidence planted on my corpse?

Again, I recoil from the thought. No one's going to kill me. I'm not worth that.

If I want to succumb to that voice whispering about my worth, then perhaps I *should* listen to it here. My lack of importance, my lack of roots, my lack of ties, all that makes me *easy* to kill. I'm single, childless, living abroad with only a school-teacher mom to care whether I die. It would be easy to get rid of me.

Is that the plan?

I honestly don't know.

There's also the possibility that my stalker is Isabella's killer. That it could even be her mystery lover. I balk at that—it doesn't fit the man from those texts. But I already consider him a potential suspect. Why couldn't it be my stalker, too?

I feel eighteen again, lost and confused and alone. So damned alone.

I could have died tonight.

That's what it comes down to. I could have died.

I sit and I stare, my coffee and pie untouched. When the sixty-something server comes by with her pot of coffee, she sees I don't need it and murmurs, "Everything okay, hon?" in a soft Southern accent, and I start to cry. I'm mortified, of course, wiping tears and stammering apologies, but she brushes them off and slides in across from me and says, "You need me to call anyone?" When I don't answer, she leans over and lowers her voice. "A friend?" She pauses. "The police?"

I shake my head.

"You sure, hon?"

I nod. "I just . . . I had a close call. I did something stupid and had a close call."

"Everyone's entitled to do stupid things, especially when they're young." Her dark eyes meet mine. "No one deserves a 'close call' for doing them."

Tears spill, and I wipe them away and thank her.

"You sure you don't want me to phone someone?"

I shake my head. "I just need a place to sit. I know I'm taking up a table." I reach into my pocket and pull out a twenty. "I can pay for more food, and you can give it to someone who needs it."

Her plump hand covers mine. "You keep your money. We're empty tonight, and I don't mind not being the only person in here. Hal in the back is too deaf to come running when there's trouble. Or that's his excuse, lazy old fart."

As she rises, she takes my pie. "This apple isn't fit for a dog. It comes straight from the freezer. You want the sweet potato pie. I make it myself. Only place in New York you can get it this time of year."

She brings me a slice, and I take a bite and pronounce it perfect, as if I am a connoisseur of the dessert. She tells me to wave if I want more, and otherwise, she'll leave me be.

Before she walks away, I make note of her name tag. Phyllis. When all this is over, I'm sending her the biggest gift basket I can find. I'm sure that, for Phyllis, this is just another shift, and I'm just another 3 a.m. customer needing a place to be for a few hours. For me, though, it's an unforgettable act of kindness when I needed it most. I won't forget that.

I eat my pie, and sip my coffee and read the paper. It contains nothing on me or Isabella's death. That would have come yesterday, and with no updates, they don't mention it. I'm fine with that.

It's barely five when PCTracy pings me.

PCTracy: Checking in. How'd last night go?

I want to say fine, but I need him to know it was not fine. I need him to have at least some inkling of what I'm facing if he's going to help me decide my next move.

PCTracy: You there?
LlamaGirl: I had a problem.
PCTracy: Are you okay?
LlamaGirl: I was accosted.

Yes, it's an odd word to use, but I'm not ready to share my theory.

Theory? You were attacked twice by the same man. That's a fact.

Doubt still whispers. Not my doubt, but the doubts of those officers when I was stabbed. The doubts of old friends who'd listened to my fears and wondered whether I might be exaggerating a wee bit. Getting paranoid.

PCTracy: What? Where?
LlamaGirl: In a park. It's okay. I'm fine.
PCTracy: That is NOT okay. I'm the one who suggested you
    stay out all night.
LlamaGirl: I'm an adult. It was still my choice.
PCTracy: Are you hurt? Are you safe?

I answer more questions, but they're all about me and my safety. He doesn't ask for details on the accosting, which seems strange. I've left the situation open for everything from attempted sexual assault to a homeless person yelling at me for taking her spot. Yet he only pushes to be sure I'm safe. He presumes that I escaped and that I'm unharmed, but doesn't ask either. It's almost as if . . .

It's almost as if he knows what happened.

LlamaGirl: I do need to go back, though. I left my
    backpack.

There's a pause. A long one.

PCTracy: You dropped it?
LlamaGirl: No, I left it where I was sleeping.

That's the obvious answer. Yet he presumes I took it. As if he *knows* I took it.

PCTracy: Are you sure?
LlamaGirl: Of course, I'm sure. How wouldn't I be?

No answer.

LlamaGirl: You seem very convinced I didn't leave my
    backpack behind.
PCTracy: Sorry. I'm freaking out. I told you it'd be safe to
    spend the night out. You could have been assaulted,
    and it would have been my fault.
PCTracy: I was an idiot, and I'm furious with myself. I was
    thinking that I could do it, and you're obviously
    resourceful and capable, so you could, too. I never
    stopped to consider the extra danger you'd face.
LlamaGirl: As a woman.
PCTracy: Right.
LlamaGirl: I never told you what happened to me. I didn't
    say it was a guy. I didn't say what he wanted. I didn't
    say anything except that I was accosted in the park.

Pause. Pause.

PCTracy: I made a presumption, and I shouldn't have. We
    need to get you a safe place to stay. A hotel room. Do
    you trust me to handle that?

I don't trust you to do anything right now.

LlamaGirl: You were there. When I was attacked.

PCTracy: You think I attacked you?

LlamaGirl: No, I think you came to my rescue. A guy woke me up. I got away. I'd escaped, and I was hiding, hoping he'd run past, when someone took him down. Beat the crap out of him, it sounded like.

PCTracy: Well, good. He deserved it, and I'd gladly have administered the beating, but I've been in my hotel room all night.

LlamaGirl: And if we met for breakfast, you wouldn't have a mark on you?

No answer.

LlamaGirl: It was you. I know it was. You're asking me to trust you. Can I? Really?

At least thirty seconds tick past.

PCTracy: It was me.

PCTracy: I wouldn't have told you it was safe to sleep out of doors unless I could watch over you.

PCTracy: I wasn't LITERALLY watching you sleep. I was just close by. I heard the guy coming. He looked like a cop. I withdrew to monitor the situation. The problem was that I couldn't hear what he was saying to you. It looked like a police interaction . . . until he grabbed you.

PCTracy: I was sneaking up when you escaped. I stayed back, hoping you'd get away on your own. I knew you were hiding behind the theater after you ran, so I took him down before he reached you.

PCTracy: I'm sorry. I should have insisted you get a hotel room, one way or another. I thought I had it under control, and I did not.

LlamaGirl: You're tracking me. You know where I am.

PCTracy: It's not like that.

LlamaGirl: No? Where am I? Right now.

Another thirty seconds. Then he names the diner.

LlamaGirl: You bastard.

PCTracy: Yes, I know where you are, but the only time I used that information was last night.

PCTracy: Okay, I used it this morning, too, but just to be sure you were safe. I'm miles away. I swear it. I have never been within a thousand feet of you before the library yesterday.

LlamaGirl: The library?

PCTracy: It's the IP address. If you're on Wi-Fi, I know how to get the IP address from the messaging app we're using. I can trace that to the location. I haven't before yesterday, though. And I won't do it again. If you're worried, use cell phone data. I can't track that.

LlamaGirl: You bastard.

PCTracy: It was a stupid thing to do. A violation of your trust. I understand that now.

LlamaGirl: And you didn't before?

PCTracy: Honestly, no. Like I said, I wouldn't have suggested you sleep outside if I couldn't be there. From my perspective, I'm guarding a client, which is part of my job. However, from your point of view, I'm a stranger tracking your movements and watching over you as you sleep. That's creepy as hell.

PCTracy: I had nothing but good intentions. But you don't know that. So I screwed up.

LlamaGirl: You did. Goodbye.

PCTracy: Wait! Tell me what I can do to make this right.

LlamaGirl: Nothing. You sent me to this app so we could chat, knowing it also meant you could track me. I'm deleting it now.

PCTracy: Please don't do that, L. Stick to data. I will make
no attempt to track you in any way.

LlamaGirl: I don't trust you.

PCTracy: Colt was definitely not at home the night of the
murder. He went to a rehearsal and then flew out on a
friend's private jet just before 3 p.m. Pacific time, 6
Eastern. I don't have the flight plan yet, but I'm
working on it. A private JET, though, suggests he wasn't
zipping up to San Francisco for the evening. If the
destination was New York, he'd have arrived around
11 p.m.

PCTracy: I also think you should see this.

He sends me a link.

PCTracy: Watch the video. You might be able to reach out
to her. We can discuss that.

LlamaGirl: I need some time.

PCTracy: Understood. Just be careful. Please.

CHAPTER THIRTY

I HAVE breakfast in the diner. I feel safe here, and that might be an illusion—by six, people are streaming in, and while I'm tucked into the corner of my booth, they could still see me if they walked past. Yet I'm still at the same point as when I walked in here. Roll the die. Accept my fate. I suppose Mom would say that I'm putting my faith in God, but God or Fate, it feels like the same thing. That moment when you look the cosmos square in the eye and say, "Do with me what you will."

I need a good breakfast, and I need to analyze how much danger I'm currently in, and I need to process what PCTracy did. If taking that time to think and eat breakfast means I get caught, so be it.

The trouble, really, is that PCTracy knows he made a mistake. I called him a bastard, and I want him to be one and belligerently defend his actions.

What? I saved you, lady. I watched over you, and I saved you, and I beat up a guy who tried to assault you. You should be thanking me.

If he said that, I could delete this app and be done with him.

Sorry, PCTracy, but I don't need a private investigator who'll cyber-stalk me and watch me as I sleep. That's creepy as hell.

Except he said it was creepy himself. He acknowledged it first and never defended himself.

Was he just saying what I wanted to hear? Talking me off the ledge?

Maybe, but if he really believed he'd done me a favor, he'd be unable to let a little of that slip in.

I can't dismiss him. But I can't trust him, either. He betrayed that trust, and he treated me like a child.

Sure, stay out all night. That's fine . . . because I'll be secretly watching over you.

I feel patronized. The question, though, is whether he'd do the same for a man, and I suspect the answer is yes. To him, I'm not a woman in jeopardy needing male protection; I'm a client in jeopardy needing professional protection.

I don't delete the app. I do close it, and I will leave it closed for a while.

It's not until I'm nearly done with breakfast that I remember the link he sent. It leads to one of the CNR-wannabe sites, where a reporter caught up with Tiana, "caught up" being paparazzi-speak for "cornered." Tiana is with Bess Tang, her mother's assistant and Tiana's ex. They're walking out of a cafe after lunch yesterday. Tiana wears oversized sunglasses and a floppy face-shadowing hat, and she reminds me so much of her mother that my heart squeezes.

When the video begins, Tiana is throwing open the cafe door and striding out, Bess at her heels, talking fast. The camera is about ten feet away, and I expect it to descend on her, but it stays where it is. A young woman with purple hair zooms up to Tiana, saying, "Oh, my God, you're *Tiana*," as if there's only one person in the world with that name.

Tiana keeps walking.

The purple-haired girl chases her, saying, "I'm sorry. I know this is a bad time. I just wanted to thank you for your work with the LGBT community."

That makes Tiana stop. She slowly pivots.

The girl thrusts out a hand. "Thank you for being out there and for representing. It means a lot to me."

Tiana can't walk away from that. She should—I know what's coming. I fell for this trick when Maureen Wilcox approached me for that article. Sure enough, after a brief exchange, the purple-haired girl says, "Shouldn't you have a bodyguard?"

"Hmm?"

The girl laughs. "Maybe you do." She nods at Bess. "Martial arts expert, right?"

"Uh, no. This is a friend. I don't need a bodyguard."

"Sure, you do. That bitch who killed your mother is on the loose."

Tiana rolls her eyes. "I'm not worried about Lucy Callahan."

"Why?" the girl presses forward. "You think she's innocent?"

Tiana's voice cools. "What I think is none of your business." She turns to continue on, but the purple-haired girl leaps into her path. The camera person, whom Tiana hasn't spotted yet, quickly walks past the trio. The purple-haired girl cuts her gaze toward the camera and then back to her quarry.

"Please move," Bess says. "Ms. Morales has a meeting with the funeral director."

"Morales? Are you switching to your mother's surname, Tiana?"

"A double-barreled surname is a pain in the ass," Tiana says. "I have used Morales for years. Now—"

"Your father thinks Lucy did it," the girl says. "He believes they had an altercation, and Lucy killed her. He's been very clear about that."

Tiana shoulders past and walks faster, Bess hurrying to catch up. Tiana says something the camera doesn't catch, under her breath presumably. As she speaks, though, words appear at the bottom of the screen, as if in translation.

Tiana: My father needs a full-time minder.

Bess: I know.

Tiana: Damn him.

I rewind a few seconds. The words fit her mouth movements, and when I look under the video, it says that a lip reader supplied the missing dialogue. A lip reader? Seriously?

The purple-haired girl catches up. "Colt thinks Lucy did it, and he knows her better than any of you."

"No, he does not." Again, Tiana mutters this, but now the camera is close enough to pick it up. She raises her voice. "I have complete confidence in the women and men of the New York Police Department. They will find my mother's killer. If that turns out to be Lucy Callahan, so be it. Now get out of my way."

The "interview" ends there with the purple-haired girl machine-gunning questions and Tiana ignoring them. A minute later, a car pulls up, and Tiana and Bess climb in. Once it's gone, the girl walks to the camera.

"Seems we have a family feud brewing," she says for her audience. "Tiana isn't convinced Lucy killed her mother, and she's not happy with Colt for saying so. It's significant that she's using her mother's surname. Let's just say the funeral should be interesting."

She grins, a hyena scenting blood. I snap the browser window shut.

PCTracy wanted me to see that video. He sees a potential ally within the family—or at least a sympathetic ear. The fact that he got that out of what I just saw only proves how desperate we both are.

Well, she didn't say you *definitely* killed her mother. That's a start, right?

I shake my head. There's no feud here.

My father needs a full-time minder.

Not "my father needs to shut his damn mouth." This isn't anger; it's exasperation. I remember Colt complaining to Isabella about Karla constantly sending him packaged soundbites and then chastising him for speaking his mind instead.

I'm honest. People like that. Karla just doesn't understand.

Karla understood just fine. She understood that Colt was indeed beloved for his honesty . . . in the same way you can't help loving a child who says whatever he thinks. It's endearing at five. At forty, though? Let's just say Karla spent a lot of time that summer cleaning up Colt's verbal vomit. She'd still been doing damage control after an impromptu interview at a spring awards show when he'd said he was happy he lost a role to a younger actor because the writing was shit and he'd have needed Isabella to rewrite the script.

When Colt claims to believe I killed Isabella, I'm not as hurt as I should be. That's just Colt looking to blame me before anyone suspects him. Just because Tiana recognizes that doesn't mean she's on my side.

I leave the money for breakfast on the table along with a twenty-dollar tip. I'm barely out the door when Phyllis comes after me with "Oh, no, you don't," and presses the extra bill into my hand.

"You need that more than I do," she says.

I flush and wonder how rough I look after a night outside. "No, really. I'm fine. I—"

"You're going to need it if you keep running, hon. And if you want my advice, you need to keep running. Just be safer about it."

I hope my face doesn't show my reaction. She only means that I seem to be living on the streets, and I'm not dressed like someone who has been doing it for long.

"Thank you," I say. "But I wanted to show my appreciation—"

"Show it later, when you're out of this mess. Right now, you need every penny you've got if you're going to keep your ass out of jail, Miss Lucy."

I go still, so still I forget to breathe.

"Oh, I know who you are. Took me a while, but I figured it out. You need to be a lot more careful, hon. I read the news. Read it all those years ago, too, and I was spitting mad at what they did to you. Just a child, you were, and with a man like that?" She whistles. "I'd have been tempted myself, and I was no child. Men like him always take advantage of pretty girls. They think they've earned them, as if you're a company bonus."

"I didn't kill—"

She shushes me and casts a quick look around. "I didn't figure you did. Not on purpose, anyway. Now my Nathaniel, he's always rolling his eyes at my conspiracy theories, but this has conspiracy painted all over it. You're the perfect scapegoat, and they're scapegoating you good. Money and power. It comes down to that. It always does."

She shakes her head. "I bet that husband of hers did it, and someone's covering it up for him. I used to like his movies, but after what happened to you, I never watched another one. He should have been run out of Hollywood, but instead, he got even more famous. Like seducing a teenage girl proved he still had it."

She eases back. "You don't need me saying any of that, not when you just want to get out of here in case I'm stalling you after I called the police." She pats my arm. "You go on then. Run, and keep running until this gets sorted out."

I pocket the twenty. "Can I at least give you a hug?"

She chuckles. "I'll take that," she says and embraces me.

I BLAME Phyllis for my next move. I'm sure she wouldn't appreciate that, but after three days of hell, she is a blazing beacon of kindness and hope, as perfect as if I conjured her from wisps of daydream. A complete stranger who understood what happened to me fourteen years ago and who understands what's happening now. Someone to pat my back and tell me everything will be okay —to tell me I'm okay.

I leave that encounter flying high and promising I truly will repay her. And, my hope and faith in humanity bolstered, I do exactly what I'd decided, mere moments before, not to do.

I call Tiana.

Well, I text her . . . after researching a way to do that online instead of text messaging.

Me: Tiana? It's Lucy.

She answers four minutes later with a two-word profanity. I expect no less.

Me: Give me five minutes. Please.

Tiana: Where did you get this number? I'll have you traced. You know that, right?

Me: Go ahead. But we need to talk.

Tiana: Oh, sure, let's do that. We'll chat. I'll bare my soul and call Lucy Callahan a monstrous bitch and wail and ask how she could have done that to me. Or should I vow vengeance instead? Which will play better online?

I read that twice, stumbling on her use of the third person for me. Then it clicks.

Me: You don't think it's me.

Tiana: Of course it's you, Lucy. Why would anyone contact me from an unknown number pretending to be Lucy Callahan? That's just silly.

Tiana: I don't know who you are, but this is harassment.

Me: 1984.

No response.

Me: That's the book you were reading when I met you. You were sitting by the pool reading 1984 while Jamie swam. He wouldn't take his swim shirt from your mom, so I jumped in, fully clothed, and gave it to him.

Silence. Dead silence. She's disconnected. I'm sure of it. Disconnected and blocked this number. Then,

> Tiana: You took my mother's phone. That's where you got my number.
> Me: I didn't kill her. I swear it.
> Tiana: And you know what, Genevieve? I don't actually care. My mother is dead. Yes, she was murdered, but right now, all I care about is the part where she's DEAD.
> Me: I'm sorry.

I get that two-word profanity again.

> Me: I deserve that. And you're right. I shouldn't be contacting you. I won't reach out again. If you want to talk to me——if you want to know what happened that night——you can e-mail me.

I give my new e-mail address. She doesn't answer. I stare at the phone for twenty minutes. Then I pocket it and move on.

CHAPTER THIRTY-ONE

I NEED to do something new with my hair. I spend twenty minutes in a family restroom with a bottle of shampoo, removing the temporary dye. I feel bad taking up space that someone with a baby may need, but it's still early, and I didn't see anyone outside with a child. I manage to wash about half the dye out, leaving my hair auburn. Then I stare in the mirror.

Does that help?

Not really.

I should cut it, but I'm not sure that would help, either. It's the obvious direction to go—like a fugitive shaving off his beard. What I really need is a wig. I know how to wear them from my filmmaking camp days. The problem is getting one without someone taking a closer look and realizing *why* I'm wig shopping.

I make another risky decision. I suppose my interaction with Tiana should have quashed that urge, but actually, she responded exactly as I expected. Honest and mature. She did not, however, rail at me, or accuse me or even threaten to report our chat to the police. So I take another chance. I open the messaging app and ping PCTracy.

LlamaGirl: I need a wig.

A reply comes in less than sixty seconds.

PCTracy: Absolutely. That's a good idea. I'm presuming
you'd like me to buy it, which is also wise.

Before I can reply, he continues,

PCTracy: It should be longer than your hair is now.
Significantly longer. Dark blond. Too light won't suit
you. A long dark blond wig.
LlamaGirl: Given this some thought, have you?
PCTracy: I've been coming up with a list of things we can
do better.
LlamaGirl: Like not tracking me without my permission?

It's a low blow, but I have to say it. Then I add.

LlamaGirl: And don't apologize again. I just want to move
forward with an understanding that you will not
track me.
PCTracy: Understood and agreed. I'll put together a bag for
you—clothing, wig and a hotel keycard.
PCTracy: Is there any chance I can give it to you in
person?
LlamaGirl: No. After last night, I need more time.

He doesn't push, just provides instructions for picking up the
bag. He's going to store it at a left-luggage facility and leave the
claim tag elsewhere.

It would, of course, have just been easier to meet in person.
After last night, though, I really am not ready. I'm skittish, and I
need space to reevaluate. Turning myself in is seeming more and
more like the right move. The smart move. But I keep thinking of
that bloody towel and the other evidence the police claim to have.
I also think of the progress PCTracy is making. If it's possible to

get a little downtime in a safe hotel, then I need that. Sleep. Rest. Think. Make clear-headed decisions.

PCTRACY PROMISED to have the bag in place by one. I wait until two to retrieve the claim ticket from a restroom. That goes off without a hitch. Same with getting the bag from the left-luggage spot—a souvenir shop in Times Square.

I resist the urge to peek inside the roller bag until I'm far enough from the pickup point. When I do, I ping PCTracy.

LlamaGirl: A stuffed dog?
PCTracy: It's part of the costume.
LlamaGirl: Uh-huh . . .
PCTracy: You're "woman who travels with small dog."
    There's a carrier for the dog. All they'll see through it is
    the white fur. I assembled the rest of the costume to fit
    the persona.
LlamaGirl: Still not getting the dog part . . .
PCTracy: It's the accessory equivalent of a facial scar or a
    bad tattoo. All people will notice is your dog. All people
    will remember is the dog. It also gives you an excuse to
    keep your head down. Talk to the dog. Coo at it.
LlamaGirl: You're having way too much fun with this.
PCTracy: You'll make a great "woman with small dog."
LlamaGirl: I don't think that's a compliment.
PCTracy: LOL. It's not an insult, either. Now, when you're
    ready, I got early check-in for your room. I'm going to
    strongly suggest that once you're in, you stay in. Get
    some rest. Let me do the legwork, and you stick to
    online research.

LOOKING at my reflection in the restroom mirror, I snort with laughter. When I picture "woman with small dog," I imagine a very chic, well-dressed woman of a certain age, striding through New York with a fluffy dog's head sticking out of her purse.

Instead, I'm wearing a long dark-blond wig with yoga pants with a barely waist-length lightweight angora sweater. For shoes, I get Keds with no socks. I also have new sunglasses and a new purse. Both are emblazoned with high-fashion names though I'm guessing they're street-vendor knockoffs.

I seriously consider changing back to my other clothes, but right now, I'm about as far as I can get from the Lucy Callahan in that hotel photo. If there's any chance my attacker from last night is in the area, he'll never recognize me in this.

The hotel PCTracy chose is the biggest one in Times Square. Again, not what I would select, but that is the point. It's also so big and so busy that I'm invisible. With the keycard in hand, I can head straight for the elevator bank.

When I step into my room, I inhale the unmistakable smell of hot food.

"Hello?" I call.

No answer. I move inside to see that I have a full suite with a sofa and a desk. A room service cart sits in front of an armchair.

Before I can retreat, I spot a sheet of paper taped to the small pyramid of silver trays. In block letters it says, "READ ME."

I ease into the room, still looking around, tensed to flee. I tug the sheet free. On the back it says, "MESSAGE ME."

I stare at it. Then I take out my phone and ping PCTracy.

LlamaGirl: Is there a "Drink me" sign somewhere, too?
PCTracy: That's why I had you text when you were ten
    minutes away. So I could get out. Yes, I was in your
    room. I left my keycard on the desk.
PCTracy: I wanted to make sure you got food without
    needing to answer the door.
PCTracy: Suitable interference? Or still creepy?
LlamaGirl: Suitable interference. Thank you. You didn't

need to do that. And I certainly didn't need a suite.

PCTracy: Free upgrade. I booked in person, and I tried to be charming in hopes of leaving a lasting impression. Apparently, I made a good one :)

LlamaGirl: Well, thank you.

PCTracy: Hope the food choices are okay, too. I went with relatively safe options. Eat. Rest. I'll touch base in a couple of hours.

I set my phone down and survey the room-service cart. There are three covered trays, plus a carafe of coffee, a small bottle of red wine, a large bottle of sparkling water and a can of Diet Coke. Under the first tray I open, there are two desserts—crème brûlée and cheesecake. The second has a salad. The third a massive burger and mountain of fries.

PCTracy said he went with safe choices, and he did. They also happen to all be things I like. That could be coincidental . . . except for the drink choices. The wine is a Pinot Noir, which is my go-to choice if I can't get a rustic Italian red. Diet Coke is my go-to for soda. Sparkling water over still? Yep.

With the drinks, there's no doubt that this is Thompson—or his investigator—and they've been in touch with my mother.

When I wheel my luggage into the bedroom, I find clothing. A couple of T-shirts, a pair of sweatpants and a nightshirt, stacked under a note reading "No underwear. Sorry. I figured I was pushing creepy with the nightshirt."

Beside the clothing there's a folded brown bag. Inside, I find cookies and chocolates along with more water and soda and two paperback novels, one a thriller and one historical fiction.

Oh, yeah, he talked to my mother.

This is all incredibly considerate. Above and beyond, really, like the perfect host contemplating what a guest might need if she's spending the next eighteen hours locked in a hotel room. It feels like an apology for last night, and while it wasn't necessary, I do appreciate it.

However this goes, I'll make sure PCTracy isn't on the hook for expenses. And I'll be sure to thank him when we talk in a few hours. Right now, though, I have a burger and fries waiting.

I EAT. I drink. I nap. Then I skim the Internet for case updates, but there's nothing new.

Next, I check for updates on my fugitive status. As expected, my sandwich shop visit did not go unnoticed. According to a source, I'd been spotted by an eagle-eyed manager, who reported it, but the police took their sweet time showing up, and I fled in the meantime.

There are more sightings, all in places I've never been, including Miami, Sydney and Toronto. One person, though, reports spotting me near Central Park last night. He didn't contact the police, fearing "repercussions." After all, I'm a dangerous criminal.

That makes me laugh, and then, mood bolstered, I do something guaranteed to bring it down. I read tributes to Isabella. It's penance, in a way, for texting Tiana earlier. She was completely right to call me on my insensitivity, and now as I read these memories of her mother, I am reminded myself that whatever personal issues I had with Isabella, I admired the hell out of her.

Tributes are, as they say, pouring in. Some are "wife of" remembrances—A-list actors and directors who only knew Isabella through Colt. I ignore those. I want the real ones, from people who knew her. I'm skimming a fan site dedicated to Isabella when I see an embedded video compilation of her acting career, and a name beneath it stops me short.

Justice Kane.

I smile. I cannot help it. I will always smile when a Justice Kane song comes on the radio. He is the one good memory from that night.

Seeing his name, I'm reminded that he'd been a friend of the Gordon-Morales clan. Apparently, he'd reached out to this

Isabella Morales fan site and asked whether they wanted to use one of his songs for their commemorative video.

When I see which one he offered, I nod in satisfaction. It's an early solo hit, and it's perfect for Isabella. A gorgeous tribute to a strong and capable woman and, quite possibly, my personal favorite of his. I can't help turning on the volume as I hit Play.

As the song begins, his rich voice starts soft, quiet words of respect and admiration beautifully underlaid with aching love, a classic admired-from-afar love song and . . .

Holy shit.

I blink, rewind and close my eyes as Justice's voice wafts from the tinny speaker. Then I hit Stop, grab my phone and redial the number of Isabella's secret lover. It goes straight to the answering message.

It's Justice's voice. That's why it sounded familiar. Because I knew it from a very long time ago.

Isabella's secret lover is Justice Kane? That doesn't make sense.

I listen to the song again, a heart-wrenching love letter to a woman who just happens to fit Isabella Morales to a tee. He'd offered this song for her memorial video on a small fan-run site unlikely to attract the attention of anyone who might put two and two together. A quiet public proclamation of love.

Justice had sent me that message of support all those years ago. And the texts from Isabella's mystery lover very clearly suggested he supported me.

So why am I doubting the connection? Because in my mind, Justice Kane is a boy that Isabella tried to set me up with. A young family friend she'd invited to her anniversary party for *me*.

Except Justice hadn't been a "boy." He'd been twenty-one. He wrote this song ten years ago when he clearly wasn't dating the woman in it. They must have gotten together later as the age difference grew less significant.

Justice Kane and Isabella Morales.

Holy shit.

My phone vibrates. It's PCTracy. I start to tell him what I've learned. Then I stop myself. This was Isabella's secret. Hers and Justice's, and neither of them deserves my betrayal.

> PCTracy: Got something for you. I've confirmed Colt's destination that night. New Haven, Connecticut. He landed at 10:10 p.m., which would get him to NYC around midnight.
>
> LlamaGirl: Damn.
>
> PCTracy: I know you aren't ready to meet in person, so I'm NOT pestering about that. But have we reached the point where I can ask for your full story? It will really help.
>
> LlamaGirl: You mean what happened to me 15 years ago?
>
> PCTracy: That is up to you. If it relates to this, then tell me whatever you're comfortable with. I mean the night of Isabella's death, though. What really happened.

It takes a moment to realize I still haven't shared that. Without knowing my side of the story, he's blindfolded, feeling his way through the situation.

> LlamaGirl: It will help to understand the beach party incident because it launched everything. That's awkward for me, though.
>
> PCTracy: No judgment here. To me, it's data. You slept with a movie star when you were eighteen. That's public record. What matters is that the affair led to you being in NYC to meet with Isabella, which led to her death.
>
> LlamaGirl: The public record is wrong. I didn't have sex with Colt. I know that doesn't matter in the larger scheme of things, but it matters to me.
>
> PCTracy: Did Isabella know the truth?
>
> LlamaGirl: I told her in a letter fourteen years ago. She never read it. So she first heard it Sunday.

PCTracy: Then it IS significant. For now, just tell me whatever you're comfortable with.

I do. When I finish my story, there's no answer for so long that I wonder whether he's declared me delusional and signed off.

PCTracy: So you're saying nothing happened before that night, during which Colt Gordon got you drunk— possibly doped you—and spirited you off to a hot tub, where he planned to seduce you, whether you wanted it or not?

LlamaGirl: I'm sorry I mentioned it. Rewind. We'll go with "I slept with a movie star."

PCTracy: What?

PCTracy: Damn it. I just reread what I wrote. Tone. That's what we're missing here, and why it would be better to meet. That wasn't skepticism, L. It was outrage. You WERE assaulted in that hot tub.

LlamaGirl: I don't see it that way. I was an adult. I made choices. Bad ones.

PCTracy: Okay. We're stepping into a quagmire, one I have no right to enter. Short version is that Isabella discovered the truth of that night. Did she think Colt was at fault for what happened?

LlamaGirl: Yes. She would agree with your interpretation. I told her I didn't, and we agreed to disagree.

PCTracy: And then?

I tell him about Isabella's plan to go public and my reaction.

PCTracy: I hate to say this, because you liked Isabella, but it could have been a ploy to get back in the spotlight. Her career suffered because of the scandal, and I wouldn't otherwise begrudge her the chance to get it back. Not at your expense, though.

LlamaGirl: I don't think she was actively planning that, but yes, it would have given her attention.

PCTracy: It could also have been about revenge. Getting back at Colt.

LlamaGirl: I don't think so. She wanted to remove him from our story. But yes, Colt would have taken it personally. Everything revolves around him. It's possible he flew in to talk her out of it. They argued. She died.

PCTracy: Yep. So what happened after you agreed to lunch?

I take him through the morning of Isabella's death. I include everything, even the fact that I have her phone and why. He knew some of this already from what I'd been okay telling him. Now he gets it all.

LlamaGirl: Taking the phone was stupid.

PCTracy: But understandable in context.

LlamaGirl: The police won't see it that way.

PCTracy: That's not giving them enough credit. The problem is that the police aren't actually the ones you need to worry about.

LlamaGirl: It's a jury, filled with people who won't put themselves in my shoes, who will only think I made a stupid choice, and therefore it's suspicious.

PCTracy: We'll deal with that. For now, are you set for food?

LlamaGirl: LOL I am very set for food. I haven't thanked you for that. It was incredibly considerate, and I appreciate it.

PCTracy: I just don't want you having any reason to leave your room tonight. You're safe there.

LlamaGirl: And here I will stay.

CHAPTER THIRTY-TWO

I EXPECT that after I tell PCTracy the story, I'll be a seething caul-dron of nervous regrets. Instead, I feel only relief—the kind that relaxes me better than any sedative. I'm in bed by ten, and thank-fully, I set my alarm for seven thirty, because otherwise, I'd have just keep snoozing. At eight sharp, there's a rap on the door. PCTracy had said he'd order my breakfast and ask them to leave the cart after a knock. I wait five minutes before wheeling the cart inside.

I'd requested coffee and a granola parfait, which does not explain the steaming covered plate beside my parfait. Two steaming plates, actually. Under one is a waffle with berry compote and melting whipped cream. Under the other is eggs Benedict with a side of bacon. And while there is coffee, there's also cappuccino.

I survey the personal breakfast buffet. Then I smile and dig in.

I eat and shower and relax, and then I settle in with my phone. I pop over to my new e-mail account, expecting nothing. Instead, there is a message from Tiana.

Lucy,

All right. Let's hear what you have to say. Meet me at the
address below for lunch at noon.

Tiana

I check the address on Google. It shows what looks like a
three-story walk-up. An office, not a condo.

I message her back.

Tiana,

I'd rather talk. Phone or text. Your choice. Meeting in person
isn't safe.

Lucy

It takes ten minutes to get a response. There's no salutation or
closing on this. Just the message body.

You have the address. You show up, or you don't.

I consider my options. Then I message PCTracy, just a quick
"I'm awake. Can we talk?"

He doesn't get back to me, and as the clock ticks past eleven, I
know I need to make a decision.

I'm lounging in a hotel room, being pampered by a guy that
I'm pretty sure is the lawyer who wants to represent me. If it's not
Thompson, then it's his investigator, and the lawyer is pulling the
strings.

Tuesday night, I was attacked in Central Park by what
PCTracy thinks is some random guy. The next day, I get this lovely
hotel suite with early check-in and all my favorite foods. It feels
like a treat.

It's not a treat. It's a cage.

I couldn't even survive a night in Central Park without PCTracy's intervention, and so I've been put in a pretty cage to rest
while he investigates. I've provided nothing useful otherwise, just

bumbling around, getting spotted by deli managers and attacked by strangers.

That's how he sees it, and I'm not sure he's wrong. In our first conversation, Thompson mocked the idea of me investigating even before I suggested doing so, and that's left me hesitant. I've been tracking the online chatter, reading Isabella's texts and trying to find clues, but I haven't actually investigated anything.

I asked PCTracy yesterday to throw me a research bone, and he brushed me off.

Thompson made me feel silly for even thinking I could try some serious detective work, and so I've been muddling about, waiting for the police to realize they're wrong or for PCTracy to solve the crime. The one real clue I've found—the existence of Isabella's mystery lover—I haven't shared. I've done nothing, really, except get myself attacked in an alley and a park.

That must stop. I need to get off my ass and take action.

Just as I think that, a message pops up.

PCTracy: Good morning! Or nearly afternoon. I hope you
    got a good sleep.
LlamaGirl: I did! Thank you! Please tell me I wasn't
    supposed to check out at eleven.
PCTracy: LOL No. You're booked for another night if you
    want it.
LlamaGirl: I want it. I really need the rest, and I'm just
    going to hole up for a bit longer if that's okay.
PCTracy: Absolutely okay.

Of course it is. Just keep sending treats my way, and I'll curl up on the king-sized bed with Netflix while you investigate.

I had wanted to ask his advice about Tiana. That urge has evaporated. I know what he'd say: just stay inside. Rest in your cage. Let me handle this.

I know what he'd say, and I know what I must do.

Get off my ass and take action.

I continue messaging with PCTracy as I get ready. Then I sign off as I slip out the door.

I have a lunch engagement to keep.

As FURIOUS AS I am about being stashed in that hotel room, I will admit that I needed the rest. I'm refreshed and clearheaded, and having not looked online today, nothing has happened to send me spiraling back into the memory quagmire. Thompson may have intended to only keep me safe while PCTracy investigated, but instead, he gave me what I needed to start moving forward with purpose.

I arrive at Tiana's building just before noon. It's in Brooklyn, and while it might have been a three-story residential walk-up once, it's been converted into a row of three-level units. All bear discreet business signs.

I survey the building from across the road, which isn't easy. In Manhattan, I'd grumbled about the crush of people and the endless skyscrapers. There'd been far fewer alleys and service lanes than a fugitive requires. At least, though, there'd been a sense of anonymity. Here I feel exposed.

I still map out an escape route.

Or you could just, you know, not walk into a potential trap.

Tiana might very well be luring me into a trap, but I need to either move forward or turn myself in. This is moving forward.

I march up and rap on the door. It opens, and there is Tiana, dressed in a white linen shirt and black jeans. Seeing her, my eyes prickle. Ridiculous phrases spring to mind.

You're all grown up.

You look amazing.

I'm so proud of you.

Instead, I say only, "Tiana," with an abrupt nod.

She returns the nod, steps back into the room and shuts the door behind me. Without a word, she leads me upstairs. As we pass the second floor, I see a meeting room with whiteboards. The third level is another meeting room, this one with couches and a windowed view. In the middle, a catered lunch waits on a table.

Tiana waves me to a seat.

As I sit, I say, "If I don't say that I'm sorry for your loss, it's because it sounds like platitudes, and I'm the last person you want to hear those from. So I'll only say that your mother was an incredible woman. She was the reason I took the job in the first place, and I never stopped admiring her."

I brace for an angry rejoinder, but Tiana only sits, her expression unreadable. One seemingly endless minute of silence, and then she says, "You were my first crush."

I must give a start at that because her lips twist in a smile.

"Not what you expected to hear?" She reaches for the linen napkin and folds it over her lap. "I'd started feeling as if I liked girls. That's why I bugged you so much about your dating. I was working through my own sexuality. Somewhere along the way, you answered my questions, not by anything you said, but because I fell for you. My first crush."

"I'm sorry."

She sputters a choked laugh, relaxing as she settles into her chair. "And that's not what I expected to hear, but oddly appropriate, under the circumstances. It screwed me up for a while. The first girl I liked slept with my father. Freud would have a ball with that one. Took me a while to get over it. I even tried boys, which did not go well."

"I *am* sorry."

She eyes me and then nods. "Well, you mentioned having a complicated relationship with my mother. I have a complicated one with you. So we start on similar ground." She takes a bite of salad and then says, casually, "Mom said you never had sex with Dad. That those photos caught the extent of it. She believed that, you know."

"Good, because it's the truth, and I suspect she believed it because your father's story matched. I can't make *you* believe it, though, Tiana. It sounds like a convenient fiction—the camera caught our one and only encounter. But it did. I made a mistake. A horrible, drunken mistake that I will never live down. I hurt your mother. I hurt you and Jamie. I cannot undo that."

She flinches at her brother's name.

"How is Jamie?" I ask, my voice softening.

"Fine," she says brusquely. She meets my gaze. "My brother had problems before you came along. You didn't help them, but you didn't cause them, either, so don't go taking credit for that."

She sips her water. "Mom said you had medical proof that you were a virgin after you left us."

I wince. "I stupidly thought that would resolve everything. I was, thankfully, convinced otherwise. If you want to hash out what happened fourteen years ago, we can do that. I'd rather not. Blame me for whatever you want—or need—to blame me for, Tiana. I'll accept it. What I came here for today was the one thing I won't accept blame for. Your mother's death."

"Then turn yourself in. Let the police sort this out."

"Right, trust that the truth will set me free just like it did the last time. No one wanted to hear my story then, Tiana. Including your mother. I poured my heart into a letter for her, and she sent me a vitriolic response that I can recite from memory. I thought that meant she rejected my apology and my explanation, but she never even read it. She judged me without opening—"

I stop abruptly. "I didn't mean that. I'm sorry. I . . ." I take a deep breath and rise. "I think I should leave now. We aren't going to get anywhere with this. We can't. Too much anger and too much bad blood, and I'm going to say things I don't want to say to you."

"If you killed my mother by accident—"

"I was nowhere near your mother when she died, Tiana."

"Then there wouldn't be a warrant for your arrest. You seem to want honesty here, Lucy, but you're obviously lying. You were in her room."

"Yes, hours after her death. I was summoned by whoever is trying to frame me."

She shoves her chair back. "Frame you? Is that where you're going with this? I thought you were smarter than that."

"I found her body. I lied about that because I panicked. I was summoned to breakfast by the killer, who was using your mom's phone and pretending to be her. When I arrived, the door was ajar. I walked in and found her, and before I could report it, the hotel staff arrived. I hid in the closet because I was about to be discovered at a murder scene holding the victim's phone."

"So you *do* have her phone. Which you just happened to be holding after finding her body . . . instead of calling the cops."

"I was confirming that she'd sent me those texts because I was freaking out. Yes, I should have called the police first, but at the time, all I could think was that I'd been summoned to a murder scene."

"I'd like her phone back."

"And I would like to stay out of prison." I take out my old cell phone, open my messages and pass it over. "This is our conversation thread. You can see her asking to switch to breakfast—and why—and me agreeing. Then you can see me texting from inside her room, saying the door was left open."

She reads the texts. Then she scrolls up, as if making sure this is part of the thread where I definitely had been speaking to Isabella earlier.

"I'm telling you my story," I say, "knowing that when I leave, you might contact the police and pass all this along, including the fact that I lied to them and fled the scene of a crime. I won't ask you not to. There's isn't a nondisclosure agreement on this conversation, Tiana. I made a mistake, one that I couldn't figure out how to undo. I still can't."

"You're digging yourself into a hole. You do realize that, don't you?"

"Of course I realize that. But from where I stand, I'm not digging a hole. I'm sliding down a slope into a fiery pit, and at any moment, I can decide to fling myself into that pit, and I'll be exactly where I would have been if I let the hotel staff find me at your mother's murder scene. I'm scrabbling up this slope, and I'm still slipping, but I'm not ready to jump to my doom."

She keeps looking at the phone. At those messages.

"A lawyer could help—" she begins.

"I tried that Monday morning. My mother found me one—and only one—lawyer who would agree to represent me, and I walked into his building to overhear him talking to the police with media there to televise my arrest."

Her head shoots up. "He can't do that."

"Well, he did, and I'm past the point—long past it—of expecting anyone to act fairly. If you doubt the veracity of those texts, contact your mother's phone company and get her records. I'd be surprised if the police haven't done that already."

"But you're saying her killer was in the suite with her body, texting you. That makes no sense."

"Was her account connected to any other devices? A laptop? A tablet? A smartwatch?"

"Her tablet is missing, too. It *was* connected to her account, so she could answer texts on it." She looks at me. "Whoever sent these used her tablet. Can that be tracked? The device identified?"

"Hopefully. Presumably."

She looks from the phone to me. Then she hands it back and says, "You need to leave."

"No lunch, then, huh?" I say with a wry smile. "Can I at least take it to go? The dining options of a fugitive are terribly limited."

She doesn't return my smile, and I falter. I'm not thrilled by the abrupt dismissal, but I understand she has what she wanted. I expect, though, that she'll have the grace to joke back and say yes, take a doggie bag.

Instead, she reaches into her purse and pulls out a wad of bills. "Take—"

"Jesus," I mutter. "I was joking. I don't need your food, Tiana, and I definitely don't need your money. You could have just skipped the whole fake-lunch invitation and said you wanted to talk."

"Please, take this," she says. "You just—you need to go. Now."

I glance at the money . . . and her trembling hand.

"You called the police," I say slowly as realization hits. "You called them before I even arrived."

"I . . ." She swallows, and in her face, I'm reminded of those rare moments when her mature veneer would crack and I'd see the ten-year-old beneath.

She straightens. "Karla was right. She told me not to turn you in, and I . . . I reminded her who paid her salary. Damn it, I don't ever learn." A sharp intake of breath as she shakes her head. "No time for that. I made a mistake, and I can't fix it now. Just go, Lucy. Quickly."

"You called me here to talk," I say. "You said you wanted to listen to me, and you summoned the police before I could say a word. Then you told me I should trust the process. Trust that people will listen to my story before they decide my fate." I look her square in the eye. "You didn't."

Her mouth opens, but I'm already sweeping past.

"Goodbye, Tiana," I say. "I hoped for better from you. I really did."

I leave her, standing in that room, money still outstretched as I clamber down the stairs.

CHAPTER THIRTY-THREE

I BARELY REACH the bottom of the stairs when the door swings open. I backpedal, hands rising.

It isn't a cop, though. It's Karla. She's a little grayer. Still dressed impeccably with that no-nonsense expression I know so well. Then she sees me. Her eyes widen. Her lips part, and she pauses. Just a split-second pause before she lets the door half close as she takes out her phone.

"I really can't talk now," she says, loudly into the phone. "I'm in the middle of something."

It takes two seconds for me to realize she's faking a call to give me a chance to run. As I dart through the next room, someone outside calls to Karla. Warns her to come outside, get away from the door.

The police.

Karla arrived just ahead of them. Maybe hoping to speak to me. Maybe hoping to change Tiana's mind about turning me in.

Our eyes meet, and she nods. Then she turns away to continue her fake call.

I jog through the lower level and find a door. Behind me, Karla's voice comes clear as she imperiously informs the police that she is Tiana's manager, and she has every right to be in this house, and they will not order her to do anything.

Thank you, Karla.

I race through the back door. It opens into a yard with a solid, six-foot wood fence. I'm about to crumple in defeat when I spot a gate.

I zoom through the gate and race along the back of the fence as Karla and the police argue, their voices wafting out to me.

Then I cut through to the next street and keep going.

It's time to end this. I'm not making progress. Not enough, anyway. As annoyed as I am about being stashed away in the hotel, I need to speak to Thompson and negotiate my surrender.

The last time I was in his building, I never got as far as his office. Now that I do, I'm surprised. I thought it'd be just another anonymous door. Instead, the tenth floor *is* his office.

To be honest, it's not what I hoped for. I guess, in my mind, I constructed a persona for Thompson, that of the scrappy, tenacious underdog. The guy who plays fast and loose ethically because he's making a name for himself. What I see here is something very different.

This isn't a lone defense attorney with a receptionist and an investigator. It's a full-fledged firm. *His* firm. Thompson's name is on the doors with other lawyers listed in smaller print.

I push aside my misgivings. Overall, PCTracy has been good to me. Really good. Time to step up and say to Thompson, "I want to hire you."

The problem is that I'd expected to walk into a tiny office and deal with a receptionist. There's no way I'm stepping into a firm where I'll instantly be recognized by a dozen people. Once I pass through those doors, I can't change my mind, and I still need that option.

I retreat to the stairwell, take out my prepaid and text Thompson.

Me: It's LC. I'd like to talk.

It takes a minute. Then he responds.

Thompson: I do not recognize this number. Please identify
    yourself more completely.
Me: Screw me over by calling the cops again, and I'll report
    you to the bar association.
Thompson: L, good to hear from you. I presume you've
    had a change of heart?
Me: I'd like to talk. Meet me in the lobby in five minutes.
    Can you do that?
Thompson: On my way.

I hurry to the floor beneath his. The first elevator to arrive is empty. I push it again. The elevator opens . . . and Thompson is there. He looks up in surprise.

I get on and then press the Stop button.

Thompson smiles, completely relaxed, brilliant white teeth flashing. "I feel like you're about to make me an offer I can't refuse."

"That depends. I presume you're still interested in representing me?"

"Very interested, but I would suggest we not talk in a stopped elevator. Let's head up to the eleventh floor. I have a private office there where we can speak undisturbed."

"One question first. Who is PCTracy?"

His smile falters. "P. C . . . ," he says, rolling the letters off like initials.

My finger freezes on the button for the eleventh floor.

"PCTracy," I say slower.

"I have the feeling the answer to this question is very important to you," he says. "That if I fail your test, I will not have you as a client after all. Which puts us in a very awkward position. I'm not at liberty to answer that question, Ms. Callahan."

Part of me leaps at his response, calling it perfectly reasonable. Whether he's PCTracy or it's an employee, the guy was aiding and abetting a fugitive. Thompson's hesitation makes sense.

Or it would if PCTracy hadn't asked multiple times for a face-to-face meeting.

"I understand," I say. "But I'm sure you understand, too, that under the circumstances, I need a guarantee that I'm speaking to the right person."

His brows knit. Again, it's a fleeting reaction, smoothed out in a blink before he says, "You think I'm P. C. Tracy?"

"No, but I need confirmation that you know him."

He eases back, smiling. "Well, of course I do. You wouldn't be here, otherwise, correct?"

Does he just not know the name his investigator is using? Possibly, but I can see in his face that he has no clue what I'm talking about. *Who* I'm talking about.

I take out my phone.

"We really should go upstairs to my office," Thompson says.

I lift a finger and ping PCTracy.

PCTracy: Perfect timing. I have something for you.

LlamaGirl: I'm with Thompson.

PCTracy: You're not in the hotel???

LlamaGirl: Daniel Thompson doesn't seem to know who you are. Is there a reason for that?

PCTracy: Well, possibly because I don't know who he is, either.

LlamaGirl: If you do, now isn't the time to be cagey. Just confirm that you're working with him.

PCTracy: I'm not.

It takes effort to turn off the app. Even more effort to hit the small *x* and delete it. Part of me screams, "What are you doing?" The other part . . . The other part keeps remembering the man in the alley, the man in the park.

The man who knew where I was.

PCTracy admitted he knew where I was. That he could track me through the app.

The only reason I didn't suspect this answer is that I was convinced PCTracy was linked to Thompson. Hell, the only reason I started *talking* to PCTracy was that I thought he was connected to Thompson. He had to be, right?

No, he just had to be an investigator who tracked down my e-mail address and reached out at a time when I was vulnerable, a time that happened to coincide with my interactions with a defense attorney. Then PCTracy mentioned he was an investigator who'd worked for defense attorneys, and I made the connection. A completely false connection.

"Ms. Callahan?" Thompson says.

Just hire him. Forget this PCTracy nonsense, and hire him. He's a good lawyer. He . . .

He tricked me. Betrayed me. Any positive impression I had of Thompson's skill came from working with PCTracy. Without that, Thompson is the same treacherous asshole I'd fled on Monday.

I've spent two days convinced that the man who was helping me worked for Thompson . . . was likely even Thompson himself.

He's not.

"Sorry," I say with a rueful smile. "I think I got my wires crossed. But it's fine. I still need a lawyer, obviously. Let's go chat in that private office."

I hit the button for the eleventh floor. When the doors open, I plan to stay on and shut the doors behind him. Only he nudges me off first. We're two paces away, and the elevator doors have just started to close when I do a wide-eyed "Oh, shit!" as if I dropped something. I dive back onto the elevator.

As the doors shut, he scrambles to catch them while I pretend to grab something from the floor. I shout, "Be right back!" and the doors close.

Even as the doors close, his footfalls pound the floor. I hit a button. The elevator starts down, and I can't help but smile, imagining Thompson's mad dash to the bottom floor. I'll be long gone by the time he—

The elevator stops, and the doors open, and a quartet of chattering office workers steps on. I hit the third-floor button before the doors shut. When they open again, I squeeze out and jog for the second stairwell.

I fly down and out the side door. I know Thompson will come after me. I know he'll call staff to come after me. I know he'll even notify the police to come after me.

When I reach the dumpster where I stashed my bag, I pull on the blond wig and quick-change my shirt. Then I walk two blocks until I find a suitable spot to pull over and breathe, just breathe.

I screwed up.

God, I screwed up so bad.

I take out my phone, navigate to the browser and log into my old e-mail so I can search PCTracy's original messages for the clues I should have picked up. I don't find any. I can berate myself all I want, but given my frame of mind when I got those messages, my mistake is forgivable. Which doesn't mean I'll forgive myself for it.

I automatically reach for the messaging app to contact PCTracy. I want his advice. Only I find my finger hovering over an empty spot on the screen.

Did I overreact by deleting the app? Possibly. But I need to pursue answers on my own. I can contact him any time I want. If I want. If I trust him again.

I'm not sure that's possible.

CHAPTER THIRTY-FOUR

AFTER I LEAVE Thompson's office, I long to return to my hotel suite. Burrow in where I can relax and think. There will be none of that now. Even if I could do it, I shouldn't. I'd needed that time—desperately needed it—but I'd been hiding, too. Hiding in a plush suite, eating all my favorite foods, and waiting for PCTracy to resolve my problem.

It's midafternoon in the busiest city on the continent. I just need to avoid the temptation to find a quiet place to hide because that's where I get myself into trouble. Empty streets and alleyways and parks. There is someone out there looking for me, and if he's tracking me right now, I can do nothing about that except stay where there are too many people for him to make a move.

Could PCTracy be my stalker? The answer seems to be a resounding yes. I know PCTracy is male, like my attacker. Our conversation makes me feel as if he's in my age bracket, same as my attacker. Most damning, though? PCTracy admitted he could track me through the app. He said he could only do it when I was on Wi-Fi, but the library was far from the first time I used that.

What about the guy in the park who went after my attacker? PCTracy could have brought in a colleague to play the role of rescuer so he could later confess to "saving" me. Or the second man could have been an actual Good Samaritan.

I don't want to believe PCTracy is my stalker. I must accept the possibility, though, which means the messaging app stays deleted.

I find myself a busy coffee shop and settle in as I check the Internet for more information on my case, busy work to calm my mind and hone my focus.

I find something right away. A site has leaked the hotel surveillance photo of me. At first, I almost ignore the link. I've seen that photograph already. Then I notice the time stamp, and my body goes cold.

The photo was captured at 3:35 a.m.

Hours before I arrived.

Reports had placed me in the hotel earlier, and I'd dismissed them because I knew I wasn't. Yet here is the alleged proof.

I open the photo.

The picture is grainy and off-center, and I exhale as I realize that even if it'd been crystal clear, there's no way anyone could prove I was this woman. She is walking past a lobby chair, and from that point of reference, I can tell she's significantly shorter than I am.

The woman has her face turned away from the camera, and she's wearing sunglasses, despite the fact it's three a.m. Her hair is red and straight, like mine. As for her figure, that's marred by a fashionable shawl.

This woman is trying to be me. I'm certain of it. That shawl conceals her figure. The glasses and hair hide her face, and she's deliberately looking away from the camera. She moved quickly through the lobby, leaving only an impression of a redheaded woman.

Tiana?

Even as my gut wonders that, I recoil. Not Tiana. She's full-figured, where I am not.

But that shawl hides the woman's figure.

Tiana's skin is darker than mine.

Not so dark that she couldn't pass for me at a glance while people are focusing on the red hair. That's always what they remember.

The woman is the right height for Tiana.

Stop that. It isn't Tiana.

Why?

Because I don't want it to be.

I take a deep breath. Then I open the e-mail box I'd asked her to use, hoping for more. Instead, I find an e-mail from PCTracy. The subject line reads: "Open Me."

I almost delete it. That would be silly, though, and when I open it, I'm glad I did. He wants to talk, of course, but for now, he's just passing on what he told me earlier he'd found.

> You mentioned Isabella might have a lover. I've been chasing that lead, and I found this. I still don't know who the guy is, but it's a start.

I already know who Isabella's lover is—Justice Kane—but I still read on in hopes of confirming that.

It's with a blind item from last fall. Such tidbits were hugely popular back in the days of gossip pages. "Blind item" means' the people involved aren't named, adding the scintillating air of a delicious mystery along with an unearned aura of veracity—if someone fears naming names, clearly it must be true. Today they're more likely to be found on social media, which is where this one turned up on Twitter.

> NYCGirl5ft2: Right place, right time. Club99 back hall. Me, lost, kinda drunk, looking for la toilette. Stumble on a couple going at it.
>
> NYCGirl5ft2: No, not "going at it" like that. Mind out of gutter, ppl. Fighting. Figured lovers quarrel. He's hot. She's hot. Must be a couple. Then I see his face
>
> NYCGirl5ft2: Boy band hottie turned grown man hottie.

Nearly wet my pants. He so fine. That's when I recognize the chick. Daddy's a movie star. Action bro. Only, she don't like dick . . . allegedly.

> NYCGirl5ft2: So I think, I got you, faker. You like dick just fine.

Then, plot twist. I realize they're fighting about her momma.

> NYCGirl5ft2: He's banging her MOM. Her MOM. And she's pissed. Spitting mad. I'm, like, I don't know who to root for. Her, for being so fired up. Or her mom, for tapping THAT. #OldLadyGoals #IGottaSecret

The details fit Tiana and Justice. But NYCGirl5ft2 is just a regular person with a couple hundred followers. Naturally, her friends want details, but she refuses—those involved are rich and famous, and she jokes she'll end up in the East River if she talks.

When her friends try to convince her to sell her story, she demurs, saying that she's not going to ruin people's lives for a few bucks. Her friends assure her she could make more than "a few bucks," and she reverts to her jokes about the East River. While she's enjoying the thrill of having a secret, she's a decent person acting decently. She finally closes the thread with a Tweet that makes me kinda love her.

> NYCGirl5ft2: Look, I can joke about dude banging her mom, but when girl got up in his face, he never fired back. He said he was in love, totes respected her mom and just wanted to make her happy. #LifeGoals #WhereDoIGetOne?

One of her friends apparently wasn't happy with that answer and posted it on a blind item site, where people have been madly guessing at those involved. Sure enough, Tiana came up a few times, given the "lesbian with action-hero father" clues. It never went beyond that, but those comments explain how PCTracy found it.

Tiana was angry with Justice for having an affair with Isabella. Is that important?

I'm not sure, but it confirms he's the mystery lover and gets me wondering whether he's still in New York. A quick search tells me yes. He's here for the funeral, which he'll attend as a family friend.

I need to talk to Justice.

The problem is finding him.

No, actually, that isn't a problem at all. In his texts to Isabella, he mentioned he's staying at the Baccarat. And I may not even need to go that far. I have the guy's phone number, and just because he isn't answering doesn't mean he's not checking texts.

"HELLO, JUSTICE," I say as I walk around the fountain in front of Lincoln Center. He's sitting on the edge, and when I walk up, he has his elbows on his knees, head down, hood shadowing his face. While the square is busy, there's a bubble around him. He might be a mega-selling rock star, but all they see today is a big Black guy in a hoodie and high-tops.

When he glances up, there's a wry twist of a smile on his face, one that shoots me back in time to that night on the beach.

"Hey, Lucy." He thumps the spot beside him.

I slide in. "How're you holding up?"

He shrugs. Then he cuts a look my way. "I presume from your text that you know about . . ."

"You and Isabella? Yes."

"So the police are right. You have her phone."

"I do, and I'm sorry about that. It's a long story."

"Well, I'd like to hear it, but I think we should talk someplace a little more private."

I shake my head. "Sorry. I've . . . had trouble with that."

His brows shoot up. "You okay?" He pauses and then shakes his head. "Dumb question. You're wanted for murder. You are definitely not okay."

"True. While a private talk makes sense, I accepted one with Tiana earlier today, and she notified the cops before I even arrived. After we spoke, she warned me, and I got out of there, but I'm being extra cautious."

"Tiana . . ." He shakes his head again and eases back, long legs outstretched. "When I was with the band, I was the 'nice guy.' That was my role, and not just in public. I was the one who made friends with every sound tech and roadie and superfan. There was this one roadie, though, an old-timer who just decided he didn't like my face. Or maybe the color of my face. Whatever his problem, I made it my personal mission to win him over. Never did, but I kept trying, like a puppy determined to get a pet from the one person who hates dogs. These days, that's me and Tiana. Even if she wasn't Izzy's kid, I'd like her, and she used to like me fine . . . until she found out about me and her mom."

"I'm sorry."

"And I'm sorry she pulled that shit on you. At least she came around in the end. Tee is complicated, like her momma. Only, with Tee, there's a prickly fence wrapped around that complicated interior, and most folks can't breach it." Another look my way. "You did, once upon a time. Which probably makes this harder on her."

I sigh, and he bumps his shoulder against mine. "That's not an invitation to a guilt trip."

I look over at him. "I didn't kill Isabella."

"If I thought you did, we would not be having this conversation. You're being set up. Any moron can see that. Someone murdered . . ." He takes a deep breath and then says, in a low voice, "I've never wanted to kill anyone before. Never even wanted to hurt anyone. But when you find out who did this, you'd better make sure they're arrested before you tell me. Or *they* won't be the one going to jail for murder."

"I'm sorry. I know . . ." I swallow. "You won't want to talk about this. I know that."

"Won't want to talk about it." He enunciates the words, rolling them out. "Lucy, you have no idea how *much* I want to talk about this. I want to stand on this fountain and shout it to the world. I love Isabella Morales, and she loved me, and what we had . . ."

He rocks back. "Shit, this isn't going to help." He puts on his sunglasses and glances over. "I don't remember ever not loving Isabella. When she invited me to that beach party, I thought . . ." A small laugh. "I was young, and hopeful and dumb enough to think she might be inviting me to her *wedding* anniversary party because she felt something for me, too. Turned out I was there . . ."

"For me," I say.

"Yeah, I wasn't sure if you knew that."

"Isabella told me."

"Of course she did. So she invited me as companionship for you. Maybe even a hookup for you. Which told me I didn't have a hope in hell of getting with her. It changed nothing. When that bullshit hit with you and Colt, I totally took advantage. I was there for Izzy. I wanted her to see me as more than a kid. And she did, eventually . . . she saw me as a friend." Another laugh. "That's all it was for years. Me, pining after her and making do with friendship. Then . . ."

He shrugs. "I don't know what happened. Maybe I hit the magic age where she wouldn't feel like a dirty old lady—her words, not mine. We got past the age barrier, and I got my dream woman, and she was everything I wanted and more. We were waiting for Jamie to get out of rehab, and then Isabella would divorce Colt, and we'd get married. I'd already given her the ring."

He folds his hands. "I have no idea where it is now. Probably hidden in a drawer, where no one will ever find it. Just like us—a secret no one will ever know."

"I'm so, so sorry. I really am."

"I always considered myself an excellent judge of character, and I remember the girl I met at that beach party. From the start, I told Izzy my theory about what really happened. Turned out, I was dead right. At least I got a chance to say I told you so."

He tries for a smile, but his lips quiver. He runs a hand over them. "We had five years together. I keep reminding myself of that. For five years, I got to hear Isabella Morales tell me I was the love of her life. I got all of her for five years, and I got her friendship for fourteen, and that is more than most people will ever have. More than I thought I'd have."

He looks at me. "Isabella died knowing the truth about that night, and she died forgiving you, and she died hell-bent on a mission to make things right. To tell your story—yours and hers. Circe and Penelope speaking out over the voice of Odysseus, that's what she called it, and it meant so much to her. She died with a fire in her belly, Lucy. With her dignity restored, and that amazing mind set on a mission, and that's something. It's really something."

I tentatively reach for his hand, and when he takes mine, I squeeze, and we sit in silence. Then he straightens and says, "So you have a story for me."

"I do."

I tell him the timeline of the morning of the murder. Nothing in that surprises him. I suspect it's like when Isabella told him what really happened fourteen years ago. It only confirmed what he'd already figured out.

"You were in New York that night," I say. "I know you were."

He nods. "I didn't see her, though. We talked for over an hour that night. We were going to meet up for breakfast. She planned to sneak over to my hotel. I expected her at ten. Instead, as I was waiting, I found out what happened."

"Tiana didn't notify you, I take it."

A short laugh. "I haven't talked to Tiana in months. When she found out about me and her mom, I held off, letting her speak to Izzy before I did. Instead, Tiana acted like she didn't know, so I played along. It was best to leave that ball in her court."

"What about Colt?"

A low rumble, almost like a growl. "Colt and I haven't been on speaking terms in fourteen years. I'm cordial to him in public for

Izzy's sake. I've wanted nothing to do with him since he messed around with you. He hurt her, and he humiliated her."

"Do you know if Isabella had any problems with him the night of her death?"

"Nothing more than you'd expect. He didn't like her talking to you. *Really* didn't like it. Unfortunately, he was in LA when she died. Otherwise, he'd be my number-one suspect."

When I don't comment, he takes off the sunglasses, and his eyes narrow. "He *was* in LA, wasn't he?"

I still stay nothing.

"Lucy . . . even if you tell me he was here, I'm not going after him. That would be critical information for the police, though."

"He flew into Connecticut around midnight."

He frowns. "Where in Connecticut?"

"New Haven."

"To see Jamie?"

When I frown, Justice says, "Ah, so we're trading valuable information here. I didn't know Colt was on the East Coast that night, and you didn't know Jamie's rehab is outside New Haven. That's not public knowledge. It explains why Colt was here, though."

"To see his son."

"Yeah. A dick move from a dick. Shocking."

I arch my brows. "Visiting his son in rehab is a dick move?"

Justice gives me a look. "That wasn't Colt being Daddy-of-the-Year. It was Colt gathering reinforcements for his battle with Isabella over you. Because that's what your kid in rehab really needs—you showing up at midnight to pull him into a fight with your mom."

"Colt wanted Jamie to side with him and agree that Isabella should stay away from me."

"Which proves Colt didn't know the first damn thing about his son, as usual. Jamie sided with you in that scandal crap. We agree on that, me and him. Always have."

"Jamie?"

"He said there was more to the story. Well, he did once he was older. At the time, he wouldn't talk about it. But when he was a teenager, if your name came up, he'd say you didn't have a fling with his father, that it was a misunderstanding. Izzy didn't argue —if he believed that, so be it."

"It affected him, though. The scandal."

Justice purses his lips. "Not really. Of the three, I think he was the least impacted. By the scandal, at least. Losing you was another thing." He glances over. "But if you think the kid was permanently traumatized? Hell, no. Jamie's problems go deeper than some silly tabloid scandal, and they all trace back to Daddy."

"His relationship with Colt? I do remember . . . issues."

"Yep, Colt had a certain set of expectations for Jamie. He was the son of Colt Gordon, action star. You gotta be a man's man to follow in those footsteps."

"And that was never Jamie."

"Toxic masculinity is toxic. Isabella did her best, but even when she made Colt shut his mouth, Jamie could sense his father's disapproval. Sports? Yes. Ice skating? No. Music? Sure. The violin? Hell, no. Colt judged, and Jamie felt that judgment. He wasn't living up to expectations. Colt was certain his son was gay. Turned out he's not . . . and Colt's Princess Tiana is. Oh, the irony."

"How's Jamie doing?"

Justice brightens. "Good. Great, actually. We're friends. Have been for years. I think he knows about his mom and me—he's hinted at it—but Izzy wanted to wait until he was released to tell him officially. Jamie has a self-medication problem, no doubt about that. But even in his addiction, he's responsible as hell. Checks himself into rehab and stays there until he's back on track."

"Good." I nod. "That's really good."

"If you were picturing some broke-down mess, that's not Jamie. He's a kid with demons, but a kid who's fighting them tooth and nail. Which is why this bullshit with Colt pisses me off.

I've been trying to talk to Jamie since Sunday. So has Tiana, from what I've heard through mutual friends. Jamie's gone into self-imposed lockdown. We're waiting him out. You remember what he's like. He needs his space, and he wouldn't appreciate either of us driving up there to hover. Now that I know Colt was there Sunday night, though, that puts a whole new angle on it. Jamie isn't just in need of alone-time to deal with his mom's death. He knows his dad was an hour from New York. He's working that through, deciding what to do about it."

"Because Colt could have seen Jamie and still had time to kill Isabella."

"Exactly."

CHAPTER THIRTY-FIVE

AFTER I LEAVE JUSTICE, I linger, making sure he walks away first. If I am identified, I don't want him pulled into it. Then, as I'm making my way out of the square, I hear a voice that has my brain perking up like a happy puppy.

Marco?

Of course it's not Marco. What I'm very obviously hearing is the contralto Italian-accented voice of a man who speaks perfect English, which is a lot more common in New York than an American speaking perfect Italian in Rome.

Still, I look. I can't help it. I even spot the back of someone who could be Marco over by the entrance to Juilliard. Dark curly hair. Athletic physique. He's wearing a tight T-shirt and cutoff jean shorts, and while he presents a very fine rear view, that is definitely not Marco's fashion style.

He's talking animatedly to a man and a woman. That's also not Marco's style despite the stereotype of the gesticulating Italian. With reluctance, I pull my gaze away to scan for who is actually speaking in that Marco-like voice. The hot-guy-in-cutoffs quarter turns, and I stop so abruptly my shoes squeak.

It's Marco.

A fantasy flits through my brain, that after e-mailing me,

Marco hopped onto a flight to New York and tracked me down to offer his help.

The problem with that story? The tracking-me-down part. I'm a fugitive, and he isn't exactly a private eye.

This is just some guy who looks enough like Marco that my brain is conflating him with another nearby tourist who sounds like Marco. Marco wouldn't be caught dead in that outfit, and he doesn't gesticulate like this.

So it's not him.

Except it is. I'm looking at the face I've woken up beside for countless nights. Which makes no logical sense.

I'm losing my mind.

Someone laughs loudly, and not-Marco glances over. I sidestep fast behind a knot of students. As he turns, I see his face full-on, and there is no doubt it is Marco, right down to the cleft-lip scar.

The woman with him turns my way. In her hand is a small video camera. I follow her gaze as it lands on the spot where I'd been sitting with Justice. The now-empty spot. She lets out a curse that has the blond man beside her jumping to attention.

They're journalists.

No, they're paparazzi. I know the look.

What is Marco doing with paparazzi?

Do I want to know?

I do. Yet the woman has realized I'm no longer where I'd been, and she's moving away from Marco, her gaze scanning the fountain square.

I withdraw. I must, as much as I want to figure out what the hell is going on here.

I slip around a restaurant and onto the sidewalk. Then I move as fast as I dare, adopting the New Yorker walk, purposeful strides that cut through the tourist clusters.

Marco.

That was Marco.

What is he doing here?

Not just in New York, but with a couple of papar—

"Keep walking," a voice says, and I'm so distracted that I inwardly exhale in relief, thinking it's Marco. Before I can even look over, I realize my mistake because I made it before, waking in a park and thinking the voice whispering in my ear was Marco's.

It's the same voice.

I stiffen, but the man's arm is already around my waist, pulling me against his side as we walk. My insides explode with panic, the air suddenly too thin to breathe.

Earlier, I thought I'd be safe in public. I *am* safe. We're surrounded by people on a busy sidewalk. I just need to be sure he doesn't take me anyplace private, and I'm not stupid enough to allow—

Cold presses against my side, and this time, it isn't a knife. It's a gun.

"Keep walking," he says in a voice so pleasant it chills me even more than that icy gun barrel.

I glance at him.

"Eyes forward, Lucy," he says. "We're just a happy couple out for a stroll." Another two steps. "I think it's time you and I had a chat, don't you?"

I look around.

"You could do that," he says, his voice still conversational. "It's a busy street. You can scream. You can run. And you can find out how serious I am about pulling this trigger."

Another two steps.

"Have you ever seen hit men in movies?" he asks. "They go through elaborate schemes to eliminate a target. It's Hollywood bullshit. A silenced gun. A busy street. A nondescript guy who shoots and keeps walking. Or maybe he'll shout for help. *Oh, my God, this woman just fell to the sidewalk! She needs medical attention!* Then as the crowd gathers, he slips away, invisible."

My heart thuds so loud I struggle to speak. "Is that what you are? A hit man?"

"Mmm, no, that's a very specific job description, and I'm much more flexible. You killed Isabella Morales, Lucy, and someone has decided they can't rely on the justice system to see actual justice done. You—"

"Excuse me," says a voice in a heavy Italian accent.

The man pretends not to hear and walks faster, but then he stops short as the speaker grabs his arm.

Marco's gaze doesn't even flick my way. He just meets my captor's glare with a disarming smile.

"Excuse me," Marco says again. "I look for . . . I look for 911 monument, yes?"

"Take your goddamn hand off my—"

"The 9/11 Memorial?" I say quickly, as if trying to get rid of this tourist.

Marco releases the man and turns my way. *"Grazie."*

I give directions. As I do, I cut my gaze subtly toward the gun. The man looks as if he has his hand casually resting on my back, jacket draped over his arm. The gun is hidden beneath it. Marco nods without even following my gaze. He's already figured that out—the jacket over an arm in June is a giveaway.

Marco asks me to repeat a few parts of my directions. My captor grows increasingly impatient, but he doesn't dare make a scene.

"Lincoln subway station, yes?" Marco says.

"Right. You want to head back to the Lincoln Center subway—"

I'm not even sure what Marco does then. It happens too fast. I'm midsentence, and he's listening intently. Then I'm shoved aside, and when I catch my balance, he's got my attacker by the arm. A sharp twist, and Marco is bouncing away, holding the jacket in a bundle.

"And I'm not going to tell you again!" Marco says, slamming his open palm into the man's chest, his accent American now. "I catch you sniffing around my girl, and I will kick your ass. You got it?"

People part around them, as if the two men are traffic cones that shot from the concrete.

Marco continues his diatribe as my stalker struggles to regain his mental footing. I spot an available cab and leap to the curb, waving. Marco doesn't seem to notice, but he has the handle before the taxi rolls to a stop, yanking open the door and bustling me inside. He climbs in behind me as I tell the driver to "just drive."

My stalker lunges for the door as the cab pulls away.

I spin on Marco. "What—?"

"PCTracy," he says, extending a hand. "Pleased to meet you."

CHAPTER THIRTY-SIX

WE'RE IN A HOTEL. I don't know which one. Some grand old dame near the park. Everything else is a blur as Marco bustles me in and up the elevator. It's only after I step into the room that I turn to him.

"You're . . . PCTracy?"

Marco steps toward me, his lips curving in a smile. When I back away, that smile twists with chagrin.

"All right," he murmurs. "Not exactly the way I imagined this." He clears his throat. "Largo di Torre Argentina."

"What?"

"It was our second date. We were looking at the Largo di Torre Argentina. You said you'd read a mystery where someone was murdered there, at the same place Caesar was presumably assassinated, but seeing it, you realized the writer had never been to Rome, because the scene made no sense. That got us talking about mysteries and then about classic mysteries and then about—"

"Dick Tracy," I say. "You'd read the old comics as a kid."

"I thought you might get the connection, but I also knew it was a long time ago, a passing conversation."

"You pretended to be a private investigator?"

His brows shoot up. "Pretended?"

I eye him and then lean back against the wall, arms crossed. "So when you said you wished you could fly out and help, but you'd just make things worse? Because you're only a tour guide and bike courier?"

"Uh . . ."

I give him a hard look.

Marco sighs. "Yes, I lied, but if I admitted I'd been an investigator, you would have still insisted I stay home so I couldn't be implicated. If I showed up anyway, you'd have blamed yourself for not making your point strenuously enough."

"You decided it was better to ask forgiveness than permission."

"More like I decided to take full responsibility for my actions. I will explain everything, but right now, I'm a little more concerned with what just happened."

"The paparazzi finding me?"

Now I'm the one getting a hard look. "You know that isn't what I mean, Gen. As for them finding you, though, that was Justice's fault."

Before I can speak, he hurries on. "No, he didn't rat you out. The paparazzi were following *him*. Then they spotted *you*. Back to the real topic of concern, though . . ." He lifts the bundled jacket and opens it to reveal a silenced handgun. "I know it takes a lot to rattle you, Gen, but the way you handled that tells me it's not the first time he's come after you. He was the guy in the park, wasn't he? I didn't get a good look at the time, but you obviously did."

I hesitate. Then I nod.

Marco sets the jacket and gun down. "Was the park the first time you'd seen him?"

"I . . . I don't think so."

I tell him about the attack outside the sandwich shop, and then about the man I'd briefly spotted the night before.

He lets out a string of curses in Italian and sinks onto the bed. "So, after you'd been held at knifepoint in an alley, I suggested you spend the night in Central Park."

"I wasn't sure the alley encounter was connected to Isabella's death. I didn't want to seem . . ."

"Paranoid. I get that. But if you'd told me, I would have been paranoid for you."

More curses as he shakes his head. "I should have told you the truth right after the park attack. Instead, I was in a panic over what happened and just wanted . . ."

"To put me safely in a hotel and shower me with goodies."

He exhales as he raises his eyes to mine. "I'm sorry, Gen. I've made a mess of this, and I could have gotten you killed."

I look at the gun. "Pretty sure you just *saved* me from getting killed."

"Pretty sure I wouldn't have needed to if I'd told you who I was two days ago."

"If you had, I'd have sent you back to Rome for your own good, like you said." I move to the bed and straddle his lap. "Let's skip the blame game. We have a lot to talk about but right now . . ."

I hug him tight and whisper in his ear, "I love you."

He gives a start at that, obviously not what he expected, and then he takes my face between his hands and tugs it in front of his. "I would say it back, but it's never quite the same in response. I think you know how I feel. At least, I hope you do."

"I kept things from you. Huge things. And when I was accused of murder, you flew across an ocean to help." I put my arms around his neck. "Yes, I think I know how you feel about me."

I bring my lips to his, and he lowers me onto the bed.

AN HOUR LATER, I'm watching Marco sleep. I'm still struggling to fully comprehend what he did. I should have figured it out. The Dick Tracy reference, the food, the fact that we got along so well . . .

The last is both unsettling and deeply, deeply satisfying. Unsettling because it makes me realize what I could have lost.

My tour guide and bike courier lover used to be a private investigator. I should be shocked. I'm not. You can't spend two years with a guy and not realize he's done more than his current jobs suggest. I knew Marco had an undergrad degree. I knew just how smart he was. I suspected something had happened to make him decide on a quieter life, careerwise. I'd done the same. So I'm fascinated by his past, but surprised? No.

I'm still watching Marco when one eyelid flutters. One eye opens and then the other.

"Are you watching me sleep?" he says. "You know that's creepy. I'd never do it to you. Especially not when you're sleeping in a park."

I kiss his cheek. "This place is a whole lot nicer than a park. A little too nice if I'm being honest." I look around the room. "Don't tell me you're also a secret millionaire."

"One quarter."

I arch my brows.

"I have a modest trust fund that makes me roughly a quarter of a millionaire. I suspect it's higher now because I haven't touched it in years and my parents are nothing if not good investors."

Marco has never talked much about his family except to say he comes from a big Italian one, but contra-stereotype, they aren't particularly close.

When he doesn't elaborate, awkward silence falls. A silence that it's my job to fill because there's something I really need to say.

"I am so sorry, Marco. I lied to you. Lied about who I was. Lied about my past. Lied about why I was coming to New York. I'm not who you thought I was."

He touches my chin. "You are Genevieve Callahan. You are from Albany. Your mother is a retired school teacher, and your dad died when you were five. You went to Juilliard for viola. I know all that, and all of it is true. You are smart. You are kind. You are funny and sweet and good. You didn't lie about who you *are*, Gen."

My cheeks heat at the compliments. "I still should have told you the rest. You suffered for that. They exposed you online and threatened your job, and you couldn't even say that you already knew about my past. I never gave you that opportunity, and I'm sorry."

"I accept the apology. But to me, you didn't lie. You just omitted things. We both avoided talking about our pasts. I kept a lot from you, too, as you may be realizing now."

"Did you sleep with a celebrity? Please tell me you did."

He chuckles. "Sorry, no. My downfall was worse . . . and far more mundane." He rolls onto his back and pulls me on top of him. "Do you want to hear it?"

"Hell, yes."

"Well, you know I got my bachelor's degree in the US. I also went to law school here. I clerked in a defense attorney's office, where I ended up doing more investigative work than clerking. After my second time failing the bar exam, I had an epiphany. If I wanted to pass, I needed to study."

I smile. "I've heard that."

"Weird, huh? The real epiphany was that there was a reason I wasn't studying. I didn't want to practice law. Never had. It was my parents' game plan. Instead, I'd discovered a career I actually enjoyed."

"Investigating."

"Yep. I gave up on law, and the firm hired me on full-time. My parents were furious. Disowned me. Did you know that's actually a thing? I figured it was just something people did in historical novels. Apparently not."

He's making light, but old confusion and hurt cloud his eyes.

"I'm so sorry, Marco."

He shrugs. "We were never close. I went to school in the US to get away from them. When I gave up law, they severed ties in hopes it'd scare me into changing my mind. Instead, I opened my trust fund, paid them back for my tuition, and stayed in America as an investigator. Fast-forward three years. We were representing this guy in court—a real son-of-a-bitch—and I met his wife. She came to me later, asking for help gathering incriminating evidence against her husband for a divorce suit."

"Ah."

"It wasn't anything to do with his less-than-legal activities. That would have been a violation of my employment contract. Still . . . let's just say I didn't tell my boss. What she wanted was evidence of infidelity. Typical PI work, and not my thing but . . ."

His cheeks heat, and he rubs a hand over his face. "I know this reflects badly on me, so I'm just going to get it out in the open. She was very pretty and very fragile, and my chivalric streak exploded."

"You had a fling with her."

"I almost wish I could say yes, because the truth seems even more embarrassing."

"That you helped her without getting any?" I waggle my brows.

"Oh, it was on offer from the start, but I was being a gentleman. I'd see her through the divorce and then hope for more than a weekend fling. I didn't want to take advantage of her fragility, especially considering she was in an abusive marriage."

"Ouch."

"The more she shared, the more I wanted to kill the guy. Then she *asked* me to kill him. Came to me in tears with fresh bruises, begging me to get rid of him so we could be together. That's when the alarm bells clanged."

"There was no abuse."

"Exactly. While I felt like a bastard for doubting her, I had to investigate. Turned out her husband was an asshole, but he wasn't abusing her. She just wanted his money, and I was the chump who'd help her get it. As I was deciding how to handle the situation, her husband wound up dead in an alley."

"Damn."

"Oh, yeah. When the cops showed up on my doorstep, I bolted back to Italy. I was in hiding for six months before they caught the actual killer. I lost my PI license for fleeing the country, and my old firm isn't ever giving me a job reference."

"And that experience totally cured your white-knight fantasies. Oh, wait . . ."

He loops his arms around my neck. "Hey, this is not the same thing. At all. I am a fully recovered white knight, who has traded in his fantasies of saving a damsel-in-distress for the much more realistic—and healthy—fantasy of supporting and aiding his capable girlfriend through a difficult time. Instead of pulling you onto my faithful steed and riding off with you, I'm standing by your side and offering the use of my lance."

I sputter a laugh.

He hesitates, as if replaying his words, and then rolls his eyes. "Get your mind out of the gutter, woman." He pulls me into a kiss and then, with a sigh, moves me aside. "And as much as I would love to distract ourselves with more of that, we need to talk strategy."

It's time to share what we know—fully and completely—and plan our next move.

THE NEXT MORNING, we're on a train to Connecticut. Yes, a train. After yesterday's encounter, we want to stick to public places as much as possible.

For a disguise, we're playing "Italian newlyweds honey-mooning in New York." Marco wears shorts, sandals and a button-down shirt, all designer wear, fitting the stereotype of the fashionable European. I'm in a linen sundress and heels with a wig of long strawberry-blond hair brushed straight. We both sport shiny wedding bands, and I have a gorgeous fake engagement ring.

We get business-class tickets and speak in Italian. When we

need to communicate with anyone, I let Marco do it—he has the properly accented English. Even in Italian, we mostly chatter about our honeymoon in case anyone nearby speaks the language.

Once on the train, we find ourselves in a half-empty car—it's midmorning, and we're traveling *out* of New York. We can relax then, and while we stick to Italian, we're not as careful with what we say unless someone's walking past.

To anyone seeing us, we maintain our personas. I sit with my shoes off and my feet curled beneath me as I lean against my new husband. The perfect picture of newly wedded bliss.

As befits a modern couple, while we're cuddling together, we're also on our separate phones. Marco assured me the train Wi-Fi is safe for what I'm doing, which is getting more information on Jamison's facility, so we're prepared. Marco is the one doing the case work—he's cultivated a few contacts by trading tidbits of my information.

He'd only traded the stuff I *want* to give away, of course. Scraps like "Look at the photo of the redhead at the hotel. Lucy Callahan is five-nine. That woman isn't more than five-three." Or "I've heard Lucy received early morning texts from Isabella. Has anyone examined Isabella's phone records?" Or "Someone called the hotel staff to Isabella's room when Lucy just happened to be on the premises. Doesn't that seem odd?"

He has traded carefully, and judiciously and entirely in my best interests.

When I finish checking out the rehab facility, I search for developments on the case. It takes a while before I find one, and when I do, I have to laugh. I expect Marco to ask what's funny. When he doesn't—presuming I'll explain when I'm ready—I finish reading the article first.

"So, get this," I say, waving the phone. "Colt gave his first post-widower interview, and the man has actually found a way to make this all about him. I'm not sure if I should be enraged by his arrogance or impressed by his ingenuity. Colt is claiming Isabella's death is part of a conspiracy against him. A conspiracy that began—get this—with our scandal."

Marco says nothing, as if waiting for me to go on.

"According to Colt," I say, "someone set him up fourteen years ago. Someone who recognized he was in a vulnerable position and foisted me on him, knowing he'd fall prey to temptation."

I snort. "Because I was *such* a temptress. According to Colt, someone sent me to him in his moment of weakness, hoping that the scandal would torpedo his career. Instead, he came back stronger than ever, which proves his talent."

Marco still doesn't answer. I lean against him and lift my phone higher so he can see the ridiculously somber picture of Colt acting the role of "mourning widower."

When Marco says nothing, I twist to look at him. He's staring into space.

"Marco?" I say.

"Hmm?"

"You missed everything I just said, didn't you?"

A faint smile as he kisses my temple. "I just got . . ." He lifts his phone. "I received information from the coroner's report. Isabella did fall and crack her skull. Enough that she probably lost consciousness, might have even suffered a concussion. But that wasn't what killed her."

He looks at me. "While she was unconscious, someone put a pillow over her face and suffocated her."

CHAPTER THIRTY-SEVEN

ISABELLA WAS MURDERED.

Yeah . . . that's the reason you're on the run, Lucy. Did you forget that?

No one is chasing me to ask whether I witnessed a fatal slip-and-fall. No one is even raising the possibility that it was an accidental shove. Yet that is what I've presumed.

When I suspect Tiana or Justice or even Colt, I envision a fight, probably about me. Accidental death or manslaughter, followed by a panicked cover-up that implicates me.

That is not what happened.

Isabella hit her head and likely lost consciousness. Did she take a tumble? Was it an accidental fall during an argument? Or did someone bash her head onto that tile step? I don't know, and it doesn't really matter. She fell. She lost consciousness. And then someone killed her.

Someone gazed down at Isabella, vulnerable and defenseless, and they saw an opportunity. Picked up a pillow, and put it over her face and smothered her.

WE RENT a car and drive to the rehab center. As one might expect, it's a country club of a hospital. This isn't where people go to serve court-mandated sentences; it's a facility that accepts voluntary—and well-paying—clients only.

From my research on the train, I know what to expect. There's a main building, which had once been a sprawling manor. That's where clients stay when they're in withdrawal. Once past that stage, they can move into a private cottage on the fifty-acre property while attending treatment sessions in the main house.

I was in touch with Justice last night, and according to him, Jamison's cottage is in a cluster far from the house. We pull off along a side road and walk through the forest. That's probably what Colt had done Sunday night, too.

We aren't even at the cottage yet when I spot Jamison in the forest, walking a toddling puff of black-and-white fur. I remember something Justice said last night.

Izzy got him a puppy. A border collie cross. It needs a lot of exercise, and that's what he wanted. Something to be responsible for, and something to get him out of his cabin . . . and out of his head. That's really what Jamie needs most. To get out of his own head, get out of his own way.

As I approach, I clear my throat, so I don't startle Jamison. He looks up, and not a flicker of surprise crosses those dark eyes.

"Lucy," he says with the faintest of smiles. "I wondered when you'd get around to me."

"You heard I've been making the rounds?" I ask as I walk over.

"Nah. But I knew you would. Tiana first, right? Then Justice?"

Those dark eyes twinkle, but it's muted, shadowed amusement and affection. He picks up the whining puppy and glances over my shoulder as Marco comes up behind me. His gaze slides over Marco, sharp and appraising. Then a small nod, as if satisfied.

He steps toward Marco and extends a hand. "Jamie."

"Marco."

"Boyfriend or bodyguard?"

Marco's lips twitch. "Both." He eases back. "Are you okay

with me being here? I can give you some privacy, but I'd prefer to stay close to Gen."

"Gen." Jamison pronounces it the way Marco does—Zhun rather than Jen. He looks at me. "Is that what you prefer?"

"Either's fine."

He lifts his free arm, as if for a hug. I step into it, and he gives me a quick squeeze. He smells of dew-damp puppy, and clean aftershave and Jamison. Mostly of Jamison, and my eyes fill with tears.

As I swipe away a tear, he shakes his head. "None of that. Also, please don't tell me I look good. I trust you can do better than that. *God, Jamie, for a recovering alcoholic and drug addict, you look awesome.*"

I smile through the tears. "I won't say it, but if I did, I wouldn't mean it like that."

He does look good, strong and healthy. A younger, slighter-built version of his father with his mother's smile and keen gaze. He's absurdly handsome, as one might expect, given his genetic inheritance. But there's none of Colt's arrogance or even Isabella's confidence. He isn't the diffident boy I remember, but there's a quietness to him, a gentle maturity.

I remember meeting Tiana at ten and thinking how much older she seemed. Now it's Jamison who acts and *feels* so much older. Unnecessarily older. He's keeping this conversation calm, light even, putting a good face on his grief, but there's an unmistakable melancholy.

"Can we take this conversation inside?" he asks.

"May I carry the puppy?" I ask.

His eyes crinkle at the corners as he passes her over. "Definitely. Her name is Molly, by the way." He falls in step beside me. "It's good to see you, Lucy. I won't add 'despite the circumstances.' It's just good to see you, and before you tell me that you didn't kill my mother, I know that. I think *everyone* knows that, really. It's just . . ." He shrugs. "It'll be resolved soon. You have nothing to worry about."

Because he knows Colt went to New York on Sunday night. He knows his father's secret, and that firm certainty in his voice says he won't let me be scapegoated for this.

I loop my arm through his. He stiffens, as if in surprise, but when I go to pull away, he keeps me there.

"I'm sorry," I say. "Obviously, for your mom. That goes without saying."

"It does."

"But the . . . rest, too. I know what happened . . . the way I left and the fallout from that for your family . . ."

He slows at the edge of the forest and glances over. "Do you think you're responsible for this?" He gestures around the grounds of the rehab facility.

"Not entirely, but what happened didn't help."

"What happened at the beach party wasn't about me. It wasn't about you and me, either. It was my dad being . . ." He makes a face, as if hating to speak against his father. "Dad being Dad. I was upset and angry. At the time, I only understood that you'd done something wrong and were sent away for it, and you weren't coming back next year, like Mom had promised. That's what I cared about. That you weren't coming back."

He opens the door to his cottage and ushers us inside. I put down Molly, and she scrambles for her bowl, careening over the hardwood floor. Jamison chuckles as he fills her water. Marco silently passes us to take a seat in the living room. I stay in the kitchen with Jamison as he feeds the puppy.

Then he says, "You aren't responsible for me being here, Lucy. That's poor life choices and even poorer DNA. Addiction runs in the family. Dad's had problems, but Mom kept him on the right path. His mother, though, was a total mess. Seems I take after her."

He waves toward the coffee maker. I nod, and he grabs three pods and pops in the first.

"Fortunately," he continues, "I seem to have inherited—or learned—a little of Mom's common sense, too. Enough for me to see the path I'm on and switch to a better one. I wasn't quite so clear-headed at eighteen. I blame testosterone." A wry smile my way. "I had my fun—and my screw-ups—but I'm clean and planning to stay that way."

I nod, saying nothing.

He searches my face and says, "You read about the suicide attempt. Or is it *attempts* now? One is far too dull." He sets out cream and sugar. "Even one overstates the matter. Technically, I suppose getting coked up and hopping behind the wheel of a friend's new Ferrari *is* suicidal, but I didn't intend to kill myself."

As he hands me the first coffee, I say, "I saw you on a movie poster at the airport. That's what you want, is it?"

He smiles. "You still have a knack for that. What you really mean is 'Do you actually want to be an actor, Jamie, or are you feeling pressured into it?'"

He hands me a second cup with a nod toward Marco. Then he says, "The answer is that I want it. Acting, yes. Action movies . . . ?" He makes a face. "That's a longer discussion. But the short one is that I really am okay, Lucy." He pauses, fingers tightening around the third mug. "Or I was last week, but again, that goes without saying."

He ushers me into the living room, where I hand Marco his coffee. The puppy gallops after us, and when Jamison sits, she vaults onto him. He absently pats her head, as if lost in his thoughts.

On the coffee table, his cell phone vibrates. He shoots it a glance of annoyance. Karla's name pops up on a text. It looks as if it isn't the first from her this morning. Notifications fill the lock screen. Jamison turns the phone facedown.

"You didn't come here to talk about me," he says.

"I do want to know how you're doing. I would have loved to see you before now. Long before now. It just wasn't appropriate."

"I know. I tried getting in touch with you a couple of years ago, just to say hello, but you'd gone into deep hiding by then. Can't say I blame you. When I was a kid, I had no idea how it affected your life. Having had my own fun with the tabloids, I understand."

He meets my gaze. "It's unfair, and it sucks, but what's happening right now is even more unfair and a whole lot worse. So ask your questions. Don't treat me with kid gloves, Lucy. You of all people know how much I hate that."

"I do. Okay, well . . ." I take a deep breath. "I won't tiptoe around it, then. I know your father came to visit you the night your mother died. He's pretending he never left LA, but he was here."

Jamison's head jerks up, his gaze meeting mine in a look of pure confusion.

"My . . . father?" A rueful laugh. "I'd ask if you mean Colt Gordon but . . ." A wave at his face. "There's no question of my paternity. My dad wasn't here, Lucy. Whatever you uncovered, it's a mistake. I haven't seen Dad in weeks."

"He caught a private jet to New Haven," I say. "He wouldn't do that if he wasn't coming here." I pause as I remember that we aren't investigating an accidental death. This is murder. "Unless he wanted to *seem* like he was coming here."

"That doesn't make sense." It isn't Jamison who speaks. It's Marco, the first words he's said since greeting Jamison. He speaks carefully. "If it was an alibi, Gen, Colt needed to show up here. To *get* an actual alibi from Jamison."

"Maybe he planned to say he came here, but Jamie was asleep."

"Then he'd have left proof. A note or something. And he wouldn't have flown back to LA and hidden the fact he was in Connecticut. The only reason he'd do that is if . . ."

Marco looks at Jamison, who hasn't said a word, who has just sat there petting Molly. The dog whines, and I look into Jamison's face. It's studiously calm, but the puppy picks up his anxiety.

"Yes," Jamison says.

"Yes . . . ?" I say.

"Yes, in answer to the possibility Marco doesn't want to raise in front of me. There's only one reason Dad would turn around, go home and pretend he never came: if I wasn't here when he arrived. If he wanted to protect me. The answer is yes. I wasn't here. I'd slipped out and driven to New York to see my mother."

My heart slams, stealing my breath. I wait for his next words, which will be that he went to see Isabella but changed his mind and turned around. Or that he saw her, but early in the evening, and she was alive when he left.

His gaze locks on mine for a split second before it drops, and he says, his voice barely above a whisper. "I'd never have let you go to jail, Lucy. Never. I wanted to turn myself in right away, but Karla insisted I wait. I've been battling it out with her. For now, I was just waiting to hear that you were arrested, and then I'd step forward."

The puppy whines, and he rises and hands her to me with a murmured thanks. Then he walks to the window and looks out with his back to us.

"This should be more dramatic, shouldn't it?" he says. "At least more drawn out. I should keep tap dancing for as long as I can, evading questions and misdirecting you. Then, when you realize it was me, I should . . ."

A one-armed shrug, his gaze still on the window. "In one of Dad's movies, I'd pull a gun. At the very least, I'd tackle Marco. Or make a run for it. You asked if I like acting. I do, but that movie poster you saw was for Dad. I don't care for action. I'm all about drama, so in my movie, I'd beg for understanding, beg you not to turn me in, maybe bribe you to take the fall, promising you won't go to prison."

He turns to me. "When Mom told me her plans for you two, I hopped on my motorcycle and drove to New York to talk her out of it. To convince her to leave you alone. She admitted you were reluctant to go public, and she needed to respect that. She needed to see that her scheme was all about *her*—assuaging her guilt and reclaiming her pride. She honestly wanted to help you, but she needed to proceed with more care, to be *sure* you wanted it."

He shoves his hands into his jeans pockets. "I asked to stay and join her lunch with you. Mom was uncomfortable with that. She knew I still cared about you, and I guess she thought I was setting myself up for disappointment. We argued. I went to leave, storming out. She grabbed my arm, and I flung her off and . . ."

His voice catches. "Those slippers. Those stupid Beast slippers. She nearly fell down the stairs in them once. I tried to get rid of them, but they were important to her." He swallows. "They slid on the bathroom floor and—"

He flinches, convulsively, as if seeing Isabella fall again, hearing her skull crack against the tiled step.

"And she hit her head and died." My voice sounds strange, hollow, because I know that isn't what happened, but he doesn't seem to catch my tone, just nods and sinks back into his chair.

"You framed me," I say.

"What?" His brow crinkles. "No. I would never do that, Lucy."

"So you didn't take your mom's tablet? Didn't send the texts luring me to her room that morning?"

He stares at me, confusion piercing the numb blankness. "Wait. You were lured . . . ?" He breaks off and curses under his breath. "Of course you were. You didn't just happen to show up that morning."

He reaches for his phone. His fingers tremble as he thumbs through the messages. He keeps talking, his gaze on his phone. "We always call Karla when we have a problem. That's her job. Fixing problems. But I'll fix this, Lucy. I'll turn myself in. Karla's apparently on her way now. I've been ducking her calls, so she's coming in person. What happened to Mom was an accident, and I should have turned myself in right away, but I called Karla and . . ." He shakes his head.

"Karla realized it wasn't an accident," Marco says. "She knew what you'd done. That's why she covered it up. That's why she framed Genevieve. She knew the coroner would uncover the truth."

Jamison looks up, blinking. "Truth?"

"Your mother died of asphyxiation. She was smothered with a pillow."

"W-what?"

Marco repeats it, but Jamison just stares, as if the words don't compute. He goes very still, his face stark white. Seconds tick past, and we let him process it. Then he shakes his head.

"That's a mistake," he says, a little too lightly, and my heart cracks. It just cracks. "They're wrong. Mom died in a fall. From hitting her head."

His phone buzzes. He stares at it, as if not recognizing the sound. Then he grabs it and shoves it into his pocket.

"Karla's here," he says. "I'm going to talk to her. Fire her, for starters. Then we'll call the police, and I'll turn myself in." He gets to his feet. "Just give me a few minutes with her alone. Please."

Marco opens his mouth, but I put out a hand to stop him.

"We'll be right here," I say. "But if you're more than fifteen minutes, we'll call the police ourselves."

He nods, as if barely hearing me. Then he heads straight to the door. Molly yips and tears after him, only to have the door clip her tiny snout, Jamison too distracted to notice her.

When Jamison is gone, Marco turns to me. "He murdered his mother, Lucy. I know you don't want to believe that, but he isn't going to confront Karla. He's going to let her fix *this* problem—by getting him out of here."

"Maybe," I say. "But I don't think so."

"Karla didn't just happen to arrive while we're here, Gen. Jamie wasn't surprised when you showed up. Justice must have warned him last night. Then Jamie called Karla, and she flew up here to spirit him away."

I don't answer that, and he continues, "Jamie knew he was safe. That's why he admitted it so readily. Admitted to *accidental* death. According to him, he didn't even shove his mother. She grabbed him, and he pulled away, and then? Those damned slippers. They killed her."

"I remember them. Very slippery slippers."

He shoots me a look for that. "Which he probably put on her feet afterward. The fall didn't do the job, so he smothered her and phoned Karla, who knows the coroner will realize it wasn't an accident. Karla framed you, but Jamie still thinks his story will set him free. Maybe the lightbulb finally flashed, and he realized he needs to run. Or maybe Karla's going to need to kick his ass into that car. Either way, the family's manager has another mess to clean up."

I nod. "Go after him, please. Stay back and listen in. I . . . I can't do it. I'm sorry."

He squeezes my arm, too distracted to see that my gaze is lowered. A quick kiss on my cheek, and he's gone.

CHAPTER THIRTY-EIGHT

THE BACK DOOR to Jamison's cabin eases open, and Karla steps inside. She shuts the door behind her and then stands just inside, listening and looking. She doesn't see me. I'm in the back closet, door opened just enough that I can see her.

In three days, I've come full circle, hiding in a closet, holding my breath as I watch and listen.

Karla takes a moment and then leans to see into the front room, where I've left my laptop playing a TV show at low volume. She nods, satisfied, and then creeps past my hiding spot. As I watch her go, my heart sinks.

I wanted to be wrong. I so badly wanted to be wrong.

I'd reflected earlier that this is the problem with Isabella's murder: so many suspects I don't want to be guilty. Tiana, Jamison, Justice . . . Even with Colt, I'd held out hope that, for Isabella's sake, he cared enough never to do this. I kept hoping that the killer would be a stranger. *Huh, she was murdered by some screenwriter I never met, who blamed her for "ruining his vision" with her script doctoring.*

Yep, that's the solution I wanted. If it had to be someone I've met, then maybe Bess. No offense, Bess, but I don't know you, and that makes it easier for you to be a killer.

Karla, though . . . ? Karla never even made it to my list of serious suspects until I heard Jamison's story, and even then, I told myself I was wrong. She was a committed employee, who'd given her professional life to the family and sacrificed, I'm sure, most of her personal life, too. No marriage. No kids. Just the job. Always the job.

I liked you, Karla. Not in the warm way I liked Tiana and Jamison and Justice. Warm wasn't your word, but I liked you for that, not in spite of it.

Before the scandal, I'd seen Isabella as my role model. After it, though? After it, I looked to Karla, even if I never quite realized it until now. Efficient and capable are not sexy adjectives, but they were what I needed post-scandal, and Karla embodied those traits. Her strength was not exactly warm and fuzzy, but it was kind. That's what I remember from that night when Karla took charge. She'd been kind when I needed kindness. Not platitudes but genuine compassion.

Maybe I'm still wrong.

That's the refrain that thuds through my head as I watch her walk toward the main room. Maybe my theory is faulty and . . .

And Jamison murdered his mother? Shoved her during a fight, and when she was knocked out, he saw his chance to murder her?

No. I don't care if I only knew Jamison for a few months as a child. Nothing I knew of him then and nothing anyone else has said of him since would allow him to be that person. His story makes perfect sense. He thought Isabella was dead, and he did what he'd been raised to do. Call Karla.

He called Karla, and she's the one who saw her chance, and I don't know why, but motive doesn't matter at this moment. I'm watching Karla sneak into Jamison's cottage, intent on that front room. She thinks Jamison is in there alone, and I don't know what she plans, but she isn't sneaking up to surprise him. She's creeping through the house, cell phone in her hand—

She twists against the wall, and my gaze falls to her hand, and what I see there is *not* a cell phone.

Karla has a gun.

Holy shit. Karla has a gun.

Even as my stomach convulses, I inwardly snarl at myself for my stupidity. I'm hiding in this damned closet, waiting for her to arrive, my gut telling me she will come for him, and yet it failed to foresee that damned gun in her hand?

Did I think Karla—fifty-something Karla, who probably doesn't even have time for spin classes—was going to confront a twenty-three-year-old action-movie star without a weapon?

I did not foresee this because I didn't want to foresee it. I wanted to believe Karla cared enough for these kids that she only came to talk to Jamison, to persuade him.

I'd planned to step from this closet and confront her myself. Now, seeing that gun, I realize my terrible mistake. I take a deep breath and ease back into the closet. I need to warn Marco and stay here—

Molly hears Karla, then. I'd put her into the bedroom with a chew toy, and she'd been quiet, but now there is clearly someone else in the building, and she wants out. Between puppy yips, Karla's shoes squeak as she halts.

She knows something is wrong, and if there was any doubt, it evaporates when Molly begins flinging herself against the door, yowling. Being locked in a room is foreign enough, but to have someone inside the house *ignoring* her? That is a mistake, and the puppy yowls her confusion and concern, telling Karla, beyond any doubt, that no one is in the front room watching TV.

I need to get out of here. Now.

I ease open the closet door and tiptoe to the back one. I twist the knob just as Karla's shoes squeak again. She's coming back my way.

I throw open the back door and run. I tear through the small yard, my gaze fixed on the woods twenty feet away—

"Stop, Lucy."

In the movie version, I'd lunge for the forest and somehow reach it despite it being at least ten feet away. Or I'd dodge and weave until I was safely in the trees. In reality, I know that if I even try that, she'll shoot me in the back.

So I turn, hands raised. Karla stands there, and I hope—I still hope—that I won't see a gun in her hand. Maybe it really was her cell phone, or maybe she's hiding the gun, hoping not to need to resort to that.

The gun is there. Right there. Pointing straight at me.

Karla came to kill me.

The thought barely settles, ice cold in my gut, before it's steamrolled by the truth, one even worse.

Karla didn't know I was here. She couldn't have come for me.

Karla came to kill Jamison.

"Suicide?" I say, and my voice is eerily calm.

Her brows shoot up. "You think I'm going to kill myself, Lucy?"

"Of course not. You came to shoot Jamison. You were just going to make it look like suicide. He has a history of it, after all. You'd shoot him and tell the police you came to talk to him because you knew he'd killed Isabella. You were coming to help Jamie turn himself in, and you arrived to discover he'd found another solution to his problem."

She doesn't answer. She doesn't need to. I see by the flicker of consternation that I'm right—or close enough to it.

"Where is he?" she says.

Now I'm the one lifting my brows. "You really think I'd tell you?"

"Yes, because you have a choice to make, Lucy. Two solutions to *this* problem. One, I can shoot you and frame him. You came to beg for his help, and—being Isabella's actual killer—he shot you. Two, I finish this, and we say Jamie took his own life. He would eventually, anyway, especially with Isabella gone. This only speeds up the inevitable."

Especially with Isabella gone.

Those words thunder in my ears. She says them offhandedly,

stating a simple fact. As if Jamison's mother died of some tragic accident or natural cause.

"You *murdered* Isabella," I say, barely able to force the words out. "She trusted you and—"

"Isabella never trusted me. She tolerated me, for Colt's sake. I spent my life working for that man, and who did he turn to? Who did he rely on? A woman too wrapped up in herself and her career to take proper care of him. That summer, he was having a midlife crisis, and she barely noticed. All she cared about was her silly show."

The hairs on my neck rise. "Is Colt actually correct? That someone set him up that summer? With me?" I step toward her. "You hired me. You didn't stop the scandal because you didn't *want* to. You wanted Colt's name in the papers again, and you wanted Isabella gone, and you thought that would do it."

"Long-suffering Isabella," Karla says. "That's the only decent role she ever played. But she couldn't even stick with that one. Hooks up with a musician half her age and intends to divorce Colt to marry him. That was bad enough. Then she brings you to New York and plans to drag Colt down by reopening the past."

"Going public with me," I murmur. "You didn't plan to kill Isabella, but when Jamie called you after the accident, you saw an opportunity. Kill her. Put Jamie in your debt. Frame me to reignite that old scandal and remind the world just how irresistible Colt Gordon is. Fourteen years later, I'm still so obsessed with him that I murder my so-called rival. Except you knew, even with the planted evidence, it was hardly an airtight case. So you hired a guy to stalk me." I meet her gaze. "You hired him to kill me."

Her lips stretch in a humorless smile. "You have quite the imagination there. Perhaps you could have been a screenwriter after all. If someone was following you, Lucy, might I suggest it had nothing to do with me and everything to do with the fact that you are a wanted fugitive."

"Possibly. That would certainly explain why you think you can get away with killing me or framing Jamie, as if there's no one else here but the three of us."

She hesitates. It's only a flicker behind her eyes, but I catch it.

"I didn't come alone," I say. "You should know that, though, if you hired the man who held a gun to me yesterday. I mean, he'd have told you, right? Told you that his attempted abduction was foiled by *my* private eye, who also took his gun."

I purse my lips. "Unless he failed to disclose that the last time you spoke. Kind of embarrassing, I guess. *My* hired guy disarming *your* hired guy in broad daylight. Tricking him with a fake tourist routine. If he is your guy, you deserve a refund."

Her expression answers for her. It is completely impassive, ice-cold with rage. Then her hand moves. I see it out of the corner of my eye, just the slightest move.

My brain doesn't even have time to tell me to dive. It screams a warning, and I twist so fast, I stumble, and the gun fires. I don't know if it's the twist or the stumble, but one of them saves my life. The bullet whizzes past, and I'm doing another awkward move, half-scrambling, half-diving for the forest. The *whoosh* of another silenced shot just as I hit the ground.

"Gen!"

Marco's shout comes from somewhere in the forest, and Karla wheels, gun raised. I scream a warning, my heart hammering as I lunge in Marco's direction.

A streak of motion flies from the other side of the house. Karla is looking the other way, scanning the forest. At the last second, she hears the sound behind her, and my mouth opens to call another warning, but Jamison is already in flight, knocking her flying. He pins her gun hand, his other hand at her throat.

"You murdering *bitch*," he snarls.

A strangled gurgling from Karla, cut short by Jamison.

"Is this what you did to her, Karla? Is this what you did to my mother?"

I race over to them. Jamison has shoved the gun aside, and he has his knee on Karla's chest, his hands around her throat as she writhes and wheezes.

"Did you think I was too stupid to figure it out?" he asks. "Or too weak to do anything about it? Too *sensitive*."

He leans his weight onto her. "Am I stronger than you expected? You're the one who insisted I do that movie with Dad. Maybe you're regretting that now. Maybe you're regretting a lot of things now."

"Jamie," I say.

He startles. Guilt and shame flood his face just like when he was a boy and I caught him destroying that script in his room.

That look vanishes in a second, replaced by hard anger and determination, his jaw setting. He does ease up on her throat, though, and Karla sputters and gasps for air.

"I called her," he says. "Called her for help. That's what we're supposed to do when we run into trouble. I used to joke I should have her phone number tattooed on my arm. Call in case of emergency. Or blackout. Or overdose." He looks down at Karla. "Or in case my mother falls, and hits her head and isn't breathing."

I glance over as Marco walks from the forest. He's moving quietly, careful not to interrupt.

I turn back to Jamison. "You thought your mother was dead. So you called Karla."

He nods, his eyes brimming with tears. "She said I had to get out of there before anyone knew I was at Mom's hotel that night. I'm an addict and an alcoholic, and if the police didn't blame me, the press would. She said that for Tiana and Dad's sake, I had to leave. She'd tidy up and slip back to her room downstairs. When the hotel staff found Mom, it'd look like an accident."

He swipes away tears as he stands. "I shouldn't have left. I just . . . I was in shock, and I kept thinking that if I left, maybe I'd wake up in an alley and realize I'd stopped to get a fix and hallucinated the whole thing."

I put my arms around him, and he falls against my shoulder. When Karla tries to rise, I slam my foot onto her throat.

"Don't give me an excuse," I say. "I won't let Jamie kill you, but I'm happy to do it myself."

Marco walks over, still quiet.

"Got my 911 text, huh?" I say.

He manages a tight smile, his gaze still on Karla, making sure she's subdued.

"Would you call the real 911 for us, please?" I ask.

"Already have. They're on their way."

I look at Jamison. "Is that okay? Are you ready for . . . ?"

"Ready to confess?" He meets my gaze. "I've been ready since Sunday night, Lucy. I just want this to be over. For all of us."

CHAPTER THIRTY-NINE

A WEEK LATER, I'm out for lunch with Tiana. Real lunch, in public —or, at least, a private dining room in a very exclusive restaurant. It's a relief not to be a fugitive, but that doesn't mean I can walk around New York just yet. If anything, I'm a bigger story now.

When Jamison and I were taken into custody, Tiana hired separate lawyers for us. Marco worked with mine, and I spent a day in lockup before they sorted everything and decided not to pursue charges. Yes, I'd tampered with the scene of Isabella's murder, but everyone seemed to decide that, under the circumstances, the optics might be better if the DA's office overlooked my panicked mistake.

Jamison is also free. Like me, he didn't do anything except make questionable choices. Looking back, though, I'm not sure either of us could have done anything different without a crystal ball to guide us.

Jamison had thought his mother was dead, so he'd brought in the person he counted on to help. At that point, realizing Isabella was alive, Karla should have called 911. Instead, she'd committed an unbelievable act of betrayal. There will be a lifetime of "what-ifs" for Jamison, but the police and DA's office were quick to see that he wasn't a killer.

Proving Karla's guilt was trickier. She admitted she was in the hotel suite that night and confessed to framing me. As for the murder weapon, she'd taken the pillowcase and shoved the insert into a closet—she could hardly walk around the hotel with a pillow under her arm. A hair on the insert matched hers, but that trivial piece of evidence wouldn't have stood up in court.

That's when the police found her accomplice. It was the private eye she'd originally set on my trail in Rome at Isabella's behest. Then she used him to plant the evidence in my hotel room and later to stalk and threaten me. Yes, threaten me. That'd been her order. Not to kill me, but to scare the crap out of me so I'd flee. She knew the evidence wouldn't hold up, but if the police were chasing me, they wouldn't be looking for other suspects. Of course, she hadn't admitted to the private eye that she'd killed Isabella herself. She pretended to be protecting Jamison. That was, after all, her job. Fixer to the stars.

No, fixer to one particular star. The only one who counted. Colt. Marco says that the DA wants to paint Karla as an obsessed middle-aged woman who couldn't get the man she loved. As much as I despise Karla, I'm almost insulted on her behalf. Just because she was a woman—and he was an attractive man—didn't make this a case of sexual obsession. He was her client. Her golden goose. The center of her career universe, which was the only universe she had.

Now her universe will be a prison cell, and I'm free, sitting across from Tiana. That's all that matters to me.

"Dad wants to see you before you leave New York," Tiana says as she cuts into a steak.

I laugh.

"I take it that's a no," she murmurs.

"I have neither the need nor the desire to see your father," I say. "This isn't his story. It never was."

She tilts her head, puzzled, before nodding. "True. Not for lack of trying on his part, though. Did you hear he's now claiming Karla set up his scandal with you?"

"I hate to give your dad any credit, but I'm not sure he's wrong."

"Really?" Tiana says. "Huh. Well, he says she gave him the champagne you drank. She handed him the open bottle and told him you were with Justice, and she was worried because she heard Justice was a player. She suggested Dad should rescue you with a drink."

"That actually *was* his excuse for taking me from Justice, who'd done absolutely nothing untoward."

"Dad claims Karla drugged you both."

When I don't answer, she says, "Dad didn't drink the champagne, did he?"

"He had a few sips and then put his glass aside. But I'm not reading anything into that. Yes, Karla wanted to get your mom out of your dad's life. She also wanted to revitalize his career, and one way to do it was to give him a scandal. One that would get his name plastered everywhere as a guy who made a mistake that, quite frankly, a lot of his fans *expect* him to make. At worst, they'd forgive him for it, and at best, it'd be a show of action-star virility."

"Whether Karla set it up or not, though, she didn't *make* him do it."

"No one made me do it, either," I remind her.

Tiana leans back, shaking her head. "I don't know what I'll do with him. Sometimes I almost hope he'll screw up so badly that I can write him off completely. Cut him out of my life."

"But he doesn't, and he *is* part of your life."

She makes a face. "A fifty-five-year-old toddler."

"Who needs to grow up," I say softly.

She nods. "I'll still be there for him, but I'm not taking Mom's place. I won't be his crutch or his caregiver. Neither will Jamie. I'll make sure of that. If anyone needs that care, it's my brother, and he's the one who's going to get it."

I keep my voice as neutral as possible. "Does he need it?"

She looks up.

"Jamie seems to be doing pretty well," I say. "At the risk of sticking my nose where it doesn't belong, I think he could do with a little *less* care. I never had a sibling, but from what I understand, sometimes they get pigeonholed into their family roles. You're the tough one. Jamie is the sensitive one. That doesn't mean he needs quite so much care." I meet her gaze. "Or that you don't need any at all."

Tiana squirms at that. I change the subject—away from her family and onto her own life and plans, more comfortable territory for her. We talk through lunch and dessert and coffee. Then someone raps on the open doorway of the private room.

Jamison ducks his head inside, puppy under his arm. "Sorry to interrupt, but Lucy isn't answering her phone, and I believe we had an ice-cream date."

I curse and scramble to my feet as he waves off my apologies.

"I could go for ice cream," Tiana says.

"Next time." Jamison gives her a sidelong glance and says casually. "Maybe we could invite Justice along, before he leaves New York."

Tiana tenses, but Jamison lets the awkward silence drag until she nods and says, "Okay. Let's do that."

"Good." Jamison gives his sister a fierce hug. "I'll catch up with you later, okay?"

He steps outside and lets me say my goodbyes to Tiana before I join him.

JAMISON and I talk as we walk to the ice cream parlor. We get some looks . . . and a surreptitiously snapped photo or two, but we ignore them. I don't ask how he's doing. I can see the answer is "not great, but coping," which is all I can ask for. He's extended his stay at the rehab center, knowing this is a dangerous time for him. He's fired his agent, and he's looking for one who wants Jamie Morales-Gordon, not "Colt Gordon's son."

He'll find his footing. I know he will.

We sit out on the parlor patio to eat our ice creams. Molly has her own—a kiddie cone, of course.

Eventually, conversation works around to me leaving the US.

"I'm going to spend a month with my mom before I go back," I say.

"Is Marco staying, too?"

"I haven't talked to him about that yet."

Jamison's look tells me to get on that—pronto.

"I know," I say. "I wanted to speak to you first and make sure you're okay with me being in the US for a while."

"Nah, hate it. Go back to Italy, please." Another look. "Are you seriously asking, Lucy? Or is it a roundabout way of asking whether it's okay to stay in contact . . . because part of the reason you're staying is to keep an eye on me."

"You don't need that."

"Mmm, not so sure. I'm doing okay, but I could probably use my Mary Poppins around for a bit as long as she has another reason to stay."

"I do."

He swirls his ice cream, licking up the drips. "I'd like that. Tiana will, too, even if she won't admit it. Mom wanted you two to go public with your story. That was her way of handling it. This is another way."

He nods at a young couple who are sneaking photos of us. "Not go public, but be seen in public. Be seen together. It says everything Mom wanted to say, if in a less dramatic fashion."

"I think she'd like that."

"I know she would."

MARCO and I are walking through the cemetery to Isabella's grave. I didn't attend the funeral service—that wouldn't have been right. As we walk, I tell Marco that I'd like to stay for a month, visit with Mom and make sure Jamison and Tiana are okay.

"Is that a subtle hint for me to get my ass back to Italy?" he asks, forcing a smile.

I take his hand. "I would be absolutely delighted to introduce you to my mom. Now that I have my luggage back, you can give her the rosary."

"That was for you to give her."

"I prefer the truth. Her absentminded daughter forgot, and her absentminded daughter's amazing boyfriend came through."

He pulls me into a kiss and then says, "We haven't talked about what comes next. You want to stay a month. And then . . . ?"

"I'd like to go back to Rome. With you, obviously. I'm also willing to consider cohabitation."

He smiles. "Your place? 'Cause I like yours better."

"Mine if the landlord hasn't kicked me out. As for my jobs, I'm sure I'll get fired from one or two, but I'll find other clients. I like what I do, and I have no intention of changing it. And while I know you enjoy being a tour guide, I kinda feel like it's not your true calling."

"I've already started looking into getting my investigator's license."

"Excellent." I smack a kiss on his lips and then hook my arm through his as we resume walking.

"At the risk of pushing my luck . . . ," he says. "After you were arrested, I made sure to get your rings back from the police."

I arch a brow. "The fake engagement ring and wedding band?"

"I threw out the wedding band. It was just tin." He reaches into his pocket and takes out the engagement one.

"A souvenir of our adventure?" I say with a laugh as I take it. I put it on my finger and wave it around. "I do like it. No one can tell it's cubic zirconia."

He says nothing. I look up at him, at his expression and . . .

"It's not cubic zirconia, is it?" I say.

He clears his throat. "Once again, these things go so much better in my head." He takes a deep breath. "I'd get down on one knee, but a cemetery is the most inappropriate place ever for that, which I should have realized before I said anything. I just wanted you to know that I kept the ring. If and when you want it, just say so, and I'll do this properly. No pressure. No rush. I want you to have all the time you need."

"And if I don't need any time?"

He inhales sharply, and I cut off his reply with a kiss that lasts until an elderly woman harrumphs at us, and we guiltily continue walking.

We find Isabella's grave. It's a simple yet gorgeous headstone. Tiana's choice, I'm sure. It's in a spot with space for her children, and maybe even for Colt. A family plot, because they were a family, however fractured.

We lay flowers at Isabella's grave, one bouquet among dozens, and then Marco steps back. I stay there, on one knee, and I remember Isabella. I remember the first time I met her, gardening in her yard. I remember playing music together under the stars. I remember lying on that bed in New York, talking into the night.

"I said I wrote you a fan letter when I was younger," I say. "Even if things hadn't gone wrong, I'm not sure I could ever have shown it to you."

I slip the letter from my pocket. "This is that letter, Isabella, from a starstruck twelve-year-old girl to her idol. There were times I wanted to say you weren't the person I wrote this letter to, that the girl who wrote it didn't know the real you. And she didn't. Because the real you was so much more."

I tuck it into the bouquet we've left. Then I touch my fingers to her headstone.

"I was always your fan, Isabella."

I push to my feet and make my way to Marco, as his arms open to pull me into a hug.

ABOUT THE AUTHOR

Kelley Armstrong is the author of the *Rockton* thriller series and standalone thrillers beginning with *Wherever She Goes*. Past works include the *Otherworld* urban fantasy series, the *Cainsville* gothic mystery series, the *Nadia Stafford* thriller trilogy, the *Darkest Powers & Darkness Rising* teen paranormal series and the *Age of Legends* teen fantasy series. Armstrong lives in Ontario, Canada with her family.

Visit her online:
www.KelleyArmstrong.com
mail@kelleyarmstrong.com

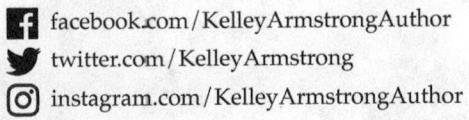

facebook.com/KelleyArmstrongAuthor
twitter.com/KelleyArmstrong
instagram.com/KelleyArmstrongAuthor

CPSIA information can be obtained
at www.ICGtesting.com
Printed in the USA
LVHW031503241220
675096LV00002B/195

9 781989 046272